BOY BANNED

Sam Stevens

PROWLER BOOKS

First published 2001 by Prowler Books,
part of the Millivres Prowler Group,
116-134 Bayham Street, London NW1 0BA

A catalogue record for this book is available from the British Library

ISBN 1 902644 36 0

Printed and bound in Finland by WS Bookwell

Prologue

The vast wave of sound that reverberated around the stadium seemed to possess a personality all its own. The deafening cacophony bounced back and forth, sometimes excited, sometimes lulled, sometimes anxious and intense, always on the verge of another loud surge of ear-shattering noise.

It filled the dressing room, the totality of the sound rattling the inferior tannoy system that hung on the mottled green wall. A number of mirrors sat on each side of the room, above flower-strewn dressing tables, surrounded by vibrant white lightbulbs, creating an endless tunnel of reflected images, growing smaller and smaller until they vanished in a series of twinkling specks. The four young members of the pop sensation BANNED stood silently in the dressing room, in a close circle, tightly holding hands, trying to blot out the violent sound that cackled from the tannoy.

None of the band members spoke, they couldn't even if they had wanted to, there seemed nothing left to say. Here they were, about to give the most important concert of their lives, to seventeen thousand screaming fans, male and female, gay and straight. They had reached the utmost pinnacle of success. Their record sales were on a constant high. They had achieved endless Number One hits, and now they stood on the verge of conquering America.

Paul believed that the idea of playing the Hollywood Bowl had come from Joe, whilst Dean held that Connor was the one who had laughingly suggested it. If Monty Python could do it, why not BANNED? No matter. They had made it. Dean looked up from the circle and noted the clock hanging above the door. 'It's eight o'clock, guys.' A tight squeezing of hands, then the boys relaxed. As Joe reached for the door handle, it swung open, banging back against the wall. Their manager, Nick De'Ath, stood framed in the doorway.

'OK guys? Have fun, go mad. And remember, they love you out there!'

Connor smiled. 'Thanks Nick,' he said. 'That's just what we needed to hear right now.' He hugged Nick, feeling the soft leather of his designer-label black jacket and inhaling the sweet citrus tones of his Boucheron aftershave. Stepping from the dressing room, Connor ran to catch the other three, who stood waiting by the steps which led up to the stage.

A slow handclap had started around the stadium, the crowd were getting restive, but it stopped as a booming southern voice drawled out over the public address system.

'Ladies and Gentlemen. The moment you have been waiting for, direct from London, England, four young guys who we know are the very best... it's time for BANNED!'

1: Dean

Beads of sweat ran down Dean's brow, and with a dismissive gesture he wiped his eyes. It had been a terrible mistake to wear so many layers of clothing, he told himself. Now here he was, wringing wet, nervous as hell, and unsure as to why he had let his friend TJ talk him into coming to these auditions.

At the time it had seemed like a good idea. Trying out for a new boy band. Why not? It would be a laugh, and who knows, someone there might like him. He stood as good a chance as any of the hopeful hunks standing around the draughty waiting room.

But just wait until he caught up with TJ – who had taken one look at the place and the various shades of attractive young man populating it and fled. Some friend he was. The next time Dean met up with TJ and his current squeeze Phil (the newest addition to TJ's catalogue of boyfriends), Phil would hear a few unpleasant truths about TJ, a certain public toilet and a road cleaner called Derek. That would show him.

The thought of toilets brought Dean out of this self-pitying reverie and he realised that his bladder was on the verge of exploding. There had to be somewhere to go.

'Er... excuse me.' Dean stammered out, tapping the shoulder of the tanned Adonis in the ripped T-shirt standing next to him. 'Do you know where the toilets are?' The hunk surveyed Dean, contemptuously eyeing his sweatshirt, jeans and trainers. His expression said 'Who the hell do you think you are?', but with a vague nod of the head he pointed to the door at the far end of the waiting room.

Stupid fucker. Dean had had much experience of that kind of man. The ones who thought themselves better than everyone else because they had good looks and a body to die for. The ones his gran called 'handsome and knows it'. He had lost count of the number of times that he had approached such a guy at his local bar and tried to engage him in conversation and been rebuffed. Still, it was their loss. They wouldn't be getting the best blow-job in years from his expert mouth. Fuck them. And fuck you Mr T-shirt, he thought as he strolled nonchalantly towards the toilet, hands in pockets, trying to look cool and hiding his slowly rising tide of nerves.

As he made his way, picking through the sprawled legs and bags of the various auditionees, he squeezed his fists tightly into a ball. You are as good as any of them, and a lot more attractive. Mentally he praised himself, and why shouldn't he? Dean was an attractive young man in his early twenties, his dark hair cut short and stylish, with large, brown eyes, and a strong face that he knew to be very masculine. He occasionally worked out, and was proud of his physique, nicely toned, and with much admired broad shoulders, tapering down to a narrow waist. He was also very happy with what he had between his legs. He had been lucky in that department... sizeable but not overwhelmingly so. A good mouthful is how he liked to put it.

As he approached the toilet, a camp voice called out from behind him, 'Number thirty-two! Who has number thirty-two?' A record company person, probably a glorified tea-boy, was standing by the door to the dance studio, clutching a clipboard and waving his arms about in a fey manner, giving the impression of a grounded helicopter. Mr T-shirt raised his hand and made his way over,

walking with a distinct swagger, his muscles bulging from the confines of the tight, white cotton, aware of the many eyes burning
into him with undisguised lust. As he approached the door, he put
out a hand to shake, but must have stood on his untied shoe-lace,
tripping up and nearly falling flat on his face, grasping at the assistant for support. A burst of relieved laughter sprang up from the
waiting auditionees, and Dean suppressed a chuckle. Serves you
right.

Pushing open the toilet door, Dean looked around the empty
convenience, small, fairly smelly, and with the obligatory condom
machine on the wall, hanging losely by one screw, at a drunken
angle. He had been in some fairly disagreeable lavatories in his life
but this one took the award for most unpleasant. Not that Dean
considered himself a cottage queen. Not at all. If he found himself
passing a public toilet he experienced a deep desire to enter. Never
one to miss the chance of finding Mr Right, he would always give
the facilities the once-over, in the hope of standing next to a gorgeous guy, who would possess a delicious dick, and who'd want to
look after him for the rest of his span on the planet.

Being raised in a small Midlands town, he had had to be careful though. If his parents ever knew that he frequented such places
they would have died of shame and embarrassment. They knew
about his homosexuality of course, he had sat them down exactly
one day after his nineteenth birthday, and told them the truth.
They had pretended to be accepting and supportive, but he knew
that they had great problems dealing with the shattering disclo-
sure. A month later he had moved down to London, found a job
in a bookshop and had been doing very nicely, thank you.

It was when he realised that life had become a little staid and
boring that he took TJ's advice and decided to audition for the new
band. Where was the problem with that? Who knows, they might
even like him. Fat chance of that, he said out loud, looking at his
reflection in the smeared mirror above the metal urinal. Standing

there, he pulled out his dick and began to piss. With one hand on the mirror in front, and the other on himself, Dean revelled in the relief of emptying his bladder, sighing softly, unaware of the opening door behind him.

'Hi. You here to audition?' Dean looked up and stared into the eyes of the guy who had entered and taken his place, standing next to Dean. Perhaps a little too close? Dean gave him a good look over. Very nice. In his mid-thirties, well-groomed, dark hair gelled back, with a strong face, dark eyes, and a firm mouth, which twitched at the corner with a slight smile. He was taller than Dean by a good twelve inches and looked down at the lad appreciatively. His leather jacket rustled slightly as he moved, unzipping his chinos and pulling out his dick. He smelt nice too.

'Yes, I guess so. I'm beginning to think it was a really dumb idea, though.' Dean finished peeing, shook himself and crossed to the dingy sink.

'Come on now. I think you stand a good chance. You are as good looking as any of those posers out there. And if you can move and sing as well as you look...' The man had also stopped pissing but he still stood at the urinal, his head turned, watching Dean washing his hands, his eyes fixed on the back of his head.

Dean wiped his hands on the back of his jeans and turned round. 'Do you really think so?' He glanced at himself in the mirror, noting his closely cropped hair and charming smile. This guy was right of course. He stood as good a chance as anyone. He had personality, a sense of humour, could move well, and had a pretty good voice. Why shouldn't he be worth considering?

The guy at the urinal hadn't moved, and Dean folded his arms, leaning back against the sink, taking the chance to look the guy over properly. He must work out, as he seemed in good shape, and his skin was smooth and slightly tanned, a very nice specimen of manhood, Dean thought, running his tongue over his dry lips. He certainly filled the tight, soft pale-blue T-shirt he was wearing, and his khaki chinos were stretched invitingly across his firm buttocks.

'Just be yourself and don't be nervous.' The guy stood back from the urinal, turning slightly so that Dean could see him shaking his cock, which was swiftly growing in size. Was this a come-on? Dean couldn't take his eyes off the monster that was now standing proudly in front of him. What if his number was called and he wasn't outside to hear it? Still, he mused, it is a very nice cock, and obviously in need of a little attention. Why not?

He crossed the tiled floor and stood a few inches away from the man. 'So what should I do to calm my nerves?' He stood, waiting for an answer, his arms crossed, his tongue flicking the corner of his dry lips.

'I think you have a very good idea, don't you?' The man turned fully facing Dean, his cock standing straight out from his body, a slight curve upwards at the end, small wisps of hair framing the monster, just poking out from the zipper.

'Should we be doing this?' Dean's voice cracked as he spoke. The man gave no reply, but put out a hand and rested it on Dean's shoulder, exerting a slight pressure downwards, pushing him to his knees.

Dean had seen some big dicks in his time, but this was one of the most impressive. Circumcised, with a huge pale head, it seemed too big to take. Reaching out a tentative hand, Dean grasped it, his fingers barely meeting around the sizeable girth. Kneeling forward he let his nose tickle the end, inhaling the scent of some medicated soap. This was obviously a clean man. Good. Dean liked men who appreciated the finer points of hygiene. A horrid memory sprang to the front of Dean's mind... a package holiday to Tunisia, a handsome young carpet seller, and a blow-job in the back-room of his shop. Enthusiastically kneeling before the Tunisian, Dean pulled out the tanned cock from the straining zip before him to be confronted with a large cheesy head. Dean shivered with disgust at the image.

11

'Anything wrong with it?' The man looked down, a puzzled expression on his face. Dean answered by letting his tongue flick across the end of the cock, lightly brushing the skin, then poking around the end slit. Lovingly he let his tongue wander about the two huge velvet lobes, following the curves around, until he had encircled the head with saliva. Now was the moment of truth. Could he fit this mammoth creation in his mouth? He would have a fucking good try.

Inhaling as he went, Dean let the head slide in, aware of the gasp of pleasure that the man gave. Loosening his jaw, Dean found he could accommodate the entire shaft, and filling his mouth with saliva, he let it slide down, the head now touching the back of his throat. Dean felt that surge of excitement, that crackle of joy, knowing that he had another man's cock in his mouth. One of his greatest loves was to suck, and here he was doing it, to an attractive man, with a huge cock, and in a public place!

Realising that time was of the essence, Dean set to, sucking for all he was worth, letting his mouth slide back and forward, pulling away to lick around the cock-head before plunging down again, feeling the discomfort of the man's fingers, clamped about his head, holding him in the suppliant position. His sucking began to increase in speed, as the solid shaft, wet with spittle, filled his very being. At this moment there was nothing but this cock and his willing mouth. Nothing but the sensation of a fantastic blow-job. Dean's eyes were tightly shut, relying totally on the feelings coming from his throat and mouth.

The man seemed to be enjoying it as much as Dean. His hips kept up the bucking motion, forcing his cock further down Dean's throat than he thought possible. He was giving out soft moans of delight, little grunts of ecstasy bursting from him, his eyes fixed on the young man kneeling before him. His fingers began to push at Dean's head with a harsh ferocity. He was about to come. Dean knew it. With a chuckle, he pulled back and stared at the dripping cock.

The man gasped. 'You bastard! What a time to stop.' Dean smiled up, his mouth ringed with spit.

'I just wanted you to hold back a bit. It would have been over too soon.'

'Fuck that!' The man grabbed the back of Dean's head and thrust his cock down his throat with one almighty push. Dean gagged at the pressure, he wanted to stop. Fingers once again held tight on his head, keeping him down on his knees, keeping his mouth full of this stranger's hardness. The rhythm of the pounding increased incredibly, until with a sudden grunt of triumph, the man threw back his head and shot his load down the throat, pulling out half-way through, splattering some of the salty semen across Dean's face.

'My God!' The man staggered back, rapidly stuffing his softening cock back inside his jeans, and staring at Dean's dripping face. 'That was incredible. You've done that before, young man!' He reached into his jacket pocket and pulled out some paper tissues, handing them to Dean with a smile. 'I should get cleaned up if I were you. You've got an audition to go to.'

Dean sank back onto his heels and grimaced. 'Don't remind me, I'm nervous enough as it is.' Then with a surge of enthusiasm and energy he sprang up and went across to the dirty, cracked mirror on the toilet wall, wiping away the streaks of spunk, then giving his face a quick splash of tepid water.

'I think I'm ready now. Do you want to go out first? We don't want people to jump to the wrong conclusion!' Dean turned round, but the man had gone.

Everyone's head turned to watch Dean as he emerged from the toilet. Shit. Was it that obvious? Did they all know what he'd just been doing? He pulled himself up and crossed to a lone plastic chair and sat, folding his arms defiantly, and looking down saw his flies were wide open. With a swift jerk, he pulled up the zip, and stared around the room. The man was nowhere to be seen. Where had he vanished to?

The camp assistant yanked open the door to the audition room and called out, his high-pitched voice ringing around the assembled auditionees. 'Number fifty-three... Dean West. Dean West? Are you here darling?'

It was now or never. Dean eased himself to his feet and stepped forward. His shoes squeaked on the tiled flooring. Oh God. What if they squeaked in the audition? Was he making a laughing stock of himself? Why not just run away?

'There you are, handsome. Come along, they don't bite you know.' The assistant took Dean's hand firmly and pulled him inside, slamming the door behind him. 'This is Dean West.' He felt hands propelling him to the centre of the polished wood flooring, and he flinched as he saw two men sat at a table, in front of a mirrored wall. It was bad enough he had to prove himself to these men, but to have to watch himself do it as well!

'Hi there.' Dean looked up, his eyes focusing on a middle-aged guy sat behind the centre of the table. He had a crooked smile, a face full and smooth and the long hair at the back of his balding head was pulled into a tight pony-tail.

'Dean, is it? OK, I'm Rudy Garland.' (If that's your real name then I'm Madonna, thought Dean.) 'This is an informal session, for us to see some guys perform with a view to forming a new boy band. We want to put together four young men, who will be the pop sensation of the twenty-first century. Young men with balls, if you'll pardon the pun, who will get the teenage girls creaming their knickers, the teenage boys wishing they were as famous, and the gay community jacking off in delight.' (A terrible way of putting it but Dean let that pass.)

'Do you think you have what it takes?' Rudy folded his arms and waited. The air was heavy with the smell of sweat. A bead broke out on Dean's forehead and he gulped. Suddenly his throat was dry, and he could taste the salt of the toilet guy's juice on his lips.

The toilet guy. Looking straight at him.

Dean stared at the other guy behind the desk, the one with sunglasses, a leather jacket and a wide smile. He focused his attention away from Rudy and returned the other guy's stare. It was him. The one he'd just sucked off. Fuck. Now I've blown it. Dean chuckled to himself at the irony of that thought, a bigger, heartier laugh bubbling up, desperate to burst out. Biting his fist, he tried to concentrate on Rudy's question.

'Yes, Rudy. I think I've got it. I'm attractive, intelligent, my voice is pretty good, and I can dance. In fact I'm really flexible.' He looked at the man, who grinned and took off his sunglasses. 'I think I'm just what you are looking for,' Dean continued.

Rudy turned to the other man who sat forward and placed his hands on the table top. 'Dean. My name is Nick, I'm the man wanting to form this new band. I think you could well be just what we are looking for. You seem a pleasant young guy, who definitely has good looks. I think you also have other hidden talents, which could be a great asset to the band. Now if you can sing and dance, you'll be in with a very good chance.'

2: Joe and Paul

'Mr De'Ath will see you now. It's the third door on the left down the corridor, just past the *Pulp Fiction* poster.' The voluptuous receptionist smiled warmly at the two lads, and went back to her computer keyboard.

'Thanks.' Joe nudged Paul in the ribs and they marched nervously down the passage. Raising a fist to knock on the door, Joe jumped as a voice called 'Come in' from somewhere in the office's interior. With a gulp, Joe pushed open the door and looked around. The office seemed to be made entirely of glass, with only the barest minimum of brick wall in evidence. The vista outside was incredible, a view over London that Joe and Paul had never thought existed.

'Fuck me!' Paul blurted out, immediately reddening with embarrassment.

'Perhaps we'll save that until after our business is finished.' Nick stood from behind his desk at the far side of the room and extended his hand in greeting. 'Welcome... er... Paul Moss and Joe Turner, isn't it?'

'That's right. Thank you ever so much for seeing us.' Joe took the offered hand and shook it. The grasp was firm but friendly. Nick smiled.

'Please sit down.' He gestured to the two tubular chairs in front of his desk, then sat back down, lacing his fingers together on the desk top. He surveyed the two young men sat across from him with interest. Working in the heady and often glamorous world of pop music, he came into contact with many wannabe stars, youngsters who believed that they had that extra something, that spark of talent and charisma to make them a success.

There was certainly something about these two. They did exude an air of confidence, and were good lookers into the bargain. Joe had an angelic air about him, his sky-blue eyes peeping out from behind the floppy strawberry blond fringe of hair, which he kept sweeping back with a strong hand. He had the look of a guy who worked out, a compact, lean, muscled body hidden beneath the bright clinging Scooby Doo T-shirt, and his trousers seemed nicely filled too, that tell-tale bulge obviously there, nestled between the muscular thighs.

Paul on the other hand was the complete opposite. Of a larger, slightly chunky build, his body not so worked on as Joe's, but an aura of friendly charm, his gaze less assured, more nervous, his voice having that sexy cockney tinge to it, implying a bit of delightful rough from the East End. He had gone for the current trends in fashion and style, his dark hair gelled down across his forehead in equal strands. Both very nice. Both equally fuckable. He smiled at them.

'Now I have your letter here. I believe you wanted to see me to ask my advice about getting on in the music industry. You know that it is a notoriously difficult business?'

Paul nodded vigorously. 'Yes, we know. But you see Mr De'Ath...'

'Nick, please.'

'Errr... Nick then, we think we have got what it takes to be really successful. We write all our own music, we play instruments, we've got personality and stage presence... And, well, we just think we should be given a chance.' He stumbled to a stop, looking down at the plush carpet, his face blushing again.

'You certainly have high opinions of yourselves, I will say that. Now, what is your band called?'

Joe crossed his arms and grinned sheepishly. 'The Big Boys.'

'Interesting name. What's the reason behind that?' Nick gazed unblinkingly at Joe, who returned the stare. 'Well... we liked the name, and it sounds good and er...'

'I hope you live up to your stage soubriquet.'

Paul looked puzzled. 'Our what?'

'Your band name. If you call yourselves big boys, it seems only right and fair that you should be.' A palpable tension seemed to be hovering in the air about the three men.

Joe broke the silence, shifting a little in his seat and spreading his legs slightly, easing himself forward an inch or two, his tight trousers emphasising the bulge within them. 'I've had no complaints so far. Eh, Paul?'

'No. It's wonderful... It's so big that I have trouble taking it...' He stopped, realising he had given the game away.

Nick sat back in his chair, his hand behind his head and smiled at the two lads. At last. He knew it. They did have that conspiratorial air of lovers. That indefinable quality that two people have when totally at ease in each other's presence.

'So we can safely assume that the two of you are on intimate terms. How long have you been together?'

Neither of the lads spoke.

'Come on. I am a very understanding man. More understanding than you would expect. You can tell me everything. An artiste has to trust his manager implicitly and there must be no secrets between them. If I am going to be your manager then you must say...'

'Our manager?' Joe burst out in a surprised shout.

'Indeed. I do think you two have a lot of potential... if guided in the right way. You won't know this but last night I popped down to the Oak Tree public house and saw your set. The audience seemed to be enjoying themselves and you performed well. You have good voices, strong and earthy... I like that. I can see the germ of success within you, but you need to be taken in hand. If you are willing of course. Are you?'

Paul turned to look at Joe, his eyes wide with wonderment and disbelief.

'Yes please!' they sang out in unison.

'Now let's get back to what we were just touching on before. I presume you are both gay, and boyfriends, yes?'

An uneasy silence fell on the two. Joe broke it by saying 'Yes, we are, and have been for the last year. We don't like to talk about it. Isn't it a terrible hindrance to a pop star? Don't people turn off you if you are found to be gay?'

'Yes and no. They tend to be supportive if you are honest with them. Look at Elton John. Or George Michael. Now that George has come out of the public lavatory and told all, he is just as popular... it's the music that sells, not what you do in bed with each other. Elton has even worked with Disney for fuck's sake.'

Paul grinned boyishly. 'I know. I love *The Lion King* to bits. Ouch.' Joe had dug him in the ribs again.

'Nick doesn't want to know about your sordid habits.'

'Oh, but I *do*.' Nick stood and crossed the room to a large glass cabinet by the door. 'Drink?' He poured out three tumblers of a clear liquid and plunked ice cubes in each from a large golden icebucket.

'Cheers.' Nick raised his glass.

'Up yours.' Joe grinned again, a charming lopsided smile that lit up his face.

'Very possibly.' Nick grinned back and perched himself on the corner of his desk, his legs spread wide, his groin somehow emphasised in the clinging black leather trousers.

'So. Who does what to whom? Which of you is passive, and

which active? Who has the biggest cock? Do you have any little kinks or peccadilloes? Do tell. I promise you it will go no further.'

Paul downed a mouthful of his drink and with a choking cry grabbed his throat. 'Fucking hell... what is this? Nearly took my tonsils out.'

Casually throwing down the last of his drink, Nick placed the glass on the desk and folded his arms. 'Slovakian Vodka. I picked it up on a video shoot in Bratislava last month. A touch rough but it grows on you.'

Joe took a sip and licked his lips. 'Hmm. Goes down nicely. And so does Paul. If you really want to know. We do everything. We both like to suck and fuck, although Paul is more passive. We occasionally use toys, dildos or vibrators, balls on a string, sometimes cock-rings. We love sex. In the time we've been together we have had no need to stray. It is one of the things that keeps us together. We know that when we get home we'll have each other, and it doesn't get any better than that. What else do you want to know?'

He stared defiantly up at Nick who had placed a hand across his crotch, lightly resting the fingers there. Joe wasn't sure but he thought the bulge was growing slowly larger. Paul looked away, his eyes not meeting Nick's.

'Interesting. So you've never played around with other guys at all?'

'No.' Joe was categorical. 'We haven't actually done that yet. But I suppose we could if we wanted to... variety is the spice of life, as some smart git said somewhere. Why do you ask? Have you got any suggestions? People we might like to meet or places we might like to go?'

Joe slid forward a little more in his seat and let his hand gently fall across his own crotch, just allowing the tips of his fingers to gently brush the end of his cock, the shape of which was becoming more obvious through the brushed cotton of his trousers.

Paul watched the two men, his eyes locked on the sight of

them playing, toying with each other. But what did it mean? Did Nick want to do it? Here and now? It looked like he did. Up to now they had always provided for each other's sexual needs... they had never wanted to have sex with anyone else. Paul rubbed his stomach which felt empty and nervous. Here was another man, an attractive one at that, offering himself.

They could end up having a threesome, and he wasn't sure if he wanted to experience that. Somehow it seemed wrong to him. He had always thought that sex should be a private act between two consenting men. But here was the chance to try it. Well, why not? With Nick's well-defined body and what appeared to be a very big cock, there was no reason why Paul and Joe shouldn't have a little bit of excitement with him. It was time to make a decision.

With one sure motion, Paul stood. If he was to do it he might as well enjoy it. He placed his glass down on the desk beside Nick's and then knelt before him. Quickly and with purpose he undid the zipper on the leather trousers, unhooked the belt and reached inside for the now hard cock.

Nick gasped at the contact and leaned back a little more, allowing Paul easier access.

'Hmmm... very nice.' Appreciation was written all over Paul's face as he leant in to the cock-head, and with one slow, practised motion he grasped it tightly, anchoring his fist about the base of the massive shaft, the trembling purple head free and unfettered.

Joe stood and came to Paul's side, watching intently as his partner got to work. He was so surprised that Paul was actually doing this... up to now he had shunned any thought of other people, and sometimes he seemed a little jealous and possessive. If Joe had inadvertently looked at another guy whilst out shopping, Paul would go quiet and, if pressed, ask if he wasn't good enough for Joe. But suddenly he had changed, become a different person. Joe wasn't sure if he liked it.

With a sigh of delight, Paul kissed the swollen head, a gentle peck with his dry lips, then running his tongue around his mouth, he did it again, leaving a small glistening trail of saliva connecting his mouth and Nick's cock. Shifting around until he was comfortable, Paul then let his tongue glide across the silky smooth head, letting the end of his tongue dart into the tiny oozing slit, before lapping with a studied intent at the bulbous end, slurping and wetting it totally.

He sat back on his heels for an instant, as if sizing up the monster before him, weighing the balls with his other hand, deciding if he could actually take it all in. He knew that he could. Swirling saliva about his warm mouth and throat, lubricated and ready, he clamped his lips about the giant head, then slowly, surely, inch by solid inch, he eased his mouth down it, feeling every vein and artery as he went, his grasp around the base not letting up.

Nick's head fell back, a gurgle of intense amazement burst from it. He couldn't believe what he was feeling, what sensations this dark-haired wonder was giving him.

'Oh, fuck! That's incredible. Oh yeah, more... more...' Nick groaned in ecstasy. For him there was now nothing else in the universe apart from his cock and the mind-shattering blow-job it was getting.

A steady rhythm had begun. Paul let his mouth pull back, easing the pressure on his stretched and aching mouth, before plunging down again, filling his throat with the fleshy rod, sucking with such power that Nick was convinced the end of his cock would burst. Gradually the speed of the sucking increased, and Nick's groans of pleasure became louder. Without warning he grabbed the back of Paul's head and began fucking his mouth, with fast, steady strokes, filling him utterly, banging against the back of his throat, provoking the need to gag. Forcing down that reflex, Paul closed his eyes and concentrated on the motion of the bucking cock, back and forth, back and forth, his grip on the hanging ball-sac tightening. It felt as if Nick was about to come. He tensed up and his breathing grew heavier.

'What about me?' Joe pulled Paul away, who sat back on his haunches, his mouth ringed with spit and pre-cum. He had seen what Paul was doing and a strange feeling overcame him. The erotic nature of the situation really made his heart beat faster, and his head swim. He needed to be involved.

'You little bastard!' Nick cried out, a slight grin on his face, wiping moisture from his eyes.

'Maybe. But I want some of that. Now strip.' There was a strange tension in his voice that neither Paul nor Nick wanted to argue with, and so with a few quick moves they had shucked their clothes and all three stood naked.

Paul looked about him. 'Shouldn't we pull the curtains or something? Or lock the door?'

'Don't worry, no one can see us up here. And my secretary is under orders not to disturb us.' Nick grabbed his dick and ran his fist up and down its length, encouraging the hard-on that stood proud before him.

'Good. Now get up on the table.' Joe gestured to Paul who clambered up, standing next to Nick, his cock rapidly swelling from its heavy semi-recumbent state. Without a word, Nick shifted his head and took Paul's now hard dick in his mouth. He sucked and sucked, taking it with pleasure, savouring the whole length of it. It was a glorious specimen, cut, very thick, not over-long, but with a large head, and a hard shaft that grew bigger towards its base.

Joe knelt and took Nick's cock in his hand, feeling it throb strongly. He wanked it slowly, sliding his fist up and down the skin from the swollen crown to the thickened base, surrounded by a thick tuft of soft pubic hair, revelling in the feel of its solidity, and the dimensions of the head where it swelled out bigger than the shaft. With his other hand he cupped the bollocks, huge and pendulous, perhaps too huge to take both in his mouth. He let his tongue start. Flicking the tip across the skin of the bollocks made Nick jump, but still he kept up the rhythm of his oral attack on Paul. Then with a deep suck Joe pulled first one then the other ball into his widening mouth, savouring their spongy hardness, stretching them away from the body, sensing the cock above twitching, desperate for more attention.

That could wait though. The balls needed attention. They needed to be worked on, and Joe was the man to do it. His tongue curled about them, sensing every nuance, pulling on one then the other, his fist grasped tightly about the cock, before sucking them both into his mouth, slippery with saliva, and fiercely stretching them away from Nick's trembling body.

God this was wonderful. And he knew that the joy of the prick was soon to come. Letting each bollock pop from his lips, he let his experienced tongue wander up to the base of the throbbing cock, then leave a shiny snail-trail of spit along the underside of the monster. Without any sign of warning he enclosed his mouth about the head, swirling his tongue, licking and smacking, and with one swift inhalation of breath, swallowed it whole.

Nick's breathing increased rapidly, he didn't want to stop working on Paul, but he wanted to savour the twin sensations of sucking a cock, while being sucked himself. He opened his eyes and looked up. Paul's face was squeezed into a mask of determination and delight, while Joe looked back at him, his blue eyes holding Nick's gaze, daring him to want to stop, knowing that he never would.

As if one entity, with only one body between them, Joe and Nick began to suck in unison, each stroke, each beat, each breath moving together, Paul responding pushing his hips forward, intent on keeping the rhythm so easily formed by the three of them.

It didn't take long. Nick could feel again that boiling sensation deep in his loins and could see that Paul wasn't too far away from coming. Joe, as before, suddenly stopped, pulling away and kneeling back.

'Shall we?' His voice was breathy, his fist pumping hard on his own sizeable, rigid dick, following the arching curve of it up to his navel. He seemed desperate for release. Without stopping, Nick nodded, speeding up his mouth, plunging faster down Paul's aching hardness. Leaning swiftly in, Joe started to suck again, wildly, passionately, willing the seed out of Nick's depths. In but a few seconds he knew he had succeeded.

A warm, salty gush of liquid shot against the back of his throat, and with several gulps Joe drank it down. Bolt after bolt poured down as Nick came. Joe raised his eyes and watched as Paul shot his load too, pulling away and letting the milky juice spatter across Nick's face, dripping from his eyelashes, coursing down the length of his nose. Nick put out his tongue and licked a few drops from around his mouth, smiling as Paul jerked out the last of his cum.

'Well... boys! That was a very nice way to meet... pass me that box of tissues, would you Paul?' He took the offered box and watched as Paul jumped down from the desk, his half-hard cock bouncing against his balls as he did so.

'Come here.' Joe reached out an arm to Paul and held him tight. Their lips met and they kissed, tongues darting into each other's mouths. Paul chuckled.

'What's up?' Joe asked, looking puzzled.

'Nothing really. It's just that I can still taste Nick's cum in your mouth. It's nice.'

Nick gave a throaty laugh, wiping the spunk from his face. 'You are an interesting couple. I can see that representing you two is going to be a real joy, not a chore – if this little escapade was anything to go by. I look forward to many such times to come. Perhaps at my flat next time... if you don't object to sex with a much older man?'

Joe grinned and ran his fingers through his hair, pushing the fringe from his eyes. 'You're not that old surely! Anyway, you've got a fucking gorgeous body, a great cock and you know what to do with it.'

'Well, here's to the future.' Nick poured out three more glasses of vodka, raising his in a mock salute. 'I think the future for you two is distinctly rosy. In fact I have a little project that I am currently working on... I recently held some auditions for a new band I am forming. They weren't particularly successful. So far I have only managed to find one member... but I think I may have found two more. Cheers!'

3: Connor

The crowd were becoming restless. Connor peeped out through the flimsy curtain and saw at least a hundred men, of all shapes and sizes, bottles and glasses in hand, a haze of cigarette-smoke hanging about them clouding his vision.

He looked down at what he was wearing, the ripped jeans, the workman's boots, the black rubber vest, and for the millionth time wondered what he was doing.

'You are making money to pay the rent,' he said to himself. 'It's only a small club. No one knows you. So what if they want to see you taking off your clothes and waving your knob in the air. You've got nothing to be ashamed of down there, in fact you should be proud of what you've got.'

He reached a hand down and grabbed his crotch, he could feel the surge of blood into his already hardened cock. 'They will like what they see, you will be the best out there and you will get the prize money. Sorted.'

Letting the curtain fall back, Connor surveyed his competition. A young lad, with a spotty complexion, dressed as a schoolboy, complete with cap, tie, and satchel containing several condoms, and rubber articles that Connor shuddered to see. He was struggling with a shoe-lace that he was trying to tie about his cock and bollocks, but his clumsy fingers were fumbling, picking

29

at a knot that had appeared. A nice cock too. Long, with a pale pink helmet.

A muscled black guy stood against the wall, quite handsome, with shaggy dreadlocks, combat trousers and a cock so large Connor couldn't imagine it ever getting hard.

Lastly himself. Connor Reid. An inexperienced guy from Dublin, with no money, no regular job, no boyfriend and no prospects. An ordinary guy, with brown eyes, brown hair, and a nice smile. A guy who'd left the family and the farm behind him with his savings in his pocket, and made his way to the bright lights of London, hoping for a fresh start. A guy who'd so far been sorely disappointed with what the capital had to offer, and had finally resorted to the dole, going through the fortnightly demeaning routine of queuing for hours to sign his name and get an insignificant cheque through the post two days later.

How on earth could he have the nerve to waltz into the amateur strip night at the Three Feathers and expect to win? It took more than a big cock. It took guts and courage and style and charm. Deep down he knew he possessed those attributes, it was just a case of making them surface before the crowd.

He ran his hands across his head, feeling the softness of just washed hair. He looked at his reflection in the grubby dressing room mirror. His deep brown eyes stared back, framed by the soft waves of his brown hair, a strong face, with full, kissable lips. His body was in good shape, and he had deliberately chosen to wear a simple outfit, black denim jeans, mountain boots and a black rubber vest, a tight white jockstrap nestling comfortably about his cock and balls. He had wondered whether to enhance their size by doing what the schoolboy had done and tying something around their base, keeping the flow of blood in the excited shaft. No. If they didn't like the look of what he had without the need for artificial help, then fuck them.

'Just get a grip.'

The black guy looked up, surprised at Connor's vocal outburst, and smiled at him.

'Sorry,' Connor was sheepish. 'Did I say that out loud?'

'You did, man. This is your first time, isn't it? I can tell. You have the look of a rabbit caught in the headlights of a car. Scared stiff, but rooted to the spot. Am I right?'

Connor laughed, the first time he had done so all day. 'Absolutely right. I've never done anything like this before... I figured it couldn't be that difficult, but now... seeing the people out there, ready to jeer at me, it doesn't seem such a good idea.'

The black guy put out a hand. 'My name's Richie.'

'Connor.'

'Scottish?'

'Irish. From the land of the bogs and the little people.'

A puzzled look corrugated Richie's face. 'Eh?'

'Dublin. You know, leprechauns and peat...'

'Yeah, whatever. Anyway, you've got nothing to worry about. The crowd here are smashing, they'll love you, nice bod, cute face and a lovely bit of meat down there... you can't fail.'

'Really?'

'Really.' Richie crossed the small dressing room and put a comforting arm around Connor's shoulders. 'You'll knock 'em dead, darling.' His fingers eased down from Connor's neck to his chest, where they dextrously tweaked his nipples, through the confining rubber vest.

'No worries. They'll love this. Just don't be afraid to show it. Be confident, imagine they are all inferior beings, not worthy of seeing your cock and it'll be a lot easier. Treat them like children... give them the tasty treat of your bits and pieces and they'll cheer you to heaven.'

His fingers grabbed Connor's crotch, wrapping themselves about the sizeable bulge. 'Hmm, very nice. I wouldn't mind a bit of that later if you are in the mood.'

Connor was shocked. 'Er... I don't know. Ask me later, after the show... I might be in a state of deep depression.'

He had never had sex with a black guy before and though the possibility was tempting, he didn't quite have the nerve to do it. If he was to be totally honest, he hadn't had that much experience of gay sex at all. Growing up in an insular Irish farming community, homosexuality wasn't even known about, let alone done. He had taken a weekend trip to Belfast on his nineteenth birthday, hoping to get a first taste of what men did with men, but had ended up in a disappointing, supposedly gay, club which only served soft drinks. The handsome young man who'd approached Connor, and engaged him in conversation, was charming and friendly, but back at Connor's hotel room had announced that he only did it for money. Shocked and disgusted, Connor asked him to leave, and so he spent a lonely, sleepless night after wanking himself off. Besides, glancing again at Richie's mammoth organ, he didn't know if he would be able to handle that much cock. And would it be a disappointment if he couldn't get that monster hard?

'I certainly will... I love a nice bit of white-boy meat. Love to get my lips about a solid white dick...' He stopped as the curtains parted and Bob, the pub's grey-haired, overweight owner stepped through.

'Right then my lovelies. It's show time. Richie, you are on first, then Davey, then you young Connor. Good luck, and don't be afraid to show them all you've got!' He patted Connor on the arse and vanished.

Connor gulped as a screech of feedback howled around the noisy bar. 'Right then everyone. Thank you for coming here tonight. This is the first in what I hope will be many such nights here at the Three Feathers. We have three gorgeous stallions for you tonight, eager and willing to show you their talents, and if I'm any judge of knob sizes they've got a lot of talent! Give them all the encouragement you can, please, so let's have a big hand for our first contestant. He comes from Wembley, he is 34 years old, and his name is Richie... let's hear it for the Dreadlock Dynamo!'

A burst of muted applause greeted Richie as he stepped through the curtains and disappeared onto the tiny, tinsel-decked stage. Connor sat on a stool, taking several deep breaths and tried to calm himself. The sounds of the bar seemed to indicate that they were enjoying Richie's performance, and the whoops and cheers grew as he shucked more of his clothes, until he stood naked and aroused. The reaction almost raised the roof, and Connor listened, downhearted, sure that this guy would win.

Five minutes later a riot of cheering greeted Richie as he bounced back into the dressing room, dripping with baby oil, his cock swinging menacingly at half-mast, the huge purple head slapping against his meaty thighs.

'Wow, that was fucking amazing!' He pounced on Connor, scooping him up in his arms. Connor could feel the semi-hard cock pushing against his own bulge. The sensation was not unpleasant.

'And now...' Bob's voice filled the air. 'We have a familiar face to a lot of you. One of our regulars has decided to show you what he's made of... I think you'll be pleased... let's hear it for our very own schoolboy, Dirty Davey!'

The other guy straightened his tie and pushed past Connor and Richie, snootily ignoring them.

'Bitch.' Richie spoke almost under his breath.

'What's up with him?' Connor pushed himself away and perched on the edge of the grimy sink, his eyes darting between the black guy's face and his bobbing prick.

'Oh, she thinks she is going to win, just because she slept with two of the judges. Slut.' Unable to contain his annoyance, Richie kicked the stool, which fell over with a loud clatter. 'Still, it's only money, isn't it? It's love that makes the world go round, or in my case a bloody good fuck. How about it then?'

33

He stood in front of Connor, gently stroking his fist up and down the length of his mammoth black tool, coaxing it to its maximum hardness, almost daring Connor not to react. Unable to move, Connor just stared at it, his mouth dry, all thoughts of the contest banished from his mind.

His hand trembled as he reached out to touch the monster. His fingers began to curl around the tremendous girth, and his eyes widened as it palpably grew in his grasp. It got harder and bigger until Connor could no longer get his fingers to meet around its hefty shaft.

'Go on. If you want to.' Richie gave a throaty chuckle and waited for Connor to sink to his knees. The Irish lad paused, his heart pounding.

Before he could go any further, the curtains parted and Davey appeared, a scowl of anger corrugating his spotty features. 'They laughed... they fucking laughed. How dare they? Bastards!' He grabbed his shoulder bag and began throwing his belongings into it, before diving into his clothes.

'Well. It's your turn, baby. Give them hell!' Richie turned and started to pull on his trousers.

The avuncular voice of Bob piped up again. 'And our last contestant is a lovely lad from across the Irish Sea. Give a big hand for the extremely well-endowed Connor!'

With a deep breath and a last look in the mirror, Connor pulled the curtains apart and stepped into the glare of the lights.

Looking back, Connor had to admit that he enjoyed himself. The crowd had seemed appreciative, and they certainly gave him a loud reception. As the track started – 'Music' by Madonna – they started to clap, encouraging him to do his best.

Swaying to the beat, moving in time to the music, Connor got into the swing of things. Shucking his boots and jeans, then peeling off his rubber vest, he posed in his pristine white jock-strap, his erection fully apparent as it stood pointing up to his stomach, hard and firm, confined beneath the thin cotton material, straining for release, the head just poking out over the elastic waistband. Bending forward, he exposed his arsehole to the audience, who whooped with delight.

'Show us your cock!' someone shouted from the back of the bar.

With one swift tug, he pulled off the jock-strap and spun round to face the audience. Something about this situation excited him. A sea of faces gazing up at him, drinking in his handsome face, well-defined body and rigid hard-on. This was a real thrill. He knew that his uncut cock was stiff and proud, curving up magnificently towards his stomach, banging against his navel as he moved.

With a swift tug he pulled back the foreskin, showing the shapely cock-head to its full advantage. Cheers and yells filled the air. They were cheering for him, and he loved it. And his big cock. It was if a switch had been clicked on inside his mind. He suddenly knew the powerful joy of performing, of being adored, of having people screaming for you. This was wonderful.

Before he could resist, a hand had reached out and grabbed his swollen dick, gripping it firmly about the shaft. Connor tried to pull away but the grasp was so firm he couldn't. What the hell? Go with it. He moved to the edge of the stage and allowed many of the watching crowd to feel and fondle his cock, which responded to the touch by jerking and twitching. Small droplets of pre-cum oozed from the tip. This was noticed by one guy who leapt up on a bar stool and suddenly took his cock into his mouth, taking it whole, with one warm wet swallow. Connor gasped and closed his eyes. The feelings of that blow-job were astounding.

'Er... thank you Tony, that's enough. Think of my licence.' Bob's voice rang over the loudspeaker. The guy leapt down, his mouth ringed with saliva, a huge grin beaming across his face. 'And a big thank you to Connor.'

Shaking his head, and bringing himself back to a semblance of reality, Connor bowed, waggled his cock from side to side and sprinted from the stage.

It had been fun. It had been exciting and it had been unbelievable when he heard the tannoyed voice announce that he had won. Scrabbling into a pair of white briefs, he dashed onto the stage, where Bob pinched his nipples and gave him the envelope containing the £100 prize money. Attached by a paper-clip to the envelope was a business card. Embossed upon it were the words 'Nick De'Ath, Music Executive', and a phone number. Scrawled below the number was a short message: 'Give me a call, You move well, and could be of use... Regards, Nick.'

Curious. Still, it was an intriguing method of introduction, and who knows, it might even be an opening for a job. Connor waved his arms triumphantly at the crowd, and grinned. This could even be the start of something really big.

4: Contacts, Contracts and Cottages

The church hall was cold and cavernous, the glow from the hanging strip-lights barely illuminating the gloom. Around the edge were wooden chairs and church pews, a bare stage at one end, and two tables at the other, one covered with polystyrene cups, a tea urn and various bottles and cartons of cold drinks. The other was bare but for a tape-deck and a large sheaf of notes, those the property of Rudy Garland, the choreographer for the newly formed boy group BANNED.

Dean, Paul, Joe and Connor sat on various chairs at one side, waiting. They had all arrived within minutes of each other, all slightly unsure of how to react to these other guys, young men who would soon be living in each other's pockets, knowing each other's secrets, aware of each other's intimate details.

'I'm Connor McEwan.' The Irish lad was the first to speak, putting out a hand to Dean, who grasped it firmly and gave a smile of relief.

'Dean West, hi. Thank God one of us broke the ice. You two must be Paul and Joe, right?'

'Yeah, that's us. How are you?' All four shook hands and smiled, relaxing for the first time that morning. The hardest part over with. They all seemed nice guys. Cute too. This could actually be fun.

'So do you know what is going to happen today?' Joe looked about the empty hall.

'I guess we'll be told what the plan of action for the band is... perhaps hear some songs...' Dean stood and stretched himself, his T-shirt riding up his body and exposing a few inches of muscled stomach. He noticed that all eyes were on him. Interesting.

The door creaked open and Nick De'Ath strode in, carrying a tanned leather briefcase, which he banged down on the table.

'Good morning boys. And what a lovely morning it is. I hope you are all ready to begin the new part of your lives. If you do as I say you can wave goodbye to poverty, struggle and obscurity for ever.

'This is the beginning of a wonderful new venture, something that will take the pop world by storm. A group which will set new standards of excellence and excitement, not to mention sex appeal and animal magnetism. I know you all have the capabilities to become world famous, and if you want it I can give it to you.

'Anyone who doesn't want this, or thinks he won't be able to stand the pace, the long days and nights, the sheer bloody exhaustion, the loss of personal freedom, and the unblinking intrusion of the media's camera lenses, then say so now. The door is behind me and you are welcome to walk through it and keep going. Well...'

The dramatic pause worked. The boys' mouths were dry, myriad thoughts of money and stardom whirling through their collective brains.

'Good. You won't regret this. I know I won't. Now before we go any further I want you to sign these.' Reaching for his briefcase, he leaned forward over the table, his leather trousers creaking as he moved, stretched tight across his arse cheeks which seemed beautifully tight and firm. Swiftly he handed out a sheaf of papers to each of the four lads.

'You are welcome to take these home and read them if you wish... if you don't trust me or believe in what I am saying and doing, or you can think of me as someone with your best interests at heart and sign them now.'

Joe raised a hand and spoke, his voice slow and deliberate. 'Nick... I think I can say that we do all want this to succeed, but we should be given the chance to know what we are signing our names to. At least give us five minutes... eh?'

Nick smiled and raised an eyebrow, his amusement obvious. 'Of course, read through the contracts by all means... there is a one page summary at the top, which explains all that is in the rest of the other twenty pages. I could summarise if you wish...'

Paul and Connor gazed at the pile of typewritten pages and turned their eyes to Nick. 'Please.' Connor flicked a strand of hair back from his forehead. 'Go ahead. I don't really feel like wading through all this technical bollocks right now.' He sat back in his chair, arms crossed expectantly.

Dean and Joe's eyes met and they exchanged a quick glance which seemed to say 'what the hell'. Sitting back, thrusting his hands in his pockets, pulling the soft material of his grey sweatpants tight across his crotch, emphasising what was lying dormant beneath, Dean waited.

'OK then, in a nutshell...' Nick paused for effect, watching the boys, their gazes staring back, '... this contract gives me the sole right to be your manager. The band we form today will be called BANNED. We will endeavour to create the hottest, most talented boy band this business has seen. You will be paid the basic wage of £200 per week, which will be paid directly into your own bank accounts. If you don't have a bank account then one will be set up for you.

'Everything that pertains to the setting up of the band will be paid for by me... costumes, sets, songs, hotels... the lot. I will be out of pocket, just remember that. The basic wage will continue until you have produced three albums. Then you will receive a percentage of the profits from that third album. Any questions so far?'

The boys looked at each other. Dean shifted in his seat, and noticed Nick's penetrating stare flick momentarily to his groin. 'Yeah. I've got a question. So we work our arses off for fuck knows how long, and you get all the money? Sounds criminal to me.'

'You might think so. But remember I shall be paying out a small fortune to get you guys off the ground... if you flop then I lose my shirt, and probably my house and my sanity too. I will only be getting back what is due to me. If you work hard there is no reason you won't be rolling in money.'

Paul spoke up. 'So how long will that take?'

'A good question. It could take years... but I want it to happen quickly. I envisage releasing the first single in a month, the first album in four months' time, the second after 18 months and the third in two years. That is a reasonable wish list. It will be fucking hard work, and you'll have no time to call your own, but you cannot expect to be famous and millionaires overnight, can you? So what do you all think? I shall leave you to chew this over for a few minutes... I have a call to make. OK?'

He pulled his mobile phone from the depths of his briefcase and slid outside, pulling the heavy wooden door shut behind him. The four boys sat unmoving and silent.

'Well, somebody say something,' Dean said.

'I don't quite know what to say.' Joe stood and scuffed the wooden parquet floor with his shoe. 'Unless we agree to what he wants then there is no way we can get to the top. And I want that badly. What about the rest of you?' He looked at the other three for a reaction.

'What the fuck!' Dean jumped up from his chair and strode to the table, picking up the pen and signing his name with a flourish on the last page of the contract. 'I'm in. It's got to be a laugh, and if it doesn't work out at least I'll have had some fun. Besides, I've always wanted to be on *Top of the Pops*!'

Paul stood and crossed to Joe, his hand outstretched. 'I want to do this. Come on... let's sign. At least if we fail we can say we had the chance.'

'Alright baby, why not!' They took the pen that Dean was holding out and signed.

'What about you, Connor?' Dean's gaze was encouraging. 'Are you with us or not?'

'Of course I am.' He smiled and reached for the pen. 'But I have one proviso. We should act as a group and look out for our own interests. I think Nick is a good guy, but we have to rely on each other for support. If there is any tough decision to be made we must all agree one hundred percent. If there is any doubt then we act against it, OK?'

'OK.' Dean put out his hand again and pulled Connor to him, his arms enfolding him in a huge friendly bear-hug. Joe and Paul joined in, the four guys group-hugging for all they were worth, all inhibitions ceased, all now determined to become the best of mates, and to make BANNED the success it deserved to be.

Dean, his arms around Joe and Connor's shoulders, squeezed tight, enjoying the shared warmth, the masculine energy that surrounded them and the feel of Joe's hand which had slowly slid down his back and was resting lightly on his buttocks. Was Joe stroking his fingers against his arse? It was difficult to tell. Cautiously Dean let his arm drop and wander its way down to the waistband of Joe's jeans, where it lingered for a moment before inching carefully south, just gently brushing the rounded cheeks, beautifully encased in the blue denim. He knew that he had done the right thing as Joe's hand gave a quick pinch, then patted his arse before he pulled away and headed to the tea urn.

This was very interesting. Up until now Dean hadn't really paid much thought to the others' sexuality. Could Joe be gay? He did call Paul 'baby' before, and they did seem close. Were they lovers? And what about Connor? There was that indefinable something about the Irish guy that said 'queer' to Dean. Surely Nick hadn't gotten together a band formed entirely of gay guys? Was that possible? He knew that Nick was gay himself, the episode in the audition room toilets had proved that, but why would he want to form

Sam Stevens

a totally gay group? Even in today's enlightened twenty-first century music business, homophobia was still rife.

The door banged open and Nick appeared, folding down his mobile phone, and slipping it into his shirt pocket. 'So do we have a band, boys?' He stood, eagerly waiting, a look of slight nervous apprehension on his face.

Joe seemed to take it upon himself to become the spokesperson for the group. 'You certainly do. When do we start?'

'Right now!' Nick banged his fist on the table in an exclamation of delight. 'No time like the present... But first there is one more thing to say to you all. BANNED will be a pop phenomenon, we will be pushing back barriers, because we will be a band that is openly gay. We will be judged on the music we make. Your looks and personalities are important too, of course, and I would be stupid not to capitalise on them.

'Now if any of you have any problems with being associated with such an enterprise, you should speak now. It's possible that we will encounter flak from the more closed-minded sections of the media, but I think we are going to win them over. Some people will say the group's sexuality is of more interest than the type of songs we release... but that is their problem. I happen to think that this is a venture worth trying, and my gut instinct tells me we will be a huge success. Any doubts?' His narrowed eyes scanned the boys, for a flicker of doubt, for the possibility that any of them wanted to leave. He saw none.

'Great. Now, have any of you seen Rudy? He'll start teaching you the steps to your first single...'

'And what is the first single?' Joe's voice was steely cool, his arms crossed, his eyes fixed on Nick. 'We have had a discussion while you were outside, and we've decided that we won't do anything we don't like.'

'It is a fantastic ballad called 'Only The Night', written by a talented youngster I am grooming to be the next Elton John. You'll love it. But you've got to work hard on this... your first gig is in a month's time.'

'What!' The cries of disbelief rang around the empty hall. 'We won't be ready.' Dean looked dismayed.

'Of course you will. I have every faith in you. Paul... could you go and check the toilets... Rudy may be in there changing clothes or something.' Nick gestured with his head to a door at the back of the hall.

'Sure, no problem.' Paul sauntered off and pushed the door which squeaked as it opened. He saw the sign 'Gents' on the grubby door opposite and went inside the darkened facilities. 'Rudy? Are you in here?'

A voice floated up from one of the cubicles. 'Yes, darling, I'm here. Just putting on my glad rags. Oh fuck...'

'What's the matter?'

'This zipper has got stuck.' The cubicle door opened and Rudy emerged in tights, legwarmers and a zip-up hooded sweatshirt. 'Give me a hand, will you?'

Paul moved forward and fumbled at the zipper which was stuck halfway up, his eyes trying to focus in the gloom.

'Hmmm... you're a cute one and no mistake.' Rudy let a finger stroke Paul's cheek.

The young guy pulled away as if burned. 'I had better get back...' He dashed for the door, letting it swing shut with a thud.

'Pity...' Rudy licked his lips and followed.

The rehearsal wasn't a great success. The song 'Only The Night' sounded unoriginal and dull through the tinny speakers on the cheap tape-deck. And Rudy's choreography was stolid and uninspired.

'That's it... left, right, left, right, now thrust those groins out... let the crowd see what you've got, boys... now turn and drop... and back to the front... hands by your sides and freeze... fabulous.'

Rudy's stream of inane movements and directions seemed unending. Nick sat at the back watching intently, making the occasional note in his thick, black filofax, now and then fielding calls on his mobile, dashing outside to avoid disrupting the rehearsal.

'Can we take a break now, Rudy? It's two o'clock and I'm starving.' Connor gave a pleading look to the choreographer.

'Alright my sweets. Back in one hour. We'll pick up where we left off. Don't be late.' Swinging his hips, he sashayed to the table, collecting his notes together, and switching off the tape-deck. Nick beckoned to Rudy and slipping an arm around his shoulder, took him outside.

'This sucks.' Connor looked about him at the other three exhausted lads. 'Can't we come up with something better than this crap?'

Joe nodded. 'I know. We'll all look like a bunch of mincing queens.' He stopped, all eyes were on him. 'Er... I hope I'm not speaking out of turn here...' he continued, 'but we are all happy with the "out" gay nature of the band, aren't we?'

Nobody else spoke. Dean raised his glance and smiled. 'Quite right, Joe. I don't care what people think of me. I came out to my folks when I was just into long trousers. If the world knows that I'm a seasoned cocksucker, I don't care. All I want to do is be the best I can. And with Rudy's fucking awful choreography I can't see that happening.'

Joe burst out laughing. 'Right on, sister! The fact we are all gay shouldn't make any difference to the act, but then again the act shouldn't make us look like a bunch of effeminate poofs. Our choreography should be hard and exciting, something to get all of our audience... boys and girls... wetting their knickers.'

'Hear, hear.' Dean agreed. 'We can't do what Rudy is suggesting, it's lame and unoriginal.' He dropped a hand and rearranged himself in his sweatpants, the movement watched closely by the other three. 'Should we have a word with Nick? If we all stick together like we said, then he will have to listen to us. Remember if we don't like what we are doing, we don't have to do it.'

'Don't have to do what?' Nick had appeared behind him, silently.

'How long have you been there?' Dean's voice quavered a little.

'Oh, long enough. I hear what you are saying about Rudy, and I agree. His style of movement isn't right for BANNED. And I have just told him so. We need something more stylish and sexual. And I know just the man to do it.

'Hang around for a while guys, I've ordered some pizza for lunch which should be here shortly... and hopefully we'll start again, afresh this afternoon. If I'm not back by three, don't panic. Sit outside, get some sun on those young skins of yours. Build up some sexy tans!' He gave Dean a reassuring pat on the back and strode off, picking up his briefcase and slamming the door behind him.

'Well, I'm parched. Tea all round?' Connor smiled at the guys and started to collect cups together, adding teabags and hot water from the urn.

'Great. I need to visit the little boys' room first. Don't wait for me.' Dean strolled toward the toilets.

'I'll make you one anyway. I'm going to drink mine outside... there are some benches across the way. Coming?' Without waiting for an answer, Connor disappeared outside. Joe and Paul picked up their cups and followed.

The toilet was smelly and dark, the two small window panes blocked up with cardboard. He pushed at the door to one of the two cubicles, pulled down his sweatpants and sat down. At least there was toilet paper, he thought.

In the darkened confinement of his surroundings he could see the walls were covered with obscene graffiti, careful anatomical studies of cocks and bollocks, drawings of mouths sucking on

45

oversized members, and many passages of illiterate writings.

'Cocks are lovly. I like to sukc them. I like bolicks too.'

'Call me for a good time. 8111 1119'

'I'm sitting here in panties. Where are you?'

The amount of this stuff was vaguely disturbing to Dean and he looked away, his gaze resting on a hole in the cubicle wall, which he hadn't noticed before. A piece of toilet paper was stuck across the hole in the other cubicle, blocking the view. What the hell. Just do what you came in here to do and get out, Dean muttered to himself, the words freezing on his lips as the outer door opened and shut with a gentle creak. Someone had entered the cubicle. He heard the sound of shuffling and unzipping. And the groan of the toilet seat as someone settled down on it.

Dean was hooked. His last experience in a public toilet had been with Nick at the audition, and the memory of it aroused him. He had only once done anything through a 'glory hole', and that was in a toilet in his home town, when he was fifteen. He had reacted to the finger that poked through the hole, beckoning him, encouraging him to push his young cock through. Eager to experience all that cottaging offered, he had done so, feeling a warm mouth fall upon his penis and suck. He hadn't much to compare it with, but he knew he had gotten a bloody good blow-job that day.

Dean waited for the current occupier of the adjacent cubicle to make a move and he shortly did. Through the dark he could see that the tissue paper was being slowly pulled away. He leant forward to see who was in the other side but could make out no details. With a shock, he backed away as the bulbous head of a hard cock emerged through the hole.

The cock was thick and rigid and barely fitted through the hole, the width of the wall's opening acting like a cock-ring, squeezing about the shaft, holding the flow of blood in the solidity of the cock's length. It was uncircumcised. And it curved up spectacularly, the head standing proud and purple, a collar of retracted foreskin tucked neatly around the head, its piss-slit large and impressive.

Dean needed no urging. Licking his lips he leaned forward and inhaled. A gentle aroma of man and soap filled his nostrils. A scent so exhilarating that his head swam. Putting out his tongue, he let the end of it flick across the tip of the cock, pushing it into the slit, and gently massaging it around. A groan came from behind the wall. Momentarily Dean wondered if he was doing the right thing. What if the owner of that cock was some horrid old tramp, come in off the streets for a bit of oral relief? That qualm passed as quickly as it came. Tramps don't have gloriously smooth skin and smell of soap, do they? Just relax and enjoy yourself.

But what if it was one of the other members of the group? Surely it couldn't be? Would Joe or Paul or Connor be doing this? Joe did get quite clingy when they had their group hug. Dean happily recalled the feel of his hand fondling the cheeks of his arse. What if it *was* Joe on the other side of this flimsy partition? With Joe's face implanted in the front of his imagination, Dean went for it. With a supreme exhalation of breath he enclosed the head of the weapon and, letting his mouth fill with lubricating saliva, let the cock slide down his throat, smelling the soap and tasting a few drops of pre-cum juice.

The cock must have been a good nine inches at least, as it filled Dean's mouth totally, with very little room for movement, it slid down until it pushed at the back of his throat. He gagged, but fought the impulse, which subsided rapidly and he continued. His lips clamped tightly about the shaft, until his nose and chin came sharply against the cubicle wall. With one swift motion he pulled back until just the head sat in his mouth, swirled with saliva, then without warning he swallowed again.

This was wonderful. Memories of sucking off Nick now flooded his mind, the happy sensations buzzed about his head. He wanted the owner of this beautiful knob, whoever it was, to have as good a time as his new manager did. Dean began to go to work, sucking and licking, pulling back and swallowing whole, the pace increasing, faster and harder, giving all he could, letting his lips feel the contours of the cock as it slid back and forth.

It seemed to Dean that the shaft was growing even bigger, forcing him to breathe through his nose. His teeth sometimes grazed the underside, eliciting quiet yelps of satisfaction from the guy next door. The cock started to pulse and buck, pushing in and out of the hole, now and then scraping against the roughness of the sides, but doing no damage because of the slippery coating of spit. Dean was ecstatic. He closed his eyes and concentrated on this mother of all blow-jobs, willing the recipient to a sensational climax. That wasn't long in arriving. He could hear heavier breaths from the guy, and a grunt as the suck-fest paid off.

Dean fell back on his heels, watching in delight as the cock spewed out its juice, several long squirts, then a couple of smaller ones, the first one shooting high and falling in an arc across Dean's face, somehow luminous in the darkened cubicle.

He sat back bemused and content. The thought of the identity of the cock's owner suddenly flashed across his mind and he knelt forward with a grunt. Too late. The door had creaked shut and the guy had gone. Reaching for a tissue, Dean sat back on the toilet seat and wiped himself down. With a deep breath he looked at his watch, pressing the little side button to illuminate its face. God, he'd been gone at least fifteen minutes. He had better finish his business and join the others before they started wondering where he'd got to.

Still, it's quite fun being a slut, he thought, and he chuckled to himself quietly.

'You took your time. Did you fall down the hole?' Joe looked up as Dean sat down on the grass by the wooden bench, leaning back to soak up the rays of the beaming sun.

'Yeah… a bit of tummy trouble actually.' Dean's voice was calm and nonchalant.

'You want to try sucking on something.' Joe crossed his arms and went back to his sunbathing.

'I'll try and remember that… if I pass a chemist on the way home.' A chuckle escaped Dean's lips. Did Joe have a conspiratorial air about him? Was it him in that cubicle? He gave no sign that it was.

The roar of a motorbike cut through the quiet glade of the churchyard, as a pizza delivery boy zoomed up with their lunch, and all four fell upon the warm, sticky wedges, gulping them down with mouthfuls of freshly made tea. A sort of lethargy took them over after they'd finished and eyes began to grow heavy, the soothing solar rays encouraging a gentle doze.

'Wake up you lazy bastards.' Nick stood over the slumbering four, hands on hips. 'Time to get back to work.' At his side stood a slim, dark-haired man, in his late twenties or early thirties. His skin was pale, but his eyes were dark, perhaps black, his gaze strong, his body obviously well cared for, the light cream coloured T-shirt he wore clung to a washboard stomach and a defined chest.

'This is Uri Pfister. He answered my SOS and came to my aid. He is one of Israel's up and coming geniuses. In the field of dance and movement he will be unsurpassed. I think his contribution to BANNED's success will be astonishing.'

'So what's happened to Rudy?' Paul sat up, shielding his eyes, trying to see more of Uri against the sun.

'He had to go. His kind of tired old choreography wasn't right for you, I see that now. Still onwards and upwards, it's only day one and we've a long way to go. If you'd care to shift those delightful arses into gear and head back, we've got some work to do.' Nick took Uri by the elbow and lead him inside.

'Come on then.' Dean leapt to his feet, brushing grass from his sweatpants, bounding after them, not waiting for the others.

The rest of that day was an improvement on the start. The twinkle in Uri's dark eyes, and his soft Israeli accent, immediately wooed the boys. They could see that he had an instinct for dance, his sinuous body seemed to have a rhythmical understanding of the music. He held their attention from the word go, and earned their immediate respect and loyalty, the first moves he suggested to them having style and grace and a macho air that screamed success. They knew that Nick had made a good choice. Even the song sounded better.

'Now just move in time to the rhythm, let yourselves go... feel it and then start to sway your hips...' Uri's voice cooed softly. 'That is good. Now just put out your hip a little bit more, Paul.' He stood behind and placed his browned hand on Paul's stomach, and as he pulled away he let his fingers brush down the crotch of Paul's trousers, a tiny, imperceptible gleam in his deep eyes.

'I want you all to watch Paul do this movement, he has a grace that you must all try to copy, I know that you all have the ability to do this. Paul, if you please.'

'I can't... you've got me all embarrassed now.' His gaze fell to the floor and his cheeks reddened, giving Paul the air of a schoolboy, caught in the middle of a naughty act.

'But you must.' Uri was insistent. 'You cannot be embarrassed. You are to be a hit group, with thousands of boys and girls screaming at you because you do this movement. If you cannot do this now for me and the group, how can you do it in the stadiums? Now pull yourself up and do it.'

Paul took a deep breath and concentrated, listening to the soft beat of the song playing on the tape machine, and began to undulate his hips.

'Very good. Now boys, see... copy him, copy him.'

Dean, Joe and Connor all started to emulate the movement, until Uri was satisfied. Throughout he stood close to each of them in turn, holding their arms or placing a firm hand on their stomachs, every time he would seem to let his touch linger about their bodies, his eyes holding theirs, sending out a look of intense sensuality. But Paul seemed to be his favourite. He earned the most praise, and the most eager fondlings. And Joe, watching every movement, saw that Paul liked it.

As six o'clock arrived, Nick reappeared from wherever he had vanished to and clapped his hands, motioning for everyone to pull up a chair around him.

'Well done everyone. I am really pleased with how you've got on. Now that Uri is part of the team, I think we are going to be a hit. But don't start expecting hordes of yelling fans yet, we have lots to do. For the rest of the week you'll be here rehearsing with Uri, getting the routine learnt, then on Saturday we'll be at the record company offices to learn the song itself. Connor, you'll be the lead singer on that.' All heads turned to the Irish guy.

Nick saw the reaction and spoke sharply. 'He has the best suited voice to this ballad. Don't go getting all jealous on me. You'll all get a chance to front the group. I want BANNED to have equality for all, and to produce songs which will utilise all your voices well. Any problems?' Nick looked about for dissension. None came.

'Excellent. Then go home, get a good night's sleep and be here fresh and fit tomorrow morning.'

5: The Studio Stud

'I can't believe I'm actually here! Abbey Road... I'm actually at Abbey Road, where the Beatles did some of their best stuff.' Paul put his arms around Joe's shoulders and gave him a wet smacker of a kiss on the lips. Startled, Joe pushed him back, a scowl corrugating his normally placid features.

'Not here you stupid fucker. People might see us.'

Paul stood back, amazed at what had just happened. It wasn't like Joe to be so harsh. From the moment they met at a local gay pub they had been inseparable. Their actions and thoughts usually as one, never arguing, never angry. But in the two weeks since the band had been formed they had hardly touched each other. After a long day they just went home exhausted, watched TV and crept into bed, with just a cursory kiss goodnight before switching off the light.

'You've changed, you know.' Paul strolled to the window and watched the traffic passing on the road outside, growling away across the famous zebra crossing. 'I don't know why. Perhaps you don't feel the same way about me as I do about you. If the band is going to split us up, then I don't want to be part of it. I need to know that we are going to be as together as we always were. If not then I might as well leave now.'

Joe crossed the room, putting his hands on Paul's shoulders.

'Look, it's just taking me a while to get accustomed to all this. I do love you, but until we get established I just think we should be a bit careful about what we do in public. Unless Nick wants to launch us from the very start as a gay band then we should just be aware of our behaviour.'

'Yeah, but that doesn't explain why we haven't made love for a week, does it?' Paul's voice cracked, a stifled sob escaped from his lips.

Unable to bear a scene, especially in the foyer at these world-famous recording studios, Joe held Paul tightly to him, wrapping his arms round his boyfriend from behind. For the first time in a week, the closeness of Paul's body and the sexy smell of his after-shave had a strange effect on him. He could feel himself becoming aroused, his slumbering cock began to slowly stiffen, pushing against the cheeks of Paul's arse, his boyfriend responding by pushing back, glad at this much needed demonstration of lust and affection. He ground his buttocks against the ever-hardening tool, rubbing the cleft up and down the ridge in Joe's trousers.

'If you've quite finished...' The two boys swung round to face Nick standing in the doorway, nonchalantly leaning against the frame, watching them, an amused grin on his handsome features. 'I should save all that for when you get home.'

Paul threw himself onto the sofa across the foyer. 'Chance would be a fine thing,' he muttered under his breath.

Dumping his briefcase by the unmanned reception desk, Nick surveyed the two lads. Something was up. He could tell. 'Now look, if there is a problem between you I should know. I cannot afford for there to be ructions within the group. Joe...?'

Saying nothing, Joe turned to face the window again.

'OK, so Paul then. What's wrong?' With a creak of his leather jacket, Nick sat at Paul's side, taking his hand and giving it a friendly squeeze. 'You know you can tell me anything. I am your manager, and I hope your mate, you can trust me totally. Come on... what's up?'

Paul opened his mouth to speak when the door was thrust open. 'Morning all, and what a lovely Tuesday it is.' Dean and Connor burst in. 'So here we all are then. I can't wait to get started. Where's the coffee?'

Glad of a positive attitude, Nick stood and walked across to the new arrivals. 'I'll order a pot immediately. Now you boys just settle down here for a few minutes and I'll see if the studio is ready.' He lowered his voice and whispered in Connor's ear. 'See if you can find out what's the matter with Paul.' With an almost imperceptible gesture of his head toward the troubled lad, he pushed at an inner swing door and disappeared.

Deciding on a direct approach, Connor smiled at Paul and playfully punched him on the arm. 'Everything alright? There's an atmosphere here I could cut with a knife...'

Paul took a deep breath and gave Connor a friendly hug. 'Course it is... I'm just tired that's all. I'm not sleeping very well at the moment...'

'Lucky bugger.' Connor gave him an affectionate squeeze. 'I wouldn't sleep much if I was married to him.' He gestured with his head towards Joe, who still stood, gazing at the passing traffic.

Joe was about to turn and answer when his attention was caught by a motorcycle courier, clad head to toe in black leather, swinging in off the road and pulling up at the steps to the studios, the sound of the growling engine penetrating the double-glazed window. The biker heaved the motorcycle onto its stand, pulled a package from the pannier and started to walk up the steps to the reception.

Beneath the rider's helmet all Joe could see was a black scarf which covered the lower part of his face, leaving the bridge of his nose and eyes free. They were a vivid blue, almost purple. He was dressed in the obligatory black leather from his boots upward, the leather trousers clinging suggestively to the contours of his legs, groin and arse. He had to be very well endowed, Joe thought, as it takes a big cock to make such thick leather bulge out in such an impressive manner.

Pushing open the door, the biker sauntered up to the desk and rang the bell, his helmet still in place, his eyes darting about the room. The leather made a sexy sound as he moved, rather like the noise of footsteps on newly settled snow. Walking with an assured manner, even with only his eyes visible, he emanated an aura of self-awareness and strength.

The receptionist appeared from a rear door and took the package with a smile. 'Hello Mark, how are you today?'

The voice from beneath the helmet was muffled, but reasonably distinct. 'Fine, just the one this morning... sign on the dotted line please.'

His voice was low and husky, with a resonant timbre that was so sexy, and perhaps, thought Joe, a slight West Country burr. The receptionist grinned appreciatively and vanished again into the inner sanctum. Mark, for that was obviously his name, picked up the pen again and scribbled something hastily on a scrap of paper, then folded it in two.

Casually, he made for the exit, pausing at the door to hand Joe the paper. His eyes shone brightly, staring intently at Joe before stepping outside, climbing onto his bike and growling away into the traffic. Joe stood amazed, transfixed by the charisma of this mystery man, unable to quite believe what had just happened, unsure of how to react to this astounding person.

He examined the piece of paper, unfolding it and reading the scrawled words, *'Call me... if you know what's good for you,'* followed by a mobile phone number. Joe hastily refolded the paper and shoved it deep into his jeans pocket, sensing that everyone in the room was watching him, including Nick who had reappeared.

'OK then, if we are all ready... the studio awaits.'

★

The session was thankfully a success. Connor's voic e handled the song well, and the others sounded great on backing vocals. Exhausted but happy the group stumbled down the front steps at the studios, to the sight of three taxis, waiting patiently. Nick appeared in the doorway and with a wave of his hand gestured to the cabs.

'You've earned these today lads, so jump in and they'll take you all straight home, don't worry about paying them, it's all on account. Just be at the rehearsal rooms at ten sharp tomorrow.' He spun on his heels and vanished inside.

Joe, Paul, Dean and Connor piled into the various taxis, slumping back on the mock-leather upholstery, gave directions and let the vehicles surge off into the traffic.

'Well, that was a great day!' Joe was bubbling with enthusiasm and excitement. 'Wasn't it?'

Paul sat silently watching the blurred images passing the cab, his eyes not focused on the world outside.

'Are you alright? Surely you're not still sulking?' Joe eased himself around to sit facing Paul, putting a friendly hand on his shoulder. 'I thought we'd sorted everything out.'

Turning his head, Paul looked back at Joe, his eyes showing a deep distrust and anger. 'YOU thought we had sorted everything out... and so did I at the beginning, but when you started throwing yourself at that courier guy...'

'For fuck's sake!' Joe exploded in a burst of untamed anger, making the cab driver swiftly look over his shoulder at his two passengers. 'When will you understand? I love you, you stupid fucker... I always have and always will. But at the moment I can't cope with this childish jealousy... this stupid reaction every time I so much as look at another man.

'I don't know what's sparked this off... or whether you were always like this and I just didn't see it, but it has to stop. I won't be treated like a possession... I want trust and respect... if you cannot give them to me, then we are in deep trouble.'

He paused waiting for a response. Paul just hugged himself tightly and looked away.

'Look Paul, we are on the brink of something big here, we could have fame and fortune, and it's you I want to share it with, but you must stop being so naïve and paranoid.'

He took Paul's hand and squeezed it. 'I am only human, so it's natural that I look at other guys, but that doesn't mean that I want to sleep with them. I have you... I only wish you'd realise that.'

Joe stroked the back of Paul's hand, wanting some reaction, some response to his heartfelt outpouring. 'Besides, you seemed to enjoy the sex we had with Nick at his office, didn't you? You seemed really keen. And you looked as if you enjoyed Uri's attentions.'

As Paul turned back to face Joe, large globular tears streamed down his face, rolling under his chin and disappearing. 'But it was different with Nick, we were both there together. Oh, I'm just being so silly I know... but I have this picture in my mind that when we get famous that you'll dump me and be off with any young bimbo that waggles his arse at you. It took me such a long time to meet anyone, and when I met you I couldn't believe that you wanted me, being so plain and fat...'

'Now that's not true... you are not plain, and you are certainly not fat. You are going to have to deal with this low self-esteem thing, because our lives together are only going to get harder... I don't understand how someone like you can be so screwed up... you have looks, personality, talent... and me! Surely everything is right with the world? Isn't it?'

The word 'hypocrite' flashed across Joe's mind. Out of his mouth were pouring words of consolation and devotion, but the image of Mark, the courier, was uppermost. He knew that he loved Paul, but the promise of a chance to unwrap that masculine leather package was irrestistible. Something about the air of that man, his totally male charisma, his confident sexuality, burned into Joe's being. He wanted him... more than he currently wanted Paul. But if Paul should find out...

The cab slowed and pulled into the kerb by their flat. 'Here we are boys... home safely.'

'Thanks.' Joe smiled at the driver, noticing for the first time that he was actually an attractive young man.

'Don't mention it... and if you'll take my advice, you'll take the boyfriend inside and give him a night he'll never forget.'

Astonished, Joe looked at the driver who gave a big grin and handed him a business card through the dividing window. 'Here... in case you ever need a cab... or some advice.'

The card bore the words 'GAY CARS – Taxis for the gay community'. Joe chuckled and tucked it into his pocket. 'Thanks Nick... nice one,' he muttered to himself.

'Now you run the bath and relax and I'll pop out for some milk... won't be long.' Joe gave Paul a hug and sprinted down the stairs towards the corner shop. As he reached the shop his eyes rested on the telephone box on the opposite corner. Pulling the folded piece of paper from his pocket and jangling a few coins in his fist, he crossed the road, opened the kiosk door and dialled the number on it.

'Hello?' The deep, brown voice spoke then paused, waiting.

'Er... is that Mark?'

'Yes.' The voice gave nothing away, except perhaps its countryside roots.

'It's Joe Turner here...'

'Yes.' He wasn't going to make this easy.

'You gave me your number at the studios today.'

'Aaah.'

'And so I'm giving you a call... like you said I should.'

'Do you want a medal for that?'

'I'm sorry... I thought you wanted me to call, but if you are just messing...'

'Don't be a wanker all your life... Come round now.'

'I can't... my boyfr... I mean I have other things to do.'

'The offer isn't indefinite. You come round now or you'll miss your chance. It's number 46 Medina Mansions, Medina Road, Wood Green.' The phone clicked and went dead.

'But...' Joe replaced the receiver, his mind now a maelstrom of thoughts and indecisions. He could get to Wood Green in half an hour, but what about Paul? He could make up some story as to why he was so long buying milk, couldn't he? And then he could make it up with Paul, surely? The bigger question was did he actually want to go through with the deception? Did he want to meet this mysterious guy, with the big bulge?

Deep down he knew that he did. Without a moment's further thought he turned and ran towards the bus-stop, seeing a bus approaching... was this a good omen?

No. 46 Medina Mansions was one of a large number of flats in a block. Joe scanned the doorway for the right bell and pressed it. That now so familiar voice answered. 'Yes?'

'It's me.' The door buzzed, inviting him to push it open. Stepping inside he slid open the ornate metal lift door and entered, jabbing at the button marked '4th floor'. The cage rose smoothly, depositing Joe in the hallway outside flat no. 46, a plain door, with just the number on it, and a small square of cardboard taped to the door with the words 'Mark Trevithick'. Raising his fist to knock at the door, Joe jumped a mile as it was sharply pulled open, Mark standing inside, his arm against the side of the door frame.

'Good. You're here. Come in.' His speech was telegraphic and slightly cold, he stood back and let Joe enter. Joe was stunned, the flat was beautiful, sparsely furnished, but with exquisite taste, although he couldn't take his eyes from his host, who stood by the door dressed only in a white towel, his hair damp, as if he'd just stepped from the shower.

Mark was the kind of man that Joe used to dream of when in adolescence... the type who he imagined would sweep him off his feet, big and silent, make love to him all night, and look after him all day. He was exceptionally good-looking, reminding Joe of one of the gorgeous American Baldwin brothers. Alec possibly? He was about six-foot tall, with lustrous dark hair, but not a hair elsewhere on his body, well none that Joe could see as yet. His eyes were the same vivid purple that Joe had seen that morning, but they seemed to complement the rest of his face, strong, with good features, a slight mouth, with thinnish lips, the hint of a smile hovering about them. His body was muscular, but not overly so, his chest and arms well defined, and glistening with droplets of water.

He closed the door and gestured to a low-slung couch across the room. 'Make yourself at home.'

Nervously, Joe sat perched on the edge of the couch as Mark disappeared into what Joe assumed was the kitchen. 'Can I get you a drink?' Mark's voice floated out through the open door.

Joe's mouth and throat were dry, but with a cracked voice he called back, 'A coffee would be good.'

'OK... won't be a minute, settle back and relax.'

Doing just that, Joe looked about the room, it certainly had style, which he guessed was all of Mark's invention. From the polished wooden floor to the Picasso and Mondrian prints on the wall, and the large vase of dried flowers in the corner, it reeked of class and money. Surely all this couldn't have been paid for on a courier's wages?

'Thirsty?' Mark appeared carrying a tray, with two mugs, milk, and a cafetiere of freshly made coffee, which he placed on the small table at the end of the couch and sat down by Joe's side, adjusting his towel, so that all he had between his legs stayed hidden.

61

'Sure... I'll take it white please.' Joe took the proffered mug and sipped at the steaming brew. 'Nice place.'

'Thanks.'

Joe watched Mark intently, unable to tear his gaze away from those beautiful eyes. 'You don't say very much do you?'

Mark smiled. 'I don't find that I have much to say generally, and if I do there are so many morons in the world unable to answer back with any degree of intelligence or wit... so I usually keep my mouth shut.' He shifted a little on the couch, his towel falling open slightly revealing a hairless thigh. 'What about you though... are you a moron?'

Clearing his throat, Joe tried to sound certain of himself. 'I don't think so. I'm reasonably intelligent and can hold my own in any conversation.'

'Good.' He paused before speaking again. 'You think I'm shallow, don't you?'

'In a way, I suppose... if you judge people in such an off-hand manner. There is more to a person than his ability to talk.'

'Well said. I think I like you. I certainly liked the look of you this morning. And I know that you liked the look of me. You couldn't keep your eyes off my cock could you?'

Joe blushed. 'What do you want me to say?'

'I want you to admit that you found the thought of this mysterious delivery guy intriguing. You liked the look of the body and were curious as to what lay beneath the leather outer shell. You wanted to know what shape the body was in, and how big the cock squashed inside would grow when aroused. Go on, admit it.'

He sat back, the towel falling aside a little more. Joe's eye couldn't help but flick down to that area, where he could just see a small area of wrinkled skin, one bollock just hanging below the towel edge.

'Alright. I admit it. You interested me. You turned me on in fact. That's why I'm here.'

Mark stretched his arms up in the air, as if showing off his torso, then clasped his hands behind his head. 'I knew it. I was right, I usually am.'

'So you are a show-off too?' Joe gave him a direct and questioning stare.

'Probably. I've got a lot to show off...' He dropped his arms and let one hand gently lie across his chest, the tips of the fingers flicking an already erect nipple. His eyes locked with Joe's, the astounding purple irises seemed to glow, a luminescent oasis of colour in his pale face.

Sounds of traffic permeated the room softly, Joe noticed it for the first time, the palms of his hands were clammy, a bead of perspiration broke out on his brow and ran down the side of his nose. Using the back of his hand he wiped it away.

'Are you hot?' Mark asked soothingly. 'You can take your jacket off, you know.'

This was it. The crunch time. Joe knew he was standing on a precipice. If he took another step he would fall head-long into what Mark was offering, he would be turning his back on his commitment to Paul, unfaithfully deserting him, doing what they always said was possible, but never thought they would do... cheating on each other. But the offer was so incredibly tempting. Mark was an Adonis, a perfect man who wanted to share himself with Joe. Would he be a fool to turn such an offer down? He knew he would.

'Thanks.' Joe sat forward and shucked his jacket, sitting back in his shirt sleeves, damp patches slowly forming under his arms.

'You really do look hot.' A spasm of concern flashed across Mark's face. 'You could have a shower if you'd like.'

Joe hesitated. Again a very tempting offer. 'I think I'm alright actually.'

'Suit yourself... I'm going to have another one.' Mark stood, adjusting his towel, which now pushed out a little from the groin, showing the enlarged outline of his semi-erect cock. It looked massive. Moving panther-like across the room, he nudged at the door next to the kitchen and walked inside, leaving it open.

Joe turned and saw the bathroom, with the shower in full view, a clear glass cubicle with no curtain. With a hiss, water started to stream down from the nozzle, and deftly Mark dropped his towel and stepped into the shower, his back to Joe. The arse was a wonder. Firm and rounded, perfectly symmetrical, leading to hairless, sturdy legs. His back was a riot of muscles, which undulated erotically beneath the downpour of steaming water, as if he was showing off his fine musculature for his guest – which he was.

Joe's mouth was dry, so he took another gulp of warm coffee, licking his lips and finally standing on trembling legs. Silently and surely he divested himself of his clothes until he stood, naked in the centre of the sitting room. A gentle breeze from somewhere played across his frame, making the hairs on his arms and legs stand up.

With a deep breath he moved toward the shower and stepped in. Mark spun round to face him, his cock now at half-mast, jutting out from his crotch, gently curving downward, the hefty weight of its mammoth head pulling it down.

The spray of the water stung Joe's skin, but he didn't notice. Mark reached out for a cake of soap which rested in a dish on the cubicle wall and with a gentle touch started to lather the soap all over Joe's body, creating foamy white bubbles across his chest, and under his arms, then moving slowly down his back to the legs, consciously avoiding the crotch and the ever-growing cock, the rush of blood to it a sign that Joe was unable to resist the tender ministrations. The heat of the water began to get to Joe, arousing a passion, arousing his stirring manhood more and more. He was growing harder and he wondered if he should stop. But a voice in his head called out to him: *Go for it.*

With a gasp he felt Mark start to soap his lower stomach with one hand while the other smoothed the lather around his arse cheeks, the first hand moving further and further downwards towards his groin, just nudging the tip of his now-solid dick, and rubbing into the skin of his bollocks, swinging tremblingly between his legs. The hand pulled on the balls, easing them down, grasping a fist about them, tightly squeezing the skin so the bollocks bulged, teasing them, pulling them away from his body, bringing another louder gasp to Joe's lips.

'Nice.' Mark's voice dripped with admiration for Joe's cock, which if anything was slightly bigger than his own. 'A real Jeff Stryker...'

Lost in a daze of intense emotion, Joe turned his face into the spray of the water, and placed his hands on the wall in front of him, content to let Mark do whatever he wanted. And he did. Replacing the cake of soap he started to wash down the body, sluicing away the soapy suds, until Joe stood, clean and fresh, the persistent water coursing over him, swirling away down the plug-hole in a gurgle.

Mark saw Joe's eyes close in delight and ecstasy, as he crouched down in front of him, his mouth open, and with one swift gulp he swallowed Joe's cock. Joe gasped, his breath coming in short, erratic bursts.

'Oh God! Yeah, that's it, suck me, Mark, suck me...'

Knowing that his new conquest was now putty in his hands, Mark went for it. His mouth closing about the cock. He knew he himself was very well endowed, but Joe's dick was certainly nothing to be ashamed of, in fact it was slightly longer, if not as thick around the shaft. With water pouring down his face he began to work at the blow-job, sliding his mouth up and down, gripping the base of the shaft, pulling back the foreskin to reveal the tender and sensitive glans beneath. The sensation of warm sucking lips upon his soft cock-head made Joe's knees buckle. He had had many blow-jobs in his time, and he thought Paul was an expert, but this was something else. The suction from Mark's mouth seemed to engulf his very being, the lips slurping as he slid back and forth, pulling away then plunging his mouth down to the very bottom, swallowing whole, totally engulfing the rigid pole, something even Paul sometimes couldn't manage, with the incredible length of the cock.

'Wow! Oh yeah!' He called out again, awash with lust and desire. He felt the tell-tale rush of adrenalin that signalled an explosion was imminent, and sensing this Mark pulled back, jumping to his feet and pushing Joe down to his knees.

Staring at the now solid monster before him, Joe gulped. He tended to be a top during his sexual encounters, and wasn't so experienced in giving head, and this whopper was scary. He wasn't given much time to think about it, as Mark grabbed his head and forced him down. His mouth stretched as it tried to accommodate the monster. It felt like the skin would rip, so big was the weapon being thrust down his throat.

Joe wanted to pull away, to call out to Mark that he had to stop, but his eyes wide with amazement, he realised he had done it, he had swallowed Mark's cock. A surge of pride and fulfilment washed over him as he proudly adjusted to the sensation of his mouth and throat being completely stuffed. OK, steel yourself, give it all you've got, Joe said to himself.

Inch after inch of solid flesh slid out of his mouth, then plunged back again, the huge tip touching the back of his throat, pushing past the tonsils, and then Mark started to fuck his mouth, in long, even strokes, savouring the incredible suction and the pure delight of Joe's lips clamped about the shaft, as it pummelled away. Joe's mouth felt every contour and raised vein on its length. The fucking became faster and more intense, Joe's mouth opening and closing as the cock pulled back and out, before feeling as if it was sliding down to the very pit of his stomach.

Joe reached down and grabbed his own cock, and began to

stroke it to its maximum state of rigidity, trying to concentrate on the blow-job and ignoring the thought of the major fucking that he was going to give Mark soon. But no. Mark pulled out of Joe's mouth and heaved him to his feet.

'I thought I was going to come... but we've got better things to do first.' He took Joe by the arm and led him towards a door on the opposite side of the room, kicking it open to reveal the double bed, covered with pristine white sheets. Forcefully he gave Joe a shove, pushing him face-forward onto the mattress, and before Joe could say or do anything his legs were yanked apart, and his arse hoisted upwards.

Kneeling quickly, Mark began to lick at the balls hanging in his face, licking and sucking them, pulling them into his mouth, then licking the underside of the cock which hung down, semi-hard now. Thrusting back, Joe knew that Mark needed no encouragement, he was superb at the art of eating butt. He flicked his tongue upwards at the ridge that led from the base of Joe's balls to the pulsing brown ring.

'Ohh, yeah, eat me out,' Joe moaned.

Mark's probing, glistening tongue moved further up, and pushed at the crack, feeling the sphincter muscles give in and pushing his tongue inside. It was almost sucked up there. Mark retreated and did it again, sliding his tongue inside, working the puckered hole, licking and slurping around its twitching, wrinkled entirety.

Joe was now so worked up that he felt that he was going to come. His fist which had wrapped itself about his own cock started to pump, but Mark sharply knocked it away.

'Not yet... I thought I told you.' There was an edge to his voice, a fierce, somewhat unpleasant note which made Joe start, his whole body tensing for a second, until the shock of what happened next took his mind from the situation. A wet finger pushed inside his arse, with a stinging jolt of pain.

Sam Stevens

'No Mark, I am a top, I don't get fucked...'

Mark ignored the plea. 'This time you do... now shut up and relax... it'll hurt less.'

Unable to believe what was being done to him, Joe realised he had no choice. He could hear Mark rummaging around beneath the bed and then the sound of tearing, followed by the slippery snap of a condom being put in its place.

He had only been fucked once before, in a remote public toilet when on holiday with his family aged 15. The guy, a trucker, had slid his cock in Joe's virgin arse, but the pain was so excruciating that he had to stop. Droplets of blood on the toilet seat had scared Joe and he vowed never to let anyone do that to him again. Again now he was in the suppliant position and Mark was in control. He had shown a dangerous side to his nature, and was obviously determined to have his way. Joe was scared.

But then he was treated to the most astounding and mind-blowing sensation yet. He winced as the meaty, lubed-up weapon was pressed against his hole.

'I thought I told you to relax... now do it.' Mark's voice had again assumed that cold edge.

Joe tried hard to let his sphincter unclench, and with one deft motion, Mark penetrated him. There was a second of blinding, searing pain, which spasmed through his whole body, and Joe cried out. Determined not to seem a total baby, he stifled his screams and bit deep into his forearm, his teeth leaving a violent crescent-shaped mark.But suddenly the pain eased and the fuck became easier. He realised he had another man inside of him, and it wasn't an unpleasurable experience.

Sensing that Joe was now accustomed to his vast cock impaling him, Mark started to fuck him for real, gripping his waist and going for it. Joe's breath came in grunts as Mark yanked back on his hips, driving his hard cock deep into him, each thrust bringing forth an even greater exhalation of breath.

He was being fucked, and the feeling wasn't bad, in fact it was amazing. To be plundered by someone who really knew what they were doing was beyond belief. Next time he fucked Paul, he would have to try and recall how it felt and imagine what his boyfriend was feeling. His boyfriend. Paul. The face of his partner flashed in front of Joe's eyes. God almighty, what was he doing here? A violent push dispelled the image and all Joe could now comprehend was the punishment his arse was getting.

Mark knelt up on the bed, and leaned forward forcing Joe down, his weight pushing him deeper into the springy mattress. The cock plunged faster and harder, each thrust rubbing against the lining of his arse, the sphincter ring expanding and shrinking back with each invasive push. The pace grew faster and more furious, and now Joe determined to give as good as he got, pushing his arse back with each inward stroke of Mark's.

His breathing getting faster, Mark tensed himself, pulling right out of Joe's tender hole with every thrust and then launching himself back in, so that both of them got the full benefit of this fuck session.

After about a minute more of this, both Mark and Joe started to gasp, and with one final, filling push they came, Joe pumping his hot spunk into his fist, spilling out onto the rumpled bed-sheets, at exactly the same moment as Mark shot his load, inside Joe, the rubbery confinement of the condom catching each drop of his juice. Joe could feel a warming glow deep within him, as his arse ring screamed for the cock to be withdrawn. Mark's head fell forward onto Joe's sweaty back, his breathing becoming slowly easier, the cock still hard, and still fully inside Joe.

'Wow!' Mark seemed more relaxed now, friendlier even, now that they had both spent themselves. 'You are a great fuck. I can feel your inside muscles twitching around my knob... how does it feel for you?'

'I can honestly say that I've never had anything like it before.

But amazing as it was... could you pull out? I am starting to feel sore.'

'Sure, sorry.' Mark lifted himself off, gently, teasingly, sliding back, letting the still hard dick emerge from Joe's arsehole, every inch's release bringing a small yelp to Joe's lips, until just the tip remained inside.

'I'm a bad boy you know...' Mark grinned, and without warning shoved the cock back inside for one last push. A cry of extreme pain and joy poured from Joe's throat, as from the almost relief of being empty he felt utterly full again, as if the cock had pushed its way up to his throat. Then with one quick movement, Mark pulled out.

Joe breathed a heavy sigh, and turned his head to watch Mark padding across to the bathroom, and turning on the shower, the filled condom still hanging tight about his cock.

'Are you going to wear that all day?' Joe called out, in a weakened voice.

'What? Oh... yeah better get rid.' Mark pulled the rubber off and wrapped it in some toilet paper, then dropped it in the waste bin. 'Are you going to join me?' he called out above the hiss of the shower spray.

Looking at his watch, Joe realised how late it had become, and how long he had been at Mark's place. Paul would be frantic, or furious... or both. Leaping to his feet, and wincing as he could still feel the phantom sensation of Mark's cock in him, Joe headed for the bathroom.

'No thanks, I'll just have quick wash, and then I'd better go.'

'Are you sure?' Mark seemed hesitant.

'Oh, yes... I should have been somewhere else an hour ago. If I don't get back my boyfriend will be out combing the streets.'

'So you do have a boyfriend then?' Crestfallen, Mark turned off the shower and watched Joe quickly scrubbing himself down in the sink. 'What a pity. Still, the gorgeous ones are never single.

I guess you're not monogamous then... if you sleep with other guys? I hope we can do this again sometime...'

Joe raised his head and stared long and hard at the reflection of Mark in the mirror in front of him. 'You probably won't believe this but this is the first time I've ever played around. It was great... better than I ever imagined it could be... but there is another person involved here, and I couldn't hurt him, I just couldn't. Give me some time to think about it. I've got your number and I'll give you a call sometime, eh?'

Mark shrugged his shoulders. 'I suppose that will have to do. Just make sure you do call me. That was the best fuck I've had in ages.'

'Thanks... I wasn't sure if I could actually do it... I mean with the size of your cock. Now I know what I must give Paul when I fuck him.' Joe towelled himself off and wandered back to the lounge, picking up his clothes and starting to dress, Mark following intently behind.

'I'm sorry if I... I mean if I got a little controlling back there. I get like that during sex. The heightened energy makes me a bit mean. I hope I didn't hurt you.'

'No... don't worry about it. In a way the whole being dominated thing was quite a turn-on. In fact I quite enjoyed it.'

Mark sank down on the couch, and reached for a small jade box with a hinged lid, which sat on the coffee table. Raising the lid, his fingers pulled out a small foil package, and some cigarettes. 'Fancy a joint?'

Drugs. Joe's eyes widened in alarm. 'No thanks. I don't do that kind of thing.'

'It's alright. It's just some harmless blow... marijuana... dope. You'll love it. It'll help relax you.'

'I think I'm as relaxed as I want to be at the moment, but thanks for the offer. Look I'd better be going... I'll give you a call.' At least the mystery of Mark's extra income was solved. Drug dealer. Joe slipped into his shoes and headed for the door, hoping that Mark only dealt in soft drugs, and wasn't involved in anything life-threatening. Flicking the latch, Joe pulled the door open, before disappearing into the cool evening, his head full of guilt and recriminations.

6: Grin and Bare It

The four members of BANNED looked at their manager with disbe-lief and dismay. Nick looked back, a cheesy grin contorting his fea-tures, pleased with the extreme reaction to the news.

'A gay club! You are joking?' Dean spluttered through a mouth-ful of hot tea. 'Our first appearance is to be at The Bare Pit? Full of queens, all ready to jeer at yet another potential boy band. I think you've lost it, mate.'

Nick poured himself a cup of steaming tea from the metal urn, his back to the boys. 'It makes perfect sense lads... just think about it for a minute. The only representatives of the press there will be the gay papers, the audience will be doubly appreciative, not only because you are all cute as fuck but because you are all gay. We'll be making that clear from the outset. And with the three numbers you've got under your belts by now you'll wow them... can't fail. The place will be packed to the rafters with the gay cognoscenti out for a fun Saturday night, plus you'll be trying extra hard to impress in case any of your mates are out there. It's a brilliant idea. So in two days you'll be showing the world what you are made of on the stage at The Bare Pit. Sorted.'

The boys' faces said it all. Horror and amazement, but tinged with a mite of excitement.

'What if we could do it?' Connor was sitting on a plastic chair, staring at the wooden flooring, scuffing it with the toe of his boot. 'Just say we could. It'd be fucking wild!'

'That's the spirit. Well said, Connor lad. Now we haven't much time. So this morning we'll be going over the three routines for the numbers, just polishing them off, and this afternoon we'll be at the studio to just add the finishing touches to the songs, before laying down the backing tracks. And then tomorrow afternoon each of you will be called by Uri for an individual session with him, to tighten up your movements. Any questions?' Nick sipped at his polystyrene cup, his eyebrows raised quizzically.

'Just one.' Joe looked grave. 'Is there a get-out clause in my contract?'

The others laughed and pushed Joe in the ribs, their laughter generally good natured, although tinged with nervousness. Joe grinned back and poured himself a cup of orange juice, his eyes on Paul, joining in with the levity.

When Joe had arrived home after his encounter with Mark, the previous Tuesday, Paul had been in bed. He had seemed to be asleep, and so Joe, thankful of the fact, slid in beside him and fell quickly asleep too. Ever since, Paul had said nothing about why Joe had stayed out so long. His demeanour was jolly as usual, but beneath the surface was this distant edge, as if he was just going through the routines, being pleasant but hiding a secret angst somewhere within him. He had said nothing when he saw the crescent-shaped bruise that appeared on Joe's arm. He just raised an eyebrow and went back to making the toast. Joe thought he had changed. Turned harder and colder. Perhaps it was what Paul needed. The music industry was a harsh place and had no vacancies for passengers or hangers-on. Maybe his being less vulnerable would be a good thing.

This morning though he appeared to be the same old Paul, happy, joking and smiling with the rest of the gang, and as tactile as he used to be with Joe himself. Perhaps all was well. Joe caught

Paul's eye and winked. Paul giggled and winked back, obviously his old self again. Crossing and standing behind him, Joe gave his boyfriend a friendly hug.

Nick turned as the hall door slammed open. 'Ah Uri, excellent timing. OK lads, let's get to work. Uri, I shall leave them in your capable hands. See you all at the studios at two.'

All was proceeding as planned. The rehearsals and recording of the tracks went without a hitch, and the boys felt at ease with their stage personas and the routines to accompany the three new numbers. All four of them had bonded, claiming a lifelong friendship, and that they would do anything for the others. They all wanted success and they now waited eagerly for the chance to see what the public reaction would be. And that chance was now only a day away. Nothing left to do but concentrate on the performance and do their utmost to impress. And of course to spend some time with Uri.

'Now just stand in the moment and gather yourself.' Uri, hands on hips, waited for Paul to relax. He was the last of the band to see their choreographer for this final check.

'That is good. Well done. Now I want you to think about each of our routines. Visualise them in your mind and see if there is any part of them that you feel nervous about. Anything that you feel you could do better. Well...?'

Paul tried to concentrate on what Uri was demanding of him, but with great difficulty. The physical closeness of the choreographer was disturbing. He had already worked out that Uri was fond of him, perhaps had fallen for him, smitten and in lust, and Paul didn't know how to deal with this notion. He had a boyfriend, someone whom he felt deeply for, but someone who at the moment maybe needed some freedom to find himself. Yes, perhaps that was what Joe needed now, a chance to see the world, to sow some wild oats and then come to the conclusion that, like

Dorothy in *The Wizard of Oz*, there is no place like home. Perhaps that was what Paul himself needed... a nice juicy affair?

As Uri placed a hand on Paul's shoulder, the youngster jumped at the contact. 'No Uri... there is nothing I can think of that I want to work on, nothing at all.'

The choreographer chuckled, deeply and with a slightly strange catch. 'I disagree, Paul.' His Israeli accent made the name sound like 'pool'.

'I think there is much to be done today. I am not so happy about your hips, they are not so loose as they should be, I am thinking. Like this...' Again placing his hands on Paul's waist, one on each hip, he encouraged a gentle and undulating movement from side to side.

'Good, now get loose, like one of those girls from Hawaii, imagine a grass skirt about you that will swish and sway. That's better. I know you can do it.' Keeping a firm grip on Paul's hips, Uri swung himself around Paul's body and knelt in front of the lad.

'Good, good. That is much better. Now I want you to totally relax. Do not react to what I do, just keep those hips moving, gently, sexily.'

Paul jumped again, as he felt Uri's face nuzzle into his crotch, his mouth open and searching for some sign of arousal. Paul pulled back and stared down at the bronze-skinned man before him. He wanted him to stop, to keep his distance, but he also had desires and wants, after all he was only human. Here was a handsome, fit guy, interested in him. Should he let him have his way?

The pressure of Uri's face nuzzling his crotch got harder, his mouth opening and licking and sucking the denim of Paul's jeans. His hand reached up and gently pulled down the zip, before fumbling around inside the crotch and levering Paul's cock free, slipping it through the soft opening of his briefs. He didn't stop to consider his actions, just took Paul's cock in his mouth, letting the rapidly hardening pole slide down his throat.

Paul's eyes rolled shut and his head fell back, it had been a good week since he'd had a blow-job and Uri was practised in the art. He licked and sucked, swallowed and slurped, giving everything to the lad's cock in his mouth. Even with the thought of Joe's probable unfaithfulness in the forefront of his mind, Paul wasn't comfortable with what he was now doing.

'I'm sorry, I can't do this.' He pulled away, his cock glistening with saliva, and hurriedly stuffed it back in his trousers. 'Uri... look this isn't right. I have a boyfriend you know.'

The choreographer stood and faced Paul, his expression open and honest. 'Of course I know... everyone knows. And everyone knows that you have jealousy. That when he looks at others you feel terrible. You see him flirt and it tears you up. Who need a boyfriend like that?'

The floodgates opened.

'I do.' Paul was suddenly awash with tears, as sobs racked his body. The full extent of his love for Joe and his anger at the deceptions finally broke through. Uri sprang to his feet and held Paul tightly, letting the heartfelt cries of anguish and relief pour out, gradually subsiding, until Paul was able to give a small smile of gratitude.

'Thanks, Uri. I needed that.'

'You are welcome. I think that you have been holding all that in for a while, yes?'

'Yes.'

'And it is much better that it is all out now?'

'Oh, yes. It's made me realise how stupid I've been. Joe loves me I am sure, and I do love him, but right now he is in a different place and has to do different things. It's not fair keeping him to myself... he has to find what he's looking for and then when he comes back I'll be waiting.'

Slowly stroking his chin, Uri watched Paul with an expression of the deepest intensity. 'And so you should be free to do different things too.'

'Possibly... er... no, I don't think so...'

'Ah, but you should be open to situations if and when they come to you... believe me.' Uri gave a huge grin, his eyes lighting up with warmth and friendliness. His arm went round Paul's shoulder, a tight hug showing his support.

'I think that is all for today. Look at the clock... it is now four. Shall we drink?'

'I don't really feel like one, thanks. I'd rather get home and sink in front of the telly.' Paul smiled back, then after a moment's hesitation hugged Uri to him, feeling the strength of his muscular, lean body, and inhaling the gentle floral scent he always seeemed bathed in. It was nice. Bodily contact was very nice. Uri squeezed back, closing his eyes and just sinking deep into Paul's embrace. Paul felt a stirring in his loins, the contact with this handsome man stirring something up again, his cock twitched slightly and began to gently swell. Perhaps he should let him finish that blowjob?

'I'd better go. Thanks again.' Pulling hurriedly away, Paul grabbed his shoulder bag and nervously rushed to the door. 'See you tomorrow?'

A deep brown chuckle was Uri's only response. He put up his hand in a mock salute and then turned away to pack up his things.

The Bare Pit seethed and writhed, the two thousand assorted punters moved and swayed almost in rhythm. From their vantage point in the back of the DJ's box, the members of the group looked down on the scene, mouths universally dry, hearts pounding, stomachs seething.

The club was housed in a disused cinema, one that had escaped the humiliation of being turned into a bingo hall for middle-aged ladies to win miniscule amounts of money in, dreaming of the fortune that would never come. The DJ's box was situated at the back of the circle, away, high above the crowds, so that they could be watched by the DJs and the management, as well as the security camera that whirred its way over the throng, perched precariously on the wall of the box.

Seats and tables populated the circle area, for those who didn't wish to mingle with the 'It' crowd downstairs on the dancefloor immediately in front of the stage. A place to sit and drink, and to watch the show, and to have assignations with those other single men wandering up and down the aisles, watching and waiting for a signal, a twitch of an eyebrow, a start of a smile, anything that said, *Hello, I fancy you, shall we fuck?*

The boys had taken refuge in the DJ's rather spacious box, nerves having overtaken them just sitting waiting in the dressing room under the stage, and so Nick and Gunther, the manager of The Bare Pit, had taken them through the back corridors, and up a flight of stairs to watch the crowd in the main club area. The two DJs for the evening, Peter Q and Jay-Vee, stood at the turntables, engulfing, black headphones perched over one ear, their faces almost covered, as they undulated to the music they provided, tapping their feet and gyrating, lost in the euphoria of the sound.

'Have a look guys. They are waiting for you.' Nick waved a hand at the multitude below. 'Don't be afraid, just give it your best shot. They will totally adore you. You've nothing to be worried about.'

'Oh yeah, what about falling arse over tit, and making a fool of myself out there.' Connor chewed on a fingernail, the sight of the people below making his nerves a hundred times worse.

'You'll be fine.' Gunther, a stockily built man with cropped hair and a combat T-shirt, leather trousers and boots, patted him on the arm. 'If Kylie can do it, so can you.'

'Kylie played here?' Connor looked amazed.

'Oh, yeah. Two weeks ago, and she was as nervous as hell. So just get on that stage and give them the fucking works.' He glanced at his watch. 'OK, it's five minutes to midnight. Showtime.'

He pulled open the door at the back of the box. 'Let's get down there, so we can start on time.'

As the boys started to leave, both the DJs turned around and smiled.

Peter Q, the taller, muscular blond, clapped Connor on the shoulder. 'Hope it all goes well. Come back up and see us sometime.' He nudged his mate, the darker, lean Jay-Vee, in the ribs, making him giggle and run his tongue over his lips. 'You'll be welcome anytime.'

Connor swallowed dryly and slipped outside to catch up with the others. What was it about this business? he wondered with a rueful grin, as he flew down the stairs. All it takes is a hint of fame and celebrity and everyone wants to know you, and everyone wants to fuck you. You'll have to be very careful, Connor, my lad. In spite of his nerves he let out a genuine burst of laughter.

'Tonight, boys and boys – and the odd fag-hag who's crept in this evening – we have a real treat in store. I want you all to give the biggest and best Bare Pit welcome for four scrumptious lads who are set to take on the pop world with their first single 'Only The Night'. I heard it in rehearsal and I think it's gonna be huge. So let's give it up for BANNED!'

Leading the tumultuous applause, Gunther ran into the wings, as the four lads ran on. Even though they'd seen the club from upstairs they were unprepared for the view from the stage. A sea of faces, a roar of deafening noise greeted them appreciatively.

Standing before their microphones, they bowed their heads and waited for the music to start.

Nick, leaning against the bar at the back of the auditorium, looked on proudly. A churning sensation deep in his stomach told him that these four stunners would be a hit, that they had the extra special something which would propel them into the spotlight and fame and stardom. He nodded to himself approvingly, glad at the simple choice of outfits the boys had chose, plain black denim jeans, and tight white T-shirts, which clung very excitingly to their chests, showing that each of them had sex appeal and was nicely shaped. That alone should get the crowd on their side, he thought. As the first bars of the song rang around the club he smiled.

The boys moved well, and sang with confidence and style. They had charisma and assuredness, their faces lighting up with the warmth of the crowd's adulation. Connor had the appearance of a real star, with the lead vocals. He held the crowd in the palm of his hand. His voice soared and fluttered, like a bird in flight. It hit the high notes and filled out the lower ones, and all the time the crowd appeared to fly with him. Something had clicked, as if a switch hidden somewhere in Connor's subconscious had been flicked on, illuminating his personality with light. A glow of satisfaction rolled over Nick. Now he knew he had a hit.

The other songs were equally well received, and after an intense roar of approval, and an encore of 'Only The Night', the boys left the stage, thunderous applause ringing in their disbelieving ears.

'We did it!' Dean yelled out in a tremulous voice, as the four lads hugged each other and jumped up and down on the spot, the infectious good humour of the crowd buoying them up on a wave of euphoria. 'We fucking did it!'

Nick appeared from the darkened recesses of the stage and threw his arms around them. 'Well done... you were incredible! I can't believe how good you were. I knew you all had talent and stage presence, but what you did tonight has completely stunned me. You boys will be the biggest pop sensation the world has known, count on it. Now who's for a drink? There is beer, wine and champagne in the dressing room, or you can feel free to go into the club and mingle. I have set up a tab at the bar... just give my name and you'll be served. What are you waiting for? Go...!'

Dean was the first to leave. With a scream of delight he rushed down the steps to the backstage area and disappeared through the pass door to the auditorium, emerging into a cacophonous deluge of cheers, kisses, pats on the back and hugs from the crowd.

It took him ten minutes to push his way through the throng and arrive at the bar. Along the way he delighted in the reaction of the adoring gay crowd, letting those who wanted to kiss him on the cheek or the lips, or feel him up as he passed, some pinching his arse or getting a good grope at his crotch. Whatever happened, he didn't care. He was floating on a cloud of adulation. Besides, there might be someone cute here that he could take home... he stood a pretty good chance. If he couldn't pull tonight then he might as well turn celibate.

'Beer, please... on Nick De'Ath's tab.' He revelled in the beaming grin of the stunning blond barman, stripped to the waist and glistening with sweat.

'Great show!' he enthused as he cracked open a bottle and passed it across. 'You were brilliant!'

'Thanks a lot...' Dean shouted across the din of the club.

'No I really mean it.' The barman leant across the top of the beer-soaked bar, ignoring the waved money and the calls for service from other customers, letting another hunky barman leap forward to pour their orders. 'And you are definitely the most attractive of the group. I bet you are hot in bed.'

Dean couldn't believe what he was hearing. Such a blatant pick-up in such a public place. He had to go with the flow, or else he might not get another chance.

'You bet. You'll have to come and find me later and see what I've got to offer...' Dean raised the bottle to his lips and swallowed deeply, glugging down the refreshing brew, until the bottle was empty. 'Fuck, I needed that.'

'Another?'

'Why not.' Grabbing the offered bottle, Dean winked at the barman, spun away through the crowd and headed for the stairs that led up to the circle, where he looked around for a table. With a sigh of elation and exhaustion he slumped down in a vacant chair, plonked his bottle on the table and sat back, observing the crowd, looking for his fellow bandmates.

He spotted Joe on the dance floor, T-shirt tied about his waist, swinging madly, gyrating to the thump of the music. Paul and Uri were standing by the stage in conversation with a group of guys, including one with a large camera about his neck. Obviously the gay press. Nick was dancing closely with a young guy in lycra shorts that left little to the imagination. Even from a distance Dean could make out the size and shape of the young guy's cock as it bounced around. Lucky old Nick. He'd be having a good night tonight for sure. But he could see no sign of Connor.

The back staircase was quite dark and Connor had to hold onto the wooden banister rail as he climbed. Without knocking he pushed at the door to the control box. It swung open noiselessly, the two DJs failing to notice him standing in the doorway. As Jay-Vee turned to grab a record, he caught sight of the lad and beckoned him over.

'Hey, look who's come to see us.' He nudged Peter Q with his elbow, who pivoted on his heels, his face lighting up with a crinkled, happy smile, putting out a hand and moving in close to talk over the pounding music, its dull thump reverberating through the control box walls.

'Hey, you came! You were great... truly. I've seen some really awful acts here over the past two years that I've been spinning the discs, but you lot were something special. How do you feel now it's over?'

'Relieved!'

'I bet!' Peter Q leant in even closer and spoke in Connor's ear. 'I reckon you'll go far. Don't forget us when you're rich and famous, living in a penthouse and shagging all the boys you can.'

Connor blushed, the red glow of his cheeks obvious even in the gloom of the box.

'Sorry, have I offended you?' Peter Q's embarrassment was acute. 'I didn't mean to say anything...'

Putting a finger to his lips and stopping him saying anymore, Connor leaned in and kissed Peter Q. Their mouths opening wide to let their tongues meet, anxiously and feverishly, darting in and out, feeling their way around the warm, moist cavern.

Peter Q pulled away and nodded at Jay-Vee. 'Put on that old party mix... it is at least twenty minutes long... long enough for us.'

Doing as requested, Jay-Vee started off the new record and moved in towards his mate and the new arrival. Peter Q and Connor resumed their passionate kissing, as Jay-Vee dropped to his knees, swiftly unzipping both pairs of trousers with ease. With both hands he reached in and pulled both the now hard cocks free from their owners' jeans. Without the slightest hesitation he nuzzled into Connor's groin and swallowed his cock down in one go.

Connor felt his knees buckle and legs go weak at the astonishing sensation from the DJ. He groaned, but the sound disappeared as Peter Q renewed his kissing with fervour, holding Connor tight about the waist. The oral onslaught continued unabated. Jay-Vee sucked with an intense dedication, he was obviously a guy who loved cock. His wet tongue slurped at the head, before giving several great cow licks at the shaft, then swallowing the whole length again, downing it with ease, taking it to the back of his throat.

Now sure of himself and growing accustomed to the attention he was getting below, Connor started to push, driving his cock harder into Jay-Vee's throat. He could feel the pressure of Peter Q's body pressed against his, their mouths and tongues still locked together. Everything seemed to be happening in slow motion, as Peter Q pulled back and easily slipped Connor's T-shirt over his head and arms, throwing it aside, and then letting his tongue flick at the rigid, quivering nipples, licking around the brown circles, nipping and biting the proud fleshy lumps.

Connor groaned ecstatically. He had had good sex before, but never experienced a threesome. This was indescribable. Jay-Vee was stroking his tongue back and forth along the underside of Connor's throbbing dick, pressing both his lips against the bulging, ribbed shaft, following the line of the veins down to the base, teasing and licking at the root, and the skin where it joined the heavy ball-sac.

From a point deep within his loins Connor felt something begin to build, and he knew that if Jay-Vee carried on blowing in such a masterful fashion he would soon pop. Stepping back a little, he pulled away from the ministrations of the DJ's mouth and pushed Peter Q's head back from his glistening chest. Flopping down to his knees, Connor knew that here was the chance to indulge in one of his top fantasy scenarios. Something he'd imagined in his mind and wanked over many times before... sucking off two cocks at the same time.

He swiftly slipped Jay-Vee's grey jogging pants down, noting that Peter Q's cock was already free, standing rigid and ready, curving upwards in a steady arc, the plum-sized uncut head trembling, its collar of skin already pulled back, a drop of pre-cum shining at the tip, picking up the changing colours of the club lights.

Jay-Vee gasped as Connor's hand pulled his dick free, and with one quick movement he shucked his joggers and stepped out of them, now standing naked and hard. His cock was cut and beautifully formed, very wide, tapering down to a rounded head. But which one to choose first?

The decision was made for him. Peter Q grabbed the hair at the back of Connor's head and pulled him forwards. 'Right you little tease, I'm gonna fuck your mouth.' The voice was almost a growl, somehow menacing, and sent a shiver down Connor's spine.

Connor gave a small yelp as the fingers entwining and yanking on his hair resulted in a sharp stap of pain. His lips faintly parted, and he ran his tongue across them, wetting them as he did so. He was being brought forward slowly until his mouth was level with the head of Peter Q's cock. Connor's tongue slid out and licked at the head, across the velvet end, and underneath to the two lobes. The head was of an enormous size, bigger than expected for such an ordinary sized shaft.

The hand on the back of his head now forced Connor to the point of no return. Opening wide, he let the knob slip in, breathing heavily through his nose, as the vast rounded end filled his mouth totally. It seemed virtually impossible that he had gotten such a huge thing in his mouth, his jaw strained wide, and at the moment that he seemed able to accommodate the monster, Peter Q pushed forward. Connor's lips closed round the narrower shaft.

Hands now moved his head around so that he was being made to work that cock, the skin of the meaty weapon rubbing against all the surfaces inside Connor's mouth, setting up an amazing frisson of excitement. He knew that Peter Q was enjoying this, as he started to moan and buck his hips, keeping up the pressure on the back of his sucker's head, now forcing himself down until it touched the back of the throat, seemingly filling his entire self. Connor's mouth now ached ferociously, as did his knees, and his balls which now screamed for release. But there was nothing he could do about that.

'Let me at him.' Jay-Vee's voice cut in over the booming music track, pushing Peter Q to one side, watching as his cock emerged solid and dripping with spit from Connor's mouth.

It took but a second for Jay-Vee to position himself in front of Connor and without hesitating he pushed his own cock against the lad's lips, which yielded and parted letting the cock slide in. As it inched down, Jay-Vee grasped the base of the shaft, feeling the head enlarge, spongy and mushroom-shaped, topping the broader shaft, that grew bigger and wider as it slid down. As the entire length lay buried in Connor's throat, Jay-Vee paused, as if letting the lad savour the full sensation. The width of the cock certainly filled him, the base seemingly twice as wide as the end of the shaft, all eight inches planted deep in the warm, wet passage.

Then suddenly Jay-Vee started to fuck Connor's face. He appeared to enter a state of overdrive, pushing and retreating, faster and faster, revelling in the attention that Connor was now bestowing on his prick, almost doubled over with pleasure.

Peter Q's cock bumped against Connor's cheek, wanting attention, feeling left out of the equation. Rocking back on his heels, Connor backed off from the dark-haired DJ's tool, and looked up with appreciation at both the attractive young guys looming over him, the chiselled features and crew-cut blond hair of Peter Q, topping a finely muscled body, and the darker, lean Jay-Vee, brooding eyes and a tight torso, his hair flopping across his face in an endearing fashion.

Their cocks now twitched in front of him, both now desperate for satisfaction. Seeing the impressive dimensions of the two weapons, Connor sensed that he wouldn't be able to get both in his mouth at the same time. Nuzzling forward, he started to lick at one then the other, trying to give equal attention to the trembling hard-ons, hearing the muffled moans of delight from both. Keeping his mouth on the task, he raised his eyes and saw the two mates kissing passionately, their arms moving about each other's bodies.

Connor plunged his mouth down on Peter Q's cock, sucking and swallowing expertly, his hand wanking the skin of Jay-Vee's upright shaft, then he swapped and began to go down on that one, whilst jerking off Peter Q, all the time aware that they were both tensing up, the feelings of a climax not too far away.

It didn't take long for both the DJs to reach an explosive end. Jacking one off then the other whilst slurping and sucking, Connor seemed to achieve what he wanted. Both guys gave a grunt and almost simultaneously they shot their loads, pumping out hot and creamy fluid, splattering across Connor's face and neck, dripping down in sticky rivulets of white juice.

Reaching down and grabbing his own cock, it took but a few seconds for Connor to come: a stream of ejaculate arched high in the air landing on the control box floor in random patterns.

It took all three of them a few minutes to recover after the exciting exertions. Peter Q seemed to get his breath back first, helping Connor to his feet, running a finger down through the blobs of spunk that covered his face and matted his hair. 'Hmm, nice.'

His voice again had the soft quality that it first had when Connor appeared, all hint of menace gone. 'Very nice. I'm glad you came back.'

'So am I.' Connor pulled a tissue from his pocket and began wiping himself down. 'I hadn't expected anything like that tonight. In fact this was my first threesome.'

'You're joking!' Jay-Vee was dressing, keeping his eyes firmly on Connor's chest. 'Well, you'll just have to come back to one of our places someday soon, and spend a bit more time. There are loads of things we can do that would blow your mind... as well as your knob!' He grabbed his shirt which he'd thrown on the desk and wiped a few rogue drops of sperm from Connor's cheek.

'That might be fun.' Connor grinned, brushing dust from his jeans. 'Don't want to give the game away, someone might see I've been on my knees.'

The party-mix track was coming to an end and so Jay-Vee quickly and smoothly set up another record, effortlessly switching from one to the other. 'No. God forbid,' he said. 'What about the headlines... "Pop Star Blew Me. Sex Shock of Gay Club!!"'

'Don't even joke about that.' Connor's face darkened, a pang of anxiety rushed through him as he realised that what Jay-Vee said could conceivably come true.

'Hey lighten up.' Peter Q squeezed his crotch in a suggestive manner, and kissed him on his lips. 'We'll keep your secret. We want to have another go with you sometime. This won't go any further.'

'Thanks. I'd appreciate that.' Grabbing up his T-shirt, Connor pushed open the door, and with a last look back at the DJs, smiled and leapt down the steps.

The music that reverberated around the club, deafening the revellers below, also covered the gentle whirr of the security camera at the side of the control box, quietly but unceasingly rotating back and forth, the giant black eye watching everybody, seeing all.

Joe surveyed the dance floor, the hordes of men, bumping and grinding to the beat, oblivious to the rest of the world, lost in the music and the haze of the inhaled aromas they carried. Scan the crowd as he might, Joe could see no sign of Paul. He had spotted Nick leaving some time ago, his arm around the shoulders of a young man, clad only in figure-hugging lycra shorts. Dean was at the back of the auditorium deep in conversation with a barman, and Connor had disappeared completely.

Oh well, Paul had probably given up and gone home. Perhaps that was what he should now do. His limbs were heavy, he'd been dancing for at least an hour, and coupled with the adrenalin rush of the performance, Joe felt exhausted. Pushing through the crowd, he waved at Dean who waved back, a slight gesture of his head showing that he knew he had clicked with the handsome and youthful barman.

Outside, the night air was cool, and pulling his coat tightly around him, Joe hailed a cab. Sinking back into its comfy seats and giving the driver directions, he let his eyes flicker shut momentarily, until with a shock he realised the driver was knocking on the partition window.

Home.

As he let himself into the flat, he saw a light from under the bedroom door. Good. Paul had got back safely. Perhaps he'd like some hot milk to unwind. Perhaps they could make love as they used to. A long, loving, tender session, drinking in each other's bodies, melting into each other, giving and receiving ultimate pleasure.

He pushed at the door and it swung open. Utterly surprised, Joe surveyed the scene before him, as Paul hastily pulled up the sheets.

Sheets on the bed he was sharing with Uri.

7: Chest is Best

'Now it's full steam ahead.' Nick beamed at the boys who sat in a semi-circle around his office. A shaft of brilliant sunlight poured through the vast picture window, the panorama of London outside seemed enormous and welcoming.

The four members of BANNED looked back at Nick, waiting patiently. They knew he had a plan mapped out for them, but were intrigued to know the next step.

'The reception and your performance on Saturday night has proved that I was right all along. I know you boys have the potential and power to get to the top. We will be releasing 'Only The Night' as soon as possible, and will need to film a video to accompany the single. I am a great believer in input where appropriate, so have any of you any ideas as to what that video should look like?' Nick watched the boys watching him. The blank expressions on their faces stared back.

After a moment's thought, Dean spoke up. 'I reckon we should have a classy image. I don't want to be one of those bands who over-dress in leather or long, poncy coats, swirling around in mist. How about just a simple video of us dressed plainly, singing the song, sort of introducing us without any arty crap?'

Nick nodded slowly and stroked the back of his neck. The beam of sun had moved inexorably across the room and was pouring down upon him, gentle motes of dust flickering in the light. Sitting back he laced his fingers together.

'Not a bad idea actually. Most of the groups I've handled seem to want to start with a bang, jet off to some exotic location, and be filmed frolicking half-naked on a beach. You may have a point. Let me have a word with our ideas men and see what we can come up with. Whatever happens we want to get it shot in the next few weeks to try and get the single out before the end of the month.'

'OK, then,' said Dean after a minute's pause. 'I think we should not try too hard and push some kind of manufactured image of something we aren't. Why can't we be four ordinary lads who sing and dance and want to be a success? Why not just be ourselves, plain and simple?'

Murmurs of agreement ran around the office, and a firm nodding of heads.

'Excellent. Simple it is then.' Nick made some notes on a pad in front of him.

The boys looked at each other approvingly. 'But what do we do in the meantime?' Joe asked earnestly.

'We get the first album together, and I plan some television appearances for you. Having a single out is fine, but unless you can plug it on national telly then you'll get nowhere with it. I want to try and get you on ROKTV, they like new bands and the producer owes me a favour... if you know what I mean.' He chuckled and let his hand sit gently on his crotch, which as ever, bulged enticingly in his plain grey slacks. 'So I want you to go home, have a few days' rest, perhaps have a look around for gear that you might want to wear, and we'll get together on Wednesday to run through some more songs. In the meantime, take it easy, anything you want just call me and I'll sort it out.'

As the boys stood and headed for the door, Nick raised his voice. 'Don't all look so downbeat... you are going to be big. I can feel it here.' Placing a hand on his chest, he smiled broadly and turned back to the paperwork on his desk.

'Fancy a coffee anyone?' Connor waited for an answer from the other three as the gleaming chrome lift sank to the ground floor effortlessly and the doors glided open.

Joe nodded. 'Sure, why not? How's about we head into Soho, grab a bite to eat and then possibly check out some clothes stores?'

'Fine by me.' Dean thrust his hands deep in his pockets and sauntered towards the reception.

'I'm in,' said Paul, jovially. Ever since Saturday night there had been a change in Paul's attitude. Somehow he seemed more relaxed, less uptight and more ready to go with the flow of what the world wanted to throw at him. Joe seemed happier too. The pair of them appeared to have stopped the sniping and bickering that they had of late constantly indulged in.

After the shock of finding Paul in bed with Uri, Joe had stayed up late with Paul, talking well into the small hours of the night, realising that at present it would best for them to have an open relationship. Paul had thoroughly enjoyed the sex with Uri, in fact he had revelled in the wonder of another man's body, one that he wasn't overly familiar with, and had loved the experience. They knew that they still had a strong bond of love and affection, but they both saw that they wanted to make the most of the wide vista of sexual opportunity that was now opening up before them.

Connor ran to catch up with Dean as they left the front of the building and looked for a cab to hail. 'They seem happier, don't they? What's up?' Connor's eyes were full of interest as he walked along, arm in arm with Dean.

'Don't know.' Dean gave a throaty chuckle. 'Perhaps he fucked the arse off him, that'd stop anyone whining!' Both lads laughed loudly, then smothered their enjoyment as Joe and Paul joined them.

The film studio was situated in a converted warehouse, on the out-skirts of London. The neighbourhood was dingy and grey, but here in Willowtree Studios magic could occasionally be found.

Joe, Paul, Dean and Connor sat in canvas director's chairs, with their names in large letters on the back, watching the crew finishing the final touches to the lighting rig. The set they were to film their first video on was large, and swathed in white muslin cloth, hanging in huge swags from the ceiling. Dotted around the back of the set were several tall columns and plinths with Grecian busts on top. In the centre sat four tall bar stools.

Three rather well-muscled young men stood with video cameras on their shoulders, focusing lenses and checking their equipment. Behind the boys' chairs sat a large Panavision camera, on a tracking crane, used for swooping shots of the performers. The atmosphere was quite light and friendly even though the temperature was exceedingly hot. The bright studio lights burned down on the set, making the white muslin glow. Any uninvited beads of sweat that appeared on one of the boys' brows was immediately vanquished with a swift pat of a powder puff, Shelagh the chief make-up artist hovering at their elbows attentively. There was a discernible buzz about the place, as preparations were almost complete, nearly ready for the first take on the music video for 'Only The Night'.

The video's director, a young, lithe bearded American called Thom, paced up and down, in intense conversation with another young man that the lads had recognised as the costume designer, Mitch. He was an excessive man, not given to living life in a small way, his very appearance shouted out 'Individual'. His jeans were ripped so much that there was hardly a stitch of denim left, his arse visible to the world at large, his flouncy, lace-edged shirt seemed an incongruous addition, not to mention the various threatening piercings about his face: ears, eyebrows, nose and mouth – all had a metal stud or ring glinting in them. Thom had his arms crossed as he listened to the demands of Mitch, occasional words floated across to the boys. He wasn't happy. They knew that the costume designer on the production was feeling as if he was a pointless addendum, the four of them having settled on the look they thought promoted them best, plain black trousers, with plain black silk shirts. Classy and tasteful.

Mitch took the opposite view. He was of the opinion that young men should dress provocatively, in stretch materials and codpieces, tight T-shirts and thongs. The boys had had the first of many arguments with him that day when they turned up on set in their chosen outfits, ignoring the boots, leather shorts and brightly coloured rubber vests that he had selected and placed in the dressing room.

'We are not wearing those, so take them away.' Joe was adamant.

'But you have to... this look is so you.' Mitch petulantly stood in the dressing room doorway, hands on hips, lips pouting.

'No, Mitch. This look is so YOU. We are not parading around like some half-baked leather or rubber queens on a Gay Pride march. You just want to see us in these so you can drool over us. Well, it won't happen, deal with it.'

A short, high-pitched scream escaped Mitch's tight, pursed lips and he flounced away, desperate for a calming menthol cigarette, and a moan at the director, who at present he was unable to find. This was the very limit. Mitch had dressed and shaped the looks of numerous bands, granted not many of them had actually made the big time, but he knew what looked good. And here was a chance to show the world another of the stunning visions of Mitch Utrillo. And now here were these four nobodies throwing his designs back in his face. Bastards. He'd show them.

'OK, then. How's about we try one for the camera?' Thom stood before the boys, his face showing nothing but calm supportiveness. In his few years in the film business he had risen swiftly to great heights, having started as a runner on an American sitcom, *Here's Mamie!*, becoming a production assistant, before being entrusted with the job of director and making his mark on the industry. As an ex-shag of Nick's, he owed him a favour and when asked if he would come over to the UK and direct a music video for a new boy band, he agreed with delight, glad of the chance to do something other than continually pander to the inflated egos of the sitcom's stars.

'Why not. Are we ready?' Everyone looked to the boys, who stood and took their places on set.

A hush settled over the studio, as all eyes focused on the lads, willing them to do the best they could.

Thom placed headphones over his ears and sat at the small TV monitor to the side of the set. 'Right. Everyone ready? Let's do one.'

'Running up to speed... speed.'

'And... action.'

The backing track started, and suddenly the boys relaxed, sliding into an assured rendition of the song. Connor seemed happy and confident, miming to the lead vocals, ignoring the swooping of the overhead crane, which sometimes seemed to rush right into him, inches from his face. The others were swaying to the music, knowing that each of the cameras was at some time focused on them, giving their best, not wanting to let the others down.

'And cut.' Thom stood and padded over to the boys. 'Excellent... great, but we need to go again. There were a few camera glitches, and Joe... can you give more of a sultry look on the line "I feel you near me"? Connor, that's good, but your lip-synch is slightly out on the first few phrases... just be aware of that. Right let's try again. Ready studio?'

The next few takes were good also, but Thom knew that the set-up wasn't right. Something wasn't working. The boys definitely looked their best, attractive and enticing, and the song was fine too, but the video lacked that certain element that would make this a 'must-see'.

'Right boys, if you all trust me I want to try something now. I know you won't like it, but so far I'm not entirely happy with the results.'

The boys waited for Thom to continue. He ran his fingers through his hair nervously. 'It's just that I want you to try the next take with... your shirts off.'

All four of the boys exploded with contempt.

'You are joking? After all we've gone through with that Mitch?' Connor sat in disbelief.

'Seriously.' Thom put a hand on Connor's shoulder placatingly. 'The video is OK at the moment, but just OK. It should sizzle, it should make the girls and boys watching feel all funny inside. I want them to be wetting themselves with desire... that is the only way that a band such as you can make their first impact. The song can be a winner, but your image needs to be astonishing. You need to provide something that the public can only dream about, that they'll fantasise over and ultimately become fans of. You are all handsome, you have charisma and talent, but I need to see those bodies. What do you say? Just for me? And if it doesn't work then we'll come up with another angle.'

Reluctantly the boys slipped off their shirts, knowing that the eyes of the entire studio were on them.

'Get used to this,' said Dean under his breath to the other three. 'From now on we'll be sex symbols, if we are lucky, and this will be a typical day's happening.'

One of the camera operators caught Dean's eye and smiled. Very cute. Dean smiled back, seeing with appreciation that he seemed a nice guy. A lopsided grin on a handsome angular face, brown hair which looked as if it had fought a losing battle with a brush that morning. Tight jeans, a scruffy plaid shirt and hiking boots completed the picture. Very nice. Unconsciously, Dean flexed his arms, showing the definition in his musculature, noticing the guy's eyes widen with admiration.

97

'So let's try another one.' Thom was again in control. 'But let's just darken the set a touch, and perhaps add a hint of colour, perhaps a pale blue gel? And can we get the smoke machine going?'

The lighting director made the required changes and the cameras started rolling again. Even the boys knew that Thom had made the right decision, and the feel of the video changed intensely. They knew that they now oozed sexuality and would get the viewers creaming themselves.

'Great! Lunch everyone. Back in one hour.' Thom stalked off to his room, muttering happily to his assistant, having given a contented salute to the boys.

'Right then, I'm starving!' Paul reached for his shirt, buttoning it up and looking around for a sign as to where the canteen might be. 'Coming?'

He waited for an answer from the others. Connor and Joe nodded heartily, but Dean was a little hesitant.

'You guys go on ahead, I'll catch you up. There's someone I want a word with.' He let his eyes wander about the set, seeing no sign of the friendly cameraman.

'OK. See you later.' Paul led the way off the set, following the stream of technicians, toward the side door.

Dean stood shirtless in the centre of the set, surrounded by Grecian busts, waiting as the studio emptied. All he could hear was the electrical hum of the lights, and a distant hubbub from the canteen, of hungry and excited people.

'Ahem.' There was the sound of someone clearing his throat, making Dean jump.

'God, you startled me!' He turned around to see the cameraman standing at the side of the set, leaning against the studio wall, his arms crossed, his face beaming.

'Sorry! I just wanted to attract your attention.' He crossed to Dean's side and put out a hand. 'Greg.'

'Dean.' They shook hands, holding the grip for as long as they dared, their eyes also holding the stare.

'Er... so you are a cameraman, then?' Dean felt a complete idiot asking such a dull question, but nerves had got the better of him. Faced with a horny young guy, he found himself in the position of tongue-tied imbecile.

'You noticed?' Amused, Greg punched Dean playfully on the arm. 'Nice definition.'

Dean realised he was talking about his muscles. 'Thanks. I try to keep in shape.'

'I should say you succeed. Is the rest of you as nice?' Greg's eyes, a dark brown, with brilliant white surround, held Dean's in a vice, daring him to look away.

'Might be.'

'I'd like to find out sometime.'

'I bet you would.'

'How about now?'

'No reason why not.'

'Good, because I'm going away tonight and I wouldn't want to miss a chance like this.'

Greg took Dean's arm and led him to the back of the set, behind the swags of curtaining, to a small room, a camera store cupboard, with shelves covered with lenses and boxes of film. On the floor were several large metal suitcases, used for transporting camera equipment to outdoor locations. The light bulb was very dim, so they had a secluded niche to themselves.

For a moment the two men stood close together, just revelling in the moment and the thought of what they might do, hardly touching, but aware of the electricity emanating from another man's body. Then Greg put out a hand and ran it across Dean's chest, slowly unbuttoning the shirt, enjoying the feel of the tightly muscled mounds of flesh, his fingertips just brushing the nipples, instantly arousing them. His hand lingered around them, before sliding down his stomach, flicking in and out of Dean's navel, then ever so slowly it reached the silken material of his trousers, inching lower until it stopped at the hardened tool beneath. The fabric was pushed out by his cock, a large bulge, and growing larger.

'Hmmm, very nice. I just knew it would be,' Greg whispered appreciatively.

'Thanks.' Dean wanted this man so much it hurt. He was genuine and friendly, and attractive. His scruffy appearance gave him the look of a cheeky schoolboy, his face constantly brightened by his appealing smile.

Greg was enjoying the feel of Dean's now hard cock through his trousers, all the while Dean was unbuttoning Greg's shirt, before slipping it off his shoulders, letting it fall in a crumpled heap on the floor. There was a light sheen of perspiration on Greg's chest, tiny droplets of sweat that mingled with the fine down of hair. Their eyes met and locked again. Dean flicked a strand of hair from Greg's eyes. All the time, Greg's hand hadn't left Dean's groin, massaging and cupping the enraged cock, and impressive bollocks. Dean pressed closer until the two stood together, and embraced, holding each other tightly. Nuzzling into Greg, Dean began to nibble at his earlobe, bringing out a groan of delight. He raised his head and their lips met. For a few minutes they kissed, deep and passionate, exploring the interiors of each other's mouths.

Reaching down with his hand, Dean fumbled around for Greg's cock, finding it and gripping hold through his jeans. He could feel it hard and ready, the length of it running down his leg, his huge balls, nestling at the top of the other leg. With a practised motion he unzipped the fly and whipped the prick free from the confines of the blue denim. It stood straight out, the cut head already hot and sticky. His cock was of a wonderful size, and his balls were enormous. Dean wondered if he'd be able to get them both in his mouth at the same time. It would be fun trying.

Greg's hands swiftly unzipped Dean, unbuckling the belt and letting the trousers fall to the ground. In two quick hops, Dean stepped out of them, placing them with care on one of the suit-cases.

'Fucking hell, I want you so much,' Greg murmured into Dean's ear, fondling his newly freed cock. 'I wanted you from the moment I saw you on set. I've never met such a beautiful man before.'

Dean knew that was his cue. 'OK then. Suck my cock.' He placed his hands on Greg's shoulders, but the cameraman needed no pushing. Greedily he sank to his knees, desperate to taste Dean's thick meat.

'Wait until I tell you!' Dean's voice was firm and unwavering. 'Now open your mouth.'

Greg stared up at Dean, his mouth now wide open, his tongue trembling with anticipation, his eyes wide and pleading. Inch after inch slid down Greg's throat, the width of the tool stretching his mouth to breaking point, his saliva-coated tongue slurping at the underside of the shaft. Dean groaned out loud, his head falling back, his hands holding tightly at the back of Greg's head, fingers entwined in his hair. He briefly held Greg in the subordinate posi-tion, before starting to fuck his mouth, watching as the guy's red lips sucked at his shaft, widening at each stroke.

Keeping watch on Dean's expression, Greg knew that he was giving pleasure. Above all else that is what he delighted in doing. Blowing to the best of his ability, serving the guy he was with, making him yearn for more and bringing him to the point of no return. He concentrated more, sucking and licking at the thick tool, which was hammering away in him, dreaming of what it would feel like up his arse.

Dean began to stiffen. Sensing that he was on the verge of com-ing, Greg pulled away. Expertly he slipped out of his jeans, until he stood naked before Dean, his own cock erect and proud.

Moving away he sat down on one of the metal suitcases, leaning his torso back, emphasising the prick's amazing dimensions.

Looking at the delicious knob waiting in front of him, Dean desperately wanted it up inside him.

'In a box up there.' Dean followed Greg's eyes, unsure what he meant, when he realised that the guy was talking about condoms. Reaching up to the box, his fingers found a condom and a sachet of lube. Now fully aroused and excited, Dean ripped the packet open and rolled the rubber down the length of Greg's cock, until it stopped at the thick base. Slathering the cock with lube, he bent over in front of Greg, who had gripped himself around the bottom of the shaft in readiness. He was still hard, the energy and thrill of the moment had made him, if possible, more erect. This was to be his first time. Up until now he had sucked cock, and been sucked, but never had the courage or nerve to fuck another guy. He steeled himself for the experience.

Positioning himself at the opening, Greg gritted his teeth and pushed. The knob-head was engulfed by the hole as it penetrated, sliding effortlessly inside, encased totally. The sphincter squeezed and tightly held the head.

'Yes, that's it... slowly.' He let the pressure ease a little so the rest of the massive girth could slide forward.

Dean winced at the flash of pain, as the cock was pushed more into him. Then Greg was totally inside. Deep in him. The width of the cock was bigger than he imagined it would be, and it stretched the muscles of his anus wide, the friction beginning to build as the strokes became faster and more regular.

Using both his arms to push down on Dean's broad back, Greg began to fuck in earnest. Unused to the sensation of forcing his dick up another guy's arse, he wanted to take his time and enjoy. This was incredible, he'd never known anything like it. It was as if Dean was somehow swallowing him, pulling his pulsing cock deep into his very self. His hips slapped wetly against Dean's arse cheeks, his bollocks swinging back and forth, banging rhythmi-cally as he fucked. He didn't know why he had never done this before. Loving the amazing feeling of being plundered perhaps meant that he had had less desire to do it to someone else.

Not wanting this to end, Greg slowed down, taking his time, pushing his weapon inch by inch into the lad, then sliding back, easing it out until just the knob-head was inside, before pushing back, resuming the slow rocking motion, burying himself deep within Dean.

The young singer grabbed his own cock and began to pump vigorously, in time with Greg's exertions, massaging its length, encouraging its own, much needed climax. The dual sensation of the exultant penetration and the sensual pulsing of his own cock pushed Dean to the heights of renewed desire. He slid his arse as far down toward Greg as he could, encouraging him further, feel-ing him swelling inside his being.

In no time they were at the moment of eruption, both feeling the surge of energy, which signalled an ejaculation. Without even touching his own cock, Dean shot his load, as Greg slipped out, pulled the rubber from him and shot also, a long stream over Dean's sweat-covered back.

'Wow! That was an eye-opener.' Greg stood, still hard, the con-dom hanging limply from his grasp, and reached for a roll of paper tissue. 'That was the first time I've ever fucked anyone.'

'You were brilliant. It felt so wonderful. I can't believe that's your first time.'

'Cross my heart. I am usually a bottom. But that was great. I'll think about it all the time I'm away.'

Dean planted a gentle kiss on Greg's cheek, and taking a wad of tissue from him, began wiping himself down. This guy looked so appealing, his hair falling in untidy swathes across his face, his boy-ish chest wet with the perspiration of effort, his semi-recumbent cock falling out from the bush of hair at his crotch.

As he wiped, he stole a glance at his watch. 'Shit. Better get a move on... they'll be back soon. Thanks Dean, that was great. Maybe we can do it again sometime, when I'm back from my trip?'

'Sure. I think we could have a lot of fun.' Dean quickly dressed, watching Greg do the same, a feeling of anxiety in the pit of his stomach, a feeling that he could become very attached to this young man. He could not bring himself to ask Greg how long he would be away.

After the cameraman slipped out the door, Dean glanced down at the used condom lying on a sheet of paper towel, on top of the skip, and something in its appearance made him examine it more closely. At the very end was a small rip. Dean went cold. If it had been ripped during the fuck, then he could have been having unsafe sex. He went out into the corridor. Greg was nowhere to be seen.

8: Revenge is a Drug

After lunch, the band managed to accomplish ten more complete takes of the song. Thom was a perfectionist, and someone that the boys immediately trusted. And so if he had wanted them to do the song naked and hanging from trapezes, they probably would have. All through the afternoon Dean was quieter than usual, not joining in with the group's jokes, something weighty on his mind.

During tea-break, Joe paid a quick visit to the toilet, head down, mind full of set-ups and lyrics, and as he pushed the door open he crashed into a guy coming out from the facilities.

'Sorry.'

'Joe, how are you? The voice had a very familiar ring to it. Joe looked up and into the grinning face of Mark Trevithick, zipping his obligatory leather trousers up.

'Hey, how's things?' Joe was genuinely pleased to see the cute delivery guy.

'Fantastic.'

'What are you doing here?'

'I had a delivery of samples for Mitch the bitch.' His face corrugated with an ironic smile.

'Oh you know her then, do you?' Joe grinned back, as he saw the designer stalking down the corridor to the dressing rooms, carrying the newly delivered paper-wrapped parcel.

'Sure. She's alright when you get to know her. You just have to agree with anything she says. Horny as fuck between the sheets though...'

Amazed, Joe stared at Mark. 'You've had sex with... with that?'

'Sure. If it's male and hung I'll do it.'

'Thanks a lot... that doesn't say much for me, does it?'

'I didn't mean that. You were... are something special. I was hoping you might like to come out with me tonight. I've been invited to a party and I wanted you to come with me.'

'Sure, why not?'

'Great. I'll swing by and pick you up about eight. And don't worry... I've got a spare helmet!'

Back on the set, Joe sat on his personalised chair next to Paul and laid a hand on his knee.

'Er... Paul, I've been invited out to a party this evening. Do you mind?'

Munching away on a cheese sandwich, Paul raised an eyebrow, a twinkle in his eye. An unspoken invitation to go and have a good time.

'Thanks.' Joe placed a kiss on Paul's forehead, knowing that the trust between them, as well as the newly found ability to stray, and to sleep around, was well formed. Paul would be OK about the party, and would know that if the opportunity to have sex with someone else cropped up, he could take it with as little guilt as Joe now had.

Swallowing hard and taking a gulp of a bottle of water at his feet, Paul squeezed Joe's hand. 'Have fun.'

As the set wrapped, at the end of a very long and exhausting day, without a word to any of the lads, Dean slipped out of the studios. He needed to think. He needed to get his mind around the possibility that he could have come into contact with one of the most pernicious viruses ever known to man. What would his life be like if he developed HIV? Could he carry on with the band? Surely no self-respecting fan would want to cheer on a guy with such a disease? Should he talk to the guys? Or should Nick be told? His brain ached with the maelstrom of nagging questions.

Dean walked the streets until he came to a small green playing field, cordoned off with a chain-link fence. Seeing a gap, he wriggled through it and headed towards the children's play area in the far corner. Sinking down onto a swing, he sat still, lost in thought, scuffing the ground with the toe of his shoe.

He didn't know what to do next. Suddenly he felt more alone than he ever had. The desire for a cuddle and words of comfort overwhelmed him. He raised his head and looked around him. At the entrance to the park stood a phone box, empty, its white light blazing out through the many panes of grafitti-covered glass. Determined, he got to his feet and crossed to the booth, yanking open the door, and searching for some coins in his jeans pocket. He deposited a coin in the slot and then his trembling fingers pushed the buttons, dialling a very familiar number. The phone was picked up.

'Hello.'

'Hello. Mum?'

'Hello Dean, love. How are you?'

'OK.'

'We haven't heard from you in ages. Everything is alright, isn't it?'

'Sort of.'

'Because you know we worry about you, your dad and me. If there's anything wrong, we hope you'd tell us.'

'I know.'

'So how is everything down there? Is the singing going well?'

'Mum, it's not just singing... it's... we are going to be a famous group.'

'Yes, love. But it's not really a proper job, is it? Now if you'd

Sam Stevens

gone into the plumbing firm with your dad you'd have had a
steady career by now.'

'Look, I don't want to get into all this again.'

'You always thought plumbing was beneath you. But it's provided very well for us and don't you forget it.'

'Mum, just give it a rest, eh? I just wanted to hear a friendly
voice. It's been a bad day and I wanted to say hello.'

'Life isn't easy, love. I should know. You should try having two
children, one dying as a baby, one who runs away from home,
leaving his mother and father, scarcely giving a thought for their
feelings. Oh but I forgot, you won't be having children, will you?'

'No.'

'So I suppose you are still keeping up this "gay" thing, are you?'

'Yes.'

'Well, I hope it's nothing that I ever said or did to you. Why my
son should grow up to be one of those is beyond me.'

'Look I've got to go. I'll ring you again sometime.'

'Just see that you do. And don't leave it so long this time.'

'Bye, Mum.'

Dean replaced the receiver with a hollow click. Unable to hold
back his emotions any longer, he fell against the side wall of the
booth and cried. Years of anguish and hurt poured out, his body
shaking with uncontrolled sobs.

The flat outside which Mark pulled up with a screech of tyres was
in a tall block, in an outer London suburb, unprepossessing and
miserable. As Joe gazed around, seeing the kids kicking cans about
for pleasure, and old ladies struggling with heavy bags of shopping, just purchased from the estate stores, he was pleased that he
lived in a nicer area.

'Come on.' Mark squatted by the bike, locking several heavy
duty chains and padlocks about the bike, thoroughly securing it
against theft. 'Scottie's flat is only on the second floor.'

As they entered the building, passing the list with the taped notice 'Out Of Order', and began to climb, Joe was curious. 'So who is this Scottie?'

'Oh, he's someone I've known for years, we were at college together. You'll like him, he's a real character.'

'Who else is likely to be there?'

'Not sure, but he has some great mates, horny too, and all very good at it.'

'Good at what?'

'You'll see. Ah, here we are... number twenty-four.' Mark gave a short jab at the bell, which rang with the alarming electronic sound of the theme tune to *Bonanza*. The door was immediately yanked open, and a short, stocky, red-headed guy stood in the doorway.

'You came!' His Scottish accent showing how his rather dull nickname originated.

'Of course... would I let you down, my darling?' Mark strode in leaving Joe to follow in his wake, pushing the door closed behind him. He stepped after Mark into the kitchen where a young Asian man was in the act of pouring drinks. He appeared to be naked under his blue striped apron, and as he turned away from Joe, it was confirmed, his pert buttocks there for all to see.

Butterflies started to turn somersaults in Joe's stomach. What kind of party had he been brought to? Please let it be a normal one... not a sex party.

Nick had given the band members strict instructions to try and be careful about their sex lives, now that fame beckoned. Although BANNED was being promoted as a gay group, the last thing they wanted was a scandal right at the beginning of their careers. Joe knew that being seen, even caught at a sex party was a very unwise thing.

He took the glass of wine that the Asian guy offered him with a cheeky smile, and looked on askance as he then raised his apron,

109

giving Joe a quick, tempting glance at what he had underneath, a long, thin cock, over pendulous bollocks, all tied round with a length of black cord. He giggled, dropped the apron and dashed out of the kitchen, leaving Joe, Mark and Scottie alone.

'So who is this tasty titbit?' Scottie put out his hand to Joe in welcome. 'Rory... otherwise known as Scottie to my friends, and I hope you'll be one of them. I can tell we'll get on... you have a generous aura.'

'Do I? Well, that's nice to know.'

'Oh yes, definitely. I can see a golden glow about you... very nice. I just know that you have a good soul, and by the look of you a high sex drive and a big cock.' He winked lasciviously and reached out, tweaking Joe's nipples which were erect and obvious through his T-shirt. Joe looked pleadingly at Mark, as if to say 'help, get me out of here'.

Ignoring the obvious, Mark took a large swig of beer from the can he was gripping, and led the way out of the kitchen. The hallway was dark, but a chink of red light shone from beneath a door at the far end of the corridor. With his free hand, Mark battered it open and entered. Inside Joe was riddled with innumerable misgivings. The spacious sitting room was peopled by youngish men, in various states of undress, entwined in each other's arms, or lying close to each other on sofas and chairs. The air was heavy with the bittersweet aroma of marijuana, some of the guys already heavily stoned.

Mark picked his way through the bodies littering the room and sank down on the floor in the far corner next to a guy he seemed to know, and took a smoking joint from his fingers. This was too much for Joe to handle. With a determined tread he strode back down the hallway to the kitchen, where Scottie was now deep in conversation with an exceedingly ugly man, heavily tattooed, balding, his face covered in greying stubble, his bare chest peppered with violent purple scars. He held out a small plastic bag, containing some small white tablets.

'Er... Scottie... I have to go now, sorry,' Joe stuttered, trying to keep his voice level, and failing.

Rapidly stuffing the bag into his pocket, Scottie turned to Joe, and put his arm around his shoulder, firmly. 'Nonsense, boy. You'll stay and at least have another drink. I insist.'

The tone of Scottie's voice had an intensity about it, a quality that defied being argued with. Joe wasn't in the mood for a fight so he nodded wearily. Turning back to the counter, Scottie poured another glass of wine, which he seemed to be hovering over for a moment, then turning back he handed it over. 'Now go in there and enjoy yourself.'

A high-pitched squawk filled the air, and as Joe spun on his heels he saw the pierced countenance of Mitch bearing down on him. 'It's one of the picky queens.' He was stumbling a little, obviously drunk and probably off his head with drugs. Grabbing Joe by the arm he pulled him toward the main room, his grip tight, his intentions unclear.

'Now you listen to me, Miss Picky, I am very angry with you...' Mitch's voice swam in and out of Joe's mind as he tried desperately to block out what the designer was screeching.

Taking a huge gulp of wine, Joe looked about him in despair, grimacing as the strangely bitter liquid ran down his throat. The whole room had assumed the air of an orgy, men were indulging in sex and drugs and alcohol, and without exception enjoying it. He stared at a couple enjoying a sixty-nine on a sofa, oblivious to the fellow party-goers in the room, sucking away at each other's cocks with gusto, entirely in that moment, aware only of the solid tools in their mouths, and the sensations they were giving and receiving.

This was becoming a nightmarish situation, and Joe knew he had to get away. He tried to shake off Mitch's attentions, and head for the door, but his legs felt weird and tremulous. Reaching out to

Mitch, he sank down on a chair, feeling distinctly woozy. His head was now spinning, images and sounds whirled around, his eyes getting blurry, a feeling of nausea in the pit of his stomach.

'How are you feeling?' Mitch seemed concerned, his face loomed in front of Joe's unfocused vision. 'It'll soon pass, and you'll feel much better. Let's get you into the bedroom. I bet you've never been drugged before, have you?'

Mitch's voice was suddenly sober and calm, as Joe gave up trying to stay awake and slumped into black unconsciousness.

Dean wiped his eyes and pushed the phone box door open, then took several large gulps of cool night air. Pulling another coin from his pocket, he dialled another number, hoping that the receiver would be picked up.

'Nick De'Ath.'

'Thank God. Nick, it's Dean. Can I come over? I need to talk to you now.'

Sensing the urgency in Dean's voice, Nick knew better than to refuse the lad. 'Of course. Come right over.'

Hailing a taxi, Dean immediately felt slightly calmer. Having someone to talk to would help, and if that someone was the ultracool Nick, then there might be a light at the end of the very long and very dark tunnel.

When Nick opened his door and saw the huddled figure, standing shivering and hunched, he took control of the situation.

'Right, come in and sit down. I'll make us some tea and you can tell me all about it.'

Dean slumped against the soft leather upholstery, curling up into a foetal ball, bringing his knees up to his chin, his arms grasping them tight.

That was how Nick found him when he reappeared with a tray of tea things. Pouring out a strengthening cup, he spoke in a soothing, encouraging tone.

'So tell me what's the matter.'

Without pause, Dean let the story out, detailing everything that happened between him and Greg, and how he had failed to find the cameraman later in the day.

'He's probably gone for good now. He kept going on about how he was going away.' Dean stopped and stared blankly at the steaming cup of tea that Nick had handed him.

'It's a tricky one.' Nick tried to sound reassuring and optimistic. 'And there is no easy answer. First thing in the morning we go to a clinic and you take the test. Then we'll know for certain. They are very quick and get the results back the same day. I'll call my doctor now and arrange it.'

He turned away and picked up the phone, jabbing the number out and waiting for a response. Dean sipped at his tea, feeling it warming and reviving him, some words of his mother's filling his head. 'If all else fails, have a cup of tea.' Words she was fond of saying. He held no grudge against his parents. When they'd been told of his homosexuality, they found it very hard to understand or accept, but over the years they had tried hard to come to terms with it. Sometimes the sadness of their situation overflowed and they would suddenly become bitter at the fact that they would probably never have grandchildren. His brother Darren had died when he was two of a brain disease that hadn't been properly diagnosed. So with Dean as their only son and heir, they found it difficult to face the truth about the end of their family line.

Dean looked up as Nick replaced the receiver, a concerned frown furrowing his brow.

'Well?'

'I'm sorry, but I don't have good news. The clinic could do a test tomorrow, but the results wouldn't show anything. We have to wait for around three months before it would become apparent if you have the virus.'

'Three months.' A tear rolled down Dean's cheek as the enormity of the situation hit him. 'How can I possibly wait that long?'

'You'll have to. I'll be there with you all the way.'

'But how can I...?' He faltered, his mind a jumble of images and worst-case scenarios.

'Just be strong. I know you can. We'll carry on with the band as if nothing happened and then we'll take the test. Then we'll know for sure. OK?'

'I guess so.' Dean was numb. How could he manage to get through the next three months, not knowing if his life was to be drastically altered?

'And look on the bright side, you may not have it. Unlike other poor bastards who are suffering right now. I'll try and track down Greg for you in the meantime – perhaps he will even be able to reassure you that you're in the clear.'

Sighing, Dean placed his cup on the coffee table and stood up, realising that what he probably needed most now was a good night's sleep. Perhaps things would look better in the morning. 'Promise you won't say anything to anyone about this... please?'

Nick drew his finger across his chest. 'Cross my heart.'

'He's coming to.'

It was Mitch's voice that Joe first heard as he started to wake from the drug-induced coma. His eyes focused slowly on his surroundings and saw that it was lit with a single red light bulb, swinging gently from the centre of the ceiling. He tried to stand up, but found that he had no strength at all. He seemed to be floating in mid-air. His arms and legs felt as if they were rock solid and couldn't move. He looked about and saw with horror that he was tied in a sling, his legs and arms fastened to the chains which hung from the ceiling, his arse and genitals there for all to see and use. He was completely naked. Someone had undressed him and whilst unconscious had played around with him – a length of twine was knotted around his cock and balls, so tightly that the second he realised the situation, Joe became erect, the blood flow to his cock swift and sure, filling out his entire length until it stood up from his lap. He tried to speak but found that he couldn't. A strip of tape had been placed over his mouth.

'I think he wants to play.' Mitch spoke again, suddenly appearing from behind Joe, also naked, his body thin, white and uninviting. His nipples and genitals were pierced, a large silver ring through the end of his knob which swung as he moved, the hefty weight of it almost stretching the cock downwards. He leaned in and whispered softly and menacingly in Joe's ear.

'Now my little prisoner... It's payback time. Ever since this morning I've wanted to have a go at one of you pissy little faggots. All you've done today is humiliate me in front of one of the biggest video production agencies in the business. I may never work for them again after today's fiasco, and so I want to get my own back... revenge I suppose you'd say. I guess in the grand scheme of things what you boys did today wasn't too nasty, but then I am a vicious queen, and I want my own back. Now we're going to have some fun... you, me and several of my friends, and there is not much you can do about it.'

Joe tried with his eyes to say that he wanted the tape taken from his mouth, but before anything further happened, someone roughly tied a scarf around his eyes, cutting him off from the rest of the scene, his only senses now available being touch, smell and hearing. And he didn't like what he then heard.

He immediately recognised the drawling accents of Scottie who spoke. 'So who wants to go first? Ooh look, it's got a lovely big prick... right, me first then.'

A hand clamped itself about Joe's cock, its grip tight and unyielding, and began to drily wank it up and down. A murmur of enthusiastic goading ran round the room. Joe thought there must be about four or five men in the room, Scottie, Mitch and some others, silent and unidentifiable. Bound and sightless like he was, there seemed no way to find out who they were. Without warning a mouth went down on his cock. The mouth was certainly an expert, it slid down the length of the shaft, sucking with exquisite pressure, the tongue moist and warm, slurping and delighting in the size of the weapon, pulling the skin back as far as possible, getting at the head, swirling it around like a giant velvet lollipop.

Twisting his head back from side to side and grunting were all that Joe could do.

'Stop that.' A firm voice cut through the room, and without warning a stinging blow was glanced across Joe's cheek. He wanted to cry out with pain and shock, but the tape over his mouth stopped him. He had never felt so helpless, being unable to move and in the hands of ruthless aggressors, men who could now do anything they wanted to him.

As the mouth continued its expert working over, two other mouths suddenly made contact with his chest, simultaneously licking and biting his nipples. Even though he was incapable of movement, Joe found the experience strangely erotic. There were three men using his body, one on his cock and two sucking at his chest, and it felt exciting. His cock stiffened, bringing an appreciative sigh from the owner of the mouth down there.

Then, all of a sudden a moistened finger began to probe at his arsehole, before being withdrawn, and a tongue manifested itself, licking with eagerness at the puckered ring. This continued, one after the other, tongue then finger, toying with him, all the while the other three kept up their oral attentions. Joe arched his body, pulling away from the leather strip he lay suspended on, the desire to cry out racking his mind and soul. Without warning, the long, probing finger thrust inside him. Again he wanted to yell, but could only manage a muffled groan. It pushed in and out with such force that his breathing increased dramatically.

In a flash, the finger withdrew and a voice spoke with a soft Cornish accent, 'I think he's ready.'

Was that Mark's voice? Surely not? That friendly, sexy man couldn't be a party to this, could he? Joe imagined Mark's muscled body standing between his legs, his cock in hand, hard and ready to penetrate his helpless hole. He felt the pressure of a cockhead at his anus, pushing and urging. Please let the guy be wearing a condom, Joe thought. There was a pause as he heard the metallic ripping noise of a packet being opened and he knew that whoever was holding him captive knew about the perils of unsafe sex.

Again the cock jabbed at his hole. Joe tried to grit his teeth ready for the invasion. With a surge of total power, the cock jammed its way inside, the huge, hardened head sliding past the tight ring of muscle. A wave of pain rippled through him, his head twisting back and forth, groans emitting from his throat. Another slap came, smacking across his face, bringing tears to his covered eyes. This was now getting way out of hand.

The other three mouths stayed at their posts, unceasing, licking and slurping, biting and nipping, giving mind-blowing sensations to every part of Joe's body. The passage of the cock up inside Joe was unstoppable. With a grunt, Joe forced his body to relax, trying to get his sphincter to ease and to let the forceful tool push inside more gently. He had been fucked before, and enjoyed it but the brutality of this situation took away some of the delight. In his mind, Joe knew he was practically being raped.

The cock was finally embedded up inside him, blazing like a fiery torch, sending out spasms of throbbing pain. Arms wrapped around Joe's torso as his dominator began to fuck his arse with a passion, thrusting deep and hard, forcing his ring to expand and contract with every pounding stroke. Gradually Joe became accustomed to the penetration, making each thrust slightly easier. In his mind he knew that he was secretly enjoying this, as the mouths worked over his tits, and his own dick was being sucked to its maximum rigidity.

The skin of his fucker was now grazing against his backside, and he could feel the dull slap as a pair of huge bollocks thumped against him with each push. The stretching pain began to subside into a feeling of warm fullness, aware of the discomfort of his position, but now relaxed enough to appreciate the excitement of the moment.

'Fuck him!' A voice floated into Joe's ears. He didn't recognise it.

Then a voice he did know spoke. 'Hurry up, it's my turn.' Mitch was wanting to fuck him too. And there was nothing he could do about it.

Whoever was fucking him started to increase his pace, and within a few more seconds came, his load shooting deep within Joe, safely caught in the strong rubber sheath. The cock was swiftly pulled out, and Joe heard the familiar sound of metal packet being ripped apart, and the crackling snap of a condom being placed over solid meat.

With no preamble, his hole was invaded again, this time without any care, just thrust upwards. He knew it was Mitch. He wasn't sure if he could feel the heavy silver Prince Albert piercing inside him or not, he just hoped and prayed that it wouldn't split the condom. The pain was equal to that of the previous solid tool, if anything it was more. Mitch's cock seemed to have grown in disproportion to the rest of him. For such a thin, wiry man, he possessed a monster organ.

He thought that things couldn't get any more intense. But he was wrong. The mouths that were working over his chest suddenly stopped, and the two strangers moved away. A moment later he heard the brisk sound of matches being struck, and the splutter of candles being lit. In another moment he writhed as blobs of hot wax fell onto his tender nipples, encasing them in the rapidly hardening substance. Again and again scalding drops fell on his chest and stomach.

Joe didn't know what hurt the most – the fucking or the wax torture. He writhed again, the agony almost overwhelming. He was totally unprepared for the hand that once more slapped his face. Joe couldn't bear it, he wanted desperately to cry, to let hot tears flow, but he couldn't. His captors had seen to that.

The fucking intensified, as did the dripping of the wax and the sucking of his cock. Another mouth materialised between his legs and started to lap at his bollocks. This was someone who knew the boundary between pleasure and pain, his attentions immeasurable. The mouth swallowed the balls in one gulp, the tongue slavering over them wetly, until Joe thought they would burst.

As if in answer to his prayers, someone ripped the tape from his mouth with a rapid yank. Joe screamed as the skin around his lips burst with stinging pain. At last he could breathe properly... and say what he thought of these bastards.

'Aaaaaah!' He screamed at the top of his voice, hoping that it would attract someone else's attention, hoping that someone would come to his aid.

'It's... no... use... screaming, petal.' Mitch's voice came in bursts, speaking in rhythm with the strokes of his unending, arse-stretching fuck. 'No one... knows... you're... here.' He gave another shuddering grunt and with an exhalation of breath, came. His juice exploding into Joe, making him wince with the thought of this vile queen's seed inside him.

Pulling out, Mitch stood away and slapped the tender skin around Joe's arse. 'Very nice. Perhaps we'll keep you here for a plaything. In fact I think that's what we will do. I've been waiting for the chance to find a nice little boy with a welcoming arse... someone to keep as a prisoner, to use whenever I want. I think you'll be perfect for the job.'

Joe panicked. He realised the sudden danger he was in. 'You can't do that. I'll be missed. The band will miss me.'

Mitch laughed, a sinister drawl, full of utter loathing and contempt.

Think. Joe concentrated hard. He had to talk his way out of here. There was no need for theatrics, just plain common-sense. Mitch had to be persuaded. Or at least some of the others did.

'Listen guys. You've had your fun... even I've enjoyed myself. I admit it was a shock to begin with, but I got used to the situation and relaxed. But you can't keep me here... that's against the law. You'll be kidnapping me and that's a serious offence. If you let me go then I'll say nothing about it to anyone. I'll even let you all fuck me now if you want.'

'Huh, like you've got any choice.' Scottie's voice piped up from behind Joe's head.

'I have got a choice,' Joe continued. 'I have the choice not to have you all arrested for grievous bodily harm or assault or some such charge. Let me go and the whole thing will be forgotten.' There was silence. Joe waited nervously for some reaction. All the while he could feel his cock still erect, still twitching, and still aching for release.

'He's right.' Joe heard Mark's voice.

Turning his head in the direction of the voice he spoke again. 'Is that you, Mark? Look, you can't let them do this to me... you aren't a criminal.' Images of Mark dealing drugs flashed across Joe's mind but he banished them quickly. It would help to get Mark on his side, sympathetic to his case.

'Mitch, you can't keep him here, he's right. It's not like he's a nobody off the street, he's an important person, and if you keep him here it'll be bad for you.' Mark's voice again had a reasonable tone. Joe prayed that it would carry some authority with Mitch.

There was a pause in the conversation. Nobody spoke. Joe wished that someone would remove the blindfold, so he could see his captors.

'I guess you're right.' Mitch said, his voice slightly disappointed. 'It could be a really stupid thing to do.' A hand slapped against Joe's arse. 'But if you ever tell anyone about this... well you know what'll happen, don't you, you faggot?' There was a new, steely, dangerous tone to what Mitch said, and Joe knew better than to argue with him.

'Of course, anything you say.'

Once more a hand slapped his buttocks, a sharp stinging sensation, which quickly subsided. 'So anyone want their go at this little tease?' Mitch spoke to the others, his fingers toying with the puckered hole.

'I'd like some of that.' Scottie piped up, as Joe heard the familiar sound of a ripping packet near his ear.

'Oh and you'd better get the other thing ready, for when we've finished.' Joe didn't know what Mitch meant by that, but a pang of anxiety shot through his stomach. As he lay in the suspended sling, his arms and legs still firmly fastened to the thick, hanging chains, Joe could feel the solidified wax on his chest and belly cracking and splitting. His arsehole ached, and his face felt sore.

A hand grabbed his face roughly and held his mouth open. A pill was dropped into his throat followed by some water. Choking, Joe had no choice but to swallow. Immediately the coughing fit had subsided, a cock slapped against his lips, pushing and wanting to gain entry to his mouth. Again Joe had no choice, as the cock slid past his dry lips. The head lay against his tongue, letting Joe give full attention to that, passing it back and forth against the underside of the full lobes.

At the same moment, another cock pushed at the entrance to Joe's arse, making him grunt again and want to cry out, but with his mouth full of cock, he couldn't. The meat in his mouth, now easing down his throat, seemed to be growing larger and larger, the skin fusing with the membrane of his throat lining. His head began to spin, until the only sensation he knew was the thrusting of the two cocks inside him, until he faded away, into a void, utter darkness swallowing him whole.

9: One Boy Down

The clock in the green room at Willowtree studios stood at 11.45am. Nick eased himself out of his chair and extinguished the cigarette he had been angrily puffing on. Paul, Dean and Connor watched every move, each of them unsure, each of them worried at the non-appearance of Joe.

Paul had told them all that Joe hadn't come home last night, even if he was out with another guy, he always came back to their flat. When Paul awoke and realised that Joe hadn't been back, he started to get anxious. He called Nick at the office who told him to come in to the studios, that there was nothing to worry about, and that he had probably crashed at a friend's place having had too much to drink at the party he'd gone to.

Now that Joe was nearly three hours late, Nick himself was beginning to get worried, this emotion superseding the intense anger he'd had so far this morning. For a member of any band he was grooming to be this late showed utter contempt, not just for Nick, but for the others who were giving their all to the future success of the group. This just wasn't done. And for it to be Joe who let them all down... Nick was very surprised. He thought that Joe was reliable and steady, and had the group's well-being at heart. This was most unlike him.

'Perhaps we should call the police.' Paul's voice was small and wavering. He picked at a loose flap of skin at his fingernail, his distress obvious.

'I don't think that's a good idea yet.' Nick remained calm now. The shooting of 'pick-up' scenes for the video would have to wait. He would go and talk to Thom and the crew and explain that Joe had been taken ill, and that everything was being put on a hiatus until after lunch. Explaining that everyone would get paid, he strode back to the green room purposefully.

'Look, I don't really know what to do next. Paul, can you go home and see if he's surfaced? Dean and Connor, can you just hang around? I know it'll be boring for you both but I'd be very grateful.'

Paul leapt to his feet, glad of the chance to actually do something rather than just sit about, helpless. 'If I have any news I'll call you on your mobile.' He nodded grimly at Nick and ran from the room.

'Right, and I'll go back to my office and see if they've heard anything yet. See you later.' He turned and left. Dean and Connor looked at each other, mystified by Joe's behaviour. Deep down they both hoped that nothing bad had happened. But they both knew that the world was a wicked place.

Dean had thankfully slept well, utter exhaustion sending him into unconsciousness as soon as his head hit the pillow. Nick had kept his word and said nothing to anyone about the scare, but he also had bad news about Greg, who had apparently given up his casual contract to go travelling. So all Dean could now do was to be optimistic and try and get through the next three months as quickly as possible.

Joe awoke, his head fuzzy, his body racked with aches. He didn't know where he was. It was dark, and as he attempted to stand up he sharply banged his head on something. Feeling about him, his hands rested on a broom handle, and several cardboard boxes.

The air was musty and smelt of polish. He realised he must be in a cupboard. There had to be a light somewhere, and so with his fingers he felt along the wall until he made contact with the small metal switch. Flicking it on he saw the rest of the confined space floodlit with brilliant illumination. He immediately recognised the janitor's cupboard at his block of flats.

Looking down he also saw that he was still naked. His stomach was covered with hardened globs of wax and all he had on were his unlaced boots. Whoever had done this to him had dumped him here while unconscious. Still, at least he was home. Pulling the door open he looked down the hallway, making sure it was empty, and with screaming muscles he limped up the stairway to his flat.

A large tub of plastic geraniums sat by the door, and pushing his hand down into the surrounding peat, his fingers made contact with the spare emergency key. Brushing the crumbs of dirt from his fingers, he inserted the key into the lock and pushed open the door to his flat.

Stumbling into the kitchen he yanked the door of the fridge open and grabbed a carton of orange juice, holding it to his lips and swallowing rapidly, like a man in a desert who has discovered a watering hole. Bolt after bolt of juice ran down his parched throat, the sweet acidity tasting like nectar.

Throwing the empty carton into the waste-bin, he made his way slowly to the bathroom, leaning over the toilet bowl and letting go with a much-needed stream of piss. As he raised his head, he recoiled in horror at his reflection in the bathroom cabinet mirror, which hung on the wall above the toilet. His face was bruised and swollen. Moving to the sink, he began picking at the wax which was set hard on his torso. It came away easily, but left a riot of reddened blotches on his skin.

With tears in his swollen eyes, he turned and stepped gingerly into the shower cubicle, roughly twisting the control, allowing a jet of steaming water to cascade over his beaten body.

The stinging, piercing needles of water started to invigorate him, and images of the previous night slowly swam before his vision. The party, a drugged drink, captive in a sling, the fucking, and Mark.

Mark. The man he thought he could trust. The man he had slept with before, but who had turned out to be a scheming, manipulative bastard. In league with that revolting creature Mitch Utrillo. But then again, Mark was the one who had talked Mitch out of keeping him locked up as a sex slave. He had to be grateful for that. A burning desire for revenge filled Joe. He had to get his own back on Mitch, that vile scum. He would denounce him to the authorites, have him locked up, and ruin him completely. Joe had never really hated anyone until now, and that sensation over-whelmed him.

He let the water slowly bring him back to some semblance of himself, and with a determined twist of the control, let it dribble to a halt, stepping out of the cubicle and onto the mat. Towelling himself dry, he watched his reflection in the half-length mirror, seeing that he looked a complete wreck, a shadow of his beautiful self, and Mitch and his cronies had done this as an act of selfish reprisal for the band's refusal to wear his pathetic costumes. He wouldn't let it rest. That cunt had it coming to him. Anger boiled up, mingled with despair and regret, he balled his fists so tight that the tips of his fingernails broke the skin of his palm. But he didn't notice this at all. Walking slowly to the bedroom, his sphincter muscles aching dully with each step, he sat on the edge of the bed, lost in thought.

His reverie was broken at the sound of the front door being opened.

'Joe, is that you?' Paul sounded worried and wavering, utter concern for his boyfriend obvious in his tremulous voice. He entered the bedroom, and seeing the hurt, crumpled frame in front of him, cried out in anguish.

'Oh my God... what's happened to you?' He sat beside Joe, cradling him in his arms, and the floodgates opened. Tears and sobs racked Joe's body, as the intensity of the ordeal and the relief at being home and with someone he loved proved too much.

Unable to speak for at least ten minutes, Joe sat, until the tears subsided, and Paul had wiped them away, holding him tight in an embrace full of love and emotion.

When he was finally calm again, Paul let Joe lie back on the bed, propping him up with some extra pillows, watching him give small winces of pain as he moved.

'So can you tell me what happened?' Paul had assumed an air of command, he was in charge of this delicate situation, and knew that he had to tread carefully.

Joe opened his mouth to speak and then shut it again, his eyes wandering to he bedroom window and the tree that was being irresistibly moved by the frenetic gusts of wind outside. He couldn't look at Paul, he had let him down, and his humiliation was utter.

'I don't know where to start...'

'Just take it slowly. You're home now and safe. Just tell me what happened... take your time.'

With a sigh Joe told all that had occurred the previous evening, from the invitation to the party, to the drugged drink, to the sling and to waking up in the janitor's cupboard. He mentioned no names. A vivid flash of memory seared across his mind, a memory of a promise, his promise to tell no one about his tormentors. But anger and despair welled up, the desire to get his own back was intense.

Paul listened to every word in silence, just holding Joe's hand, stroking the skin, offering mute support.

When he'd finished his tale, Joe closed his eyes and sighed, a mixture of relief and exhaustion.

'You just lie there, try and get some sleep if you can.' Pulling the covers up over Joe's recumbent frame, Paul gave a small peck on his cheek and slowly eased the bedroom door closed. Absently, he picked up the phone and dialled Nick's number. As he pushed the buttons and heard the pulsing of the tones, Paul was lost in a reverie of thoughts, a maelstrom of unpleasant images.

Never in his wildest dreams did he think that their now open relationship could lead to such a terrible occurence. Pictures of Joe trussed up floated viciously before him, and he couldn't shake them off. Pictures of his boyfriend helpless and in pain, abused, tormented and totally dejected. It was horrible. But what if it had been himself? Paul didn't know how he would have survived such an ordeal, the notion was too ghastly to contemplate.

'Nick De'Ath.' The voice was firm and resolute.

'It's me. He's here. But I think you'd better come over.'

Suddenly concerned, Nick pressed for more information. 'What's happened? Is he alright?'

'I can't say too much as he's in the next room. Just come over and you'll see.'

As the connection was cut, Paul could distinctly hear Nick swearing profusely under his breath. Still, at least he was on his way. He'd know what to do.

'Christ Almighty.'

Joe woke with a start, as Nick banged open the door and stood looking at him, at his swollen face. He had been submerged in a dream, where he was floating in a dark place, and naked little devils were stabbing him with their sharpened pitchforks. He tried to scream for help but his mouth had vanished. Shaking the images away, Joe sat up, pulling the covers about his neck for warmth and safety.

'There's more, I'm afraid,' he said, vaguely aware of the tinge of black humour in the situation. Letting go, he allowed the covers to drop and to reveal the red marks on his chest and stomach. Nick gaped at him.

'You stupid fucker.' Anger erupted from the manager in a boiling stream. 'What the hell did you get up to? I told you to stay clear of dangerous situations, didn't I? And what do you go and do? Have some sordid S&M session, resulting in you looking like you've been in a road accident. How dumb can you get?' He gritted his teeth and stormed from the room.

'I'll deal with this.' Paul suddenly had an air of calm authority, and he pulled the bedroom door shut behind him, and took Nick into the kitchen.

'Now you listen to me, Nick. Joe has had a terrible time. It was not his fault, so before you start going ballistic, let me tell you what happened.' Paul unfolded the story, watching Nick intently, who stood leaning on the kitchen counter, his knuckles white as he gripped the counter edge. All the while he kept his head down, his breathing slow and sure, and when Paul finished, he looked up and stared at the boy with a strange look on his face, impossible to read. Nick didn't speak for what seemed like hours. Without asking, he took a bottle of milk from the fridge and swigged it down in one. Brushing his mouth with the back of his sleeve, he turned to Paul.

'If any of you boys pull any more stunts like this... first Dean...' He realised what he could have said and stopped short. 'Right, OK. Damage limitation.'

'What do you mean?' Paul was puzzled.

'I mean we have to sort this fucking mess out quickly and with no fuss. He is going to be in no state to appear on the ROKTV show. Two days won't be enough recovery time for that. So we'll have some story... perhaps we can say he actually has been in a road accident, that would account for the state of his face. No one will see his chest if he keeps his shirt on.

'But we won't be able to do any more on the video for a while, and that'll mean putting the release date of the single back. Still that can't be helped. OK, you make sure he rests, we'll have to take the rest of the week off. I will send a car for you on Thursday morning, the interview will go ahead with the three of you. Right, I'd better get back to the studio and tell everyone what the situation is.'

As he placed his hand on the door latch, Nick turned back to Paul and lowered his voice. 'Did he say who did this to him?'

'No, but I get the feeling he wants to do something about it... I reckon he'll want to get even with them.'

'Make sure he stays silent. If the truth gets out... well, let's just say that the future of the band could be in the balance. I don't want lurid headlines in the Sunday papers. Just keep mum, OK?'

'Sure, whatever you say. And... er... what were you going to say about Dean?'

'Nothing at all.'

Paul closed the door on Nick and sank down on the sofa, relieved at Joe's reappearance, but completely dismayed by the circumstances. What if the news did leak out? The band would be finished, before they'd even got going. Their future would be unemployment and failure. Spending the rest of their lives knowing that they could have had the world.

The studios of ROKTV were housed in a five-storey building in a cul-de-sac in the heart of London's Soho. A few doors down from the studios a neon sign flickered and flashed its welcoming message: 'Pussy Galore – Nude Girls, Hot Chicks, Cheap Drinks.' Outside stood a bored bouncer, clothed in black, his baleful glare frightening the intrigued stares of passing businessmen and Japanese tourists.

The limousine pulled up at the front of the ROKTV building, and the capped chauffeur sprinted round to open the door, allowing Paul, Dean, Connor and Nick to step out onto the rain-washed pavement.

'Now remember what we discussed?' Nick stopped short of entering the building, rounding on the three lads with a stern expression. 'Just answer the simple questions, anything that sounds like it might be designed to catch you out, ignore. I'll be there with you, as well as my new press officer, who should be here to meet us. Ah, there she is.'

A tiny purple-haired woman tottered out from the reception area to the side of the car, clutching sheaves of papers, wearing a shiny plastic coat, with her feet encased in towering, knife-edge stiletto heeled shoes.

'Oh, there you are.' Her voice had a dreadful nasal twang and a small gobbet of spit leapt from her lips as she spoke. The three boys looked at each other, the desire to laugh was immense. 'I wondered where you'd got to. Better get inside.'

She pushed at the huge, owl-like spectacles that kept sliding down her sizeable nose, and gave a good hard stare at the boys. 'Ooh, 'ello, I'm Melanie... Melanie Splasche. Nice to meet you all at last.' She put out a bejewelled hand and limply shook the boys' firm grips, the myriad bracelets on her wrist jangling like an alarm clock.

'I can tell we'll all get on like a house on fire.' Unsteadily turning on her heels, she sailed into the building, leaving the four men to follow in her wake. As Nick held the door for the boys to enter he said, 'Don't judge by appearances. Melanie is shit-hot. The best press officer I've ever had. If anyone can get you noticed, she can. So give her every support possible. Oh and remember... any questions about Joe, I'll answer them.'

The studio itself was tiny, with barely enough room for the orange, low-slung sofas and the cameras to cohabit comfortably. A far cry from the vast expanse of space at Willowtree. The sofas on which they were to be interviewed had their backs to the large picture window, which faced onto the street, where occasional passers-by would stop and wave, or pull faces at the camera, or mouth the obligatory 'hello mum', before a security guard would move them along. Nick often wondered why they filmed onto the street, if they didn't want disruption from the great unwashed.

People. Sometimes people really pissed Nick off. Those sad specimens who blocked your way, or who scratched your car, or who stood in front of you in the supermarket paying for one Mars Bar with a cheque. Sometimes he despaired of the human race.

'You can sit there, please.' The dizzy blond, queeny floor manager was placing the band on set, squeezed up against each other as if they were sardines, his screeching voice bringing Nick out of his reverie. 'And if you'd like to perch on the end there... Mr Death.'

Nick sighed. 'It's De'Ath, you moron, not death. It's simple enough.'

Taking slight umbrage, the floor manager minced away to tell the director that all was ready. All they needed now was the star of ROKTV, the jewel in their crown, the most important, up and coming interviewer of the day. Jodi Thorogood.

Paul and Joe were avid viewers of ROKTV, sitting down for Jodi's Sunday afternoon chart show with a plate of biscuits and a pot of coffee. Enjoying the weekly appearance of the station's resident wonderboy, who would beam at them from the screen, his persona oozing sex and charm. Paul tugged at Dean's sleeve as a discernible hum of chatter started up around the studio. Jodi was on his way.

'Boys, hello, how are you all? And Nick... how good to see you again.' Jodi descended on them, looking immaculate. He shook hands with all four, before settling down on the far end of the sofa, clipboard in hand.

His heart beating with a nervous clamour, Paul took the chance to get a good look at one of his heroes. Jodi was tall, and with a lean frame, not thin, and with a body that was clearly well looked after. He was wearing a green woollen roll-neck sweater that seemed to capture the glow of his sea-green eyes and magnify it. He had on a pair of baggy trousers that were covered in zipped pockets, giving no hint of the size of his genitalia. His skin was smooth and slightly tanned, his face quite long but defined with a strong chin and nose, all helped by his smile, lips pulled back to show a set of perfect, snow-white teeth. Teeth that seemed to sparkle when he talked. Paul's heart began to beat even faster at the realisation that Jodi was even more beautiful in the flesh. And here he was sitting next to him, their knees touching.

'I think I've got everything I need for the interview, guys.' Jodi gave each of them in turn a devastating smile, then looked down at his notes. 'It'll be quite a short piece, to insert in the Sunday show, in a segment about emerging talent. Nick seems to think you have potential... and he's never let us down yet.'

Nick leaned forward. 'That's right, Jodi. These guys are going to be huge. They have talent, as well as personality and sex appeal, and they aren't hiding behind any false claims. They are honest about themselves and what they stand for.'

'Excellent.' Jodi gave another hyena grin and patted Paul on the knee. 'Then let's do it! I'm ready, Malcolm.' He waved at the floor manager who blew him a kiss back and the recording began.

'BANNED are a new boy group who are hoping to storm the charts. I'm here with Dean, Paul and Connor from the group as well as their manager, the infamous pop impresario Nick De'Ath. Welcome all of you. So Nick, first of all... what's the aim of putting yet another boy band on the road to stardom?'

'Well, Jodi, can I just say first of all that BANNED won't be just another bland, featureless boy band. These guys can really sing and move. They don't have to fall back on using other secret vocalists, or shy away from performing live. They all have superb voices, as well as having great personalities. They are just four of the nicest guys I know.'

'Four, but if I'm not mistaken I can only see three of them here on the sofa today. Who's missing?'

'That's our other member, Joe Turner. Unfortunately he was involved in a road traffic accident a few days ago, and is at home recuperating.'

'I hope it's not serious.'

'No it isn't, and he's feeling fine, but not up to a TV interview just yet.'

'So what happened?'

'I don't have full details of the accident, Jodi. This may surprise you, but unlike some managers, I don't keep total control over the group's lives.'

'I see. But if I can leap to the crux of your angle... if I can use such a phrase, BANNED is completely open about the fact that all of the members are gay, isn't that right?'

'Yes it is, Jodi. We have formed a band with the best gay talent around. We are now living in the 21st century, an age where bigotry should be eradicated. These guys are going to get to the top because they are the very best. We don't want to hide behind lies and speculation about their private lives... everything will be out in the open. We won't be like certain stars, cowering in the closet until they are forced to step out into the limelight. The record-buying public will know all there is to know about these great lads. We want people to go out and buy their records because they love the music, because after all that is what this business is about... music. There will be no secrets.'

'No secrets, Nick? So tell me the truth about Joe, who is unable to be here today. Is it true that he was gay-bashed because he tried to pick up some young innocent impressionable boy in a public lavatory?'

'That is utter rubbish, and I am disappointed in you, Jodi, for even deigning to mention it.'

'So it isn't true?

'It most certainly isn't. And can I just say that this is typical of the kind of homophobic journalism that is dragging this country into the mud, the mire of tabloid sleaze, where people's abilities and strengths are ignored and their human frailties are magnified.'

'But where did the rumour come from then?'

'I have no idea.'

'And have any of the other members of BANNED tried to pick up young boys in public lavatories?'

'Jodi... that is an offensive question.'

'A question which none of you are answering... it seems.'

'Because we don't wish to get involved with such a pathetic and sordid subject. Can we talk about the new single now?'

'Yes, I believe it is called 'Only The Night', and will be available in the shops next month, right?'

'That's right, Jodi. Look out for it everyone...'

Malcolm, the floor manager, drew his finger across his throat in a silent signal to Jodi. Time up.

The four studio guests looked at each other in amazement, even Nick was surprised at the angle of questioning. 'What was that all about, Jodi? I thought we were here to promote a new band, not get involved in a stupid argument about cottaging.'

Jodi gave yet another face-splitting grin. 'Yes, Nick, old love, but this sort of thing helps the ratings. No one is in the slightest bit interested in some goody-goody, insubstantial bunch of cute no-hopers.'

He turned to Paul. 'No offence. The audience want gossip and dirt. And today you've done us proud. Thanks.' He patted Paul on the knee again, giving it a little squeeze, winking at the lad. So none of the others could hear him, Jodi leant in and whispered in

Paul's ear. 'And if you ever want to have a prowl round a toilet sometime, do let me know.'

Paul was stunned. Up until now Jodi had never given the slightest hint to anyone about his sexuality. He was never seen in the press with either a girlfriend or boyfriend. Not an iota of gossip and rumour stuck to him, giving him the nickname in the industry of 'Teflon Man'. But right here and now was he coming on to Paul, or just fishing for a story? The youngster was intrigued to find out.

'Do you recommend any good toilets, then?' He stood and walked with Jodi off the set, and towards the coffee machine in the corridor, leaving Nick and the others chatting loudly, annoyed at their treatment, calling for the show's producer.

'Possibly... coffee?' Jodi deftly pressed the right combination of numbers and waited for the plastic cup of tepid, white, sweetened liquid to fill. Taking the overflowing cup, he turned to Paul who stood leaning against the wall, his arms crossed, the hint of a crooked smile on his rounded face. He seemed to be waiting for some sign from Jodi, who just sipped at his coffee, his gaze intent on Paul's wide eyes. Then saying nothing, Jodi spun round and strolled off down the corridor, until he reached a door at the far end, his fingers resting lightly on the handle. He looked back at Paul and gave a tiny, almost imperceptible gesture with his head, motioning for him to follow.

This was it. Paul gave a gulp and nonchalantly strolled after him, entering Jodi's dressing room, and with a purposeful twist of his wrist turned the key in the lock, keeping all intruders out. Should he take the upper hand? Paul wasn't sure. Jodi had settled himself on a low couch which stood against the far wall, his coffee placed on a table at his elbow. The blinds were closed over the window, darkening the room slightly. The sounds of traffic and people filtered in from outside. Jodi had sat back, his arms stretched wide along the back of the couch, his legs also spread, but with still no clue as to what lay beneath. Paul wanted to find out.

Taking a deep, steadying breath, he crossed and sat beside Jodi. 'So what were you saying about toilets?'

Jodi giggled, and ran a hand over his beautifully coiffeured hair. 'It's just there.' He nodded to a small room, through an open door. 'There's the toilet. Need to go?'

Unsure of what game Jodi was playing, Paul shook his head. 'Not now thanks.' He could see that Jodi had shifted slightly and had put a hand gently on his lap, the elegantly manicured fingers just touching his crotch area. Noticing Paul's eyes wander downwards, Jodi let his fingers wander also. He slowly, and with great care, started to massage himself through the material of his baggy trousers.

'Do you like what you see?' His voice was quiet and cracked a little with nervous tension. 'Are you sure you don't want to use the toilet?'

'Should I want to?'

'Perhaps... I'd like it if you did.' So that was his game. A penchant for piss.

'Would you?' Paul just sat still, waiting for Jodi to make the first move. The atmosphere had an electric charge, and Paul was on tenterhooks. For him this was an amazing scenario. To even be in the presence of the gorgeous Jodi was fantastic, but to be this close, and to have him offering his body, with the prospect of sex ahead, he could scarcely believe it. Ever since he and Joe had relaxed things within their relationship he had been open to offers. Uri had been the first and the sex he had experienced with him had been really great. But now here was this Adonis, adored by the public, talented and rich, squeezing himself, and wanting sex.

Without another word, Jodi stood and crossed to the toilet door, pushing it almost closed. He flicked a switch and a narrow shaft of light beamed out from behind the door. Paul was puzzled. He didn't know what to do next. Was he invited in or should he stay seated?

The answer came quickly.

'Are you coming in then?' Jodi's voice floated out, an obvious invitation.

With a deep steadying breath, Paul stood and slowly advanced, pushing the door open, his eyes widening in surprise.

The room was a lavatory and shower, and Jodi was standing in the shower cubicle, naked. His clothes had been flung randomly on the floor. Paul stared in confused admiration at the man before him. His body was astonishing, with a very well-muscled chest, his nipples standing hard, his torso tapered down to a V-shape, the ridges of his washboard stomach the finest Paul had ever seen. His body was almost hairless, except for a sooty black tuft around his groin.

And the centrepiece of all was the cock. It stood up from the groin, cut, tremendously thick at the base, getting slightly narrower towards the top, the shaft curving beautifully until the head stood against the lower ridges of his stomach. Paul just looked at it with a mixture of adoration and lust, the perfect cock for the perfect man.

'Well?' Jodi asked, hands on hips, a radiant smile on his face.

'Beautiful.' Paul had nothing else to say. He took a faltering step closer, and put out a hand. Dare he even touch such a treasure? Jodi's eyes held his in a strong gaze, seemingly daring him to make his move. Reaching out he grasped the cock, wrapping his trembling fingers around it, finding with delight that they barely met around the weighty shaft. It was rigid, as if it had been carved out of solid rock, a sight to inspire worship. As Paul gazed down at it, he pondered that some guys have all the luck – not just good looks and talent, but a dick to die for. Life could be extremely unfair with its distribution of goodies.

With a small shake of his head, he cleared his mind of all thoughts except this creation in his hand. He stroked it a few times, enjoying the contact, watching Jodi's eyes narrow and his breath get imperceptibly faster. His own penis was growing bigger, the mound at the front of his trousers sizeable.

Then Paul sank to his knees, and took the massive head between his lips. The skin of the head was so silken and smooth that it felt almost unreal. He clamped his mouth about it, letting it completely fill his mouth. Knowing that this would be a challenge, Paul let the cock start to slide down his throat, pulling it further and further into the warm, moist passage, feeling it rubbing against the sides of his mouth and teeth. Then in an instant, it was buried, deep inside Paul's throat, the ultimate contact between the two men, Paul burying his nose in the dark mass of pubes.

He inhaled and breathed in the clean smell of soap. Jodi gasped as Paul inched away, sliding his mouth back up the monstrous weapon, revelling in the astounding smoothness of the pole, until his lips bumped against the underside of the head, the two fleshy mounds stopping the cock from emerging into the daylight.

Tears sprang to Paul's eyes, tears of joy and wonder, mingled with tears of exertion and effort, as he began to suck the cock. He ran his lips up and down the dick's length, exploring every inch, now slower, now faster, working Jodi into heights of ecstasy. Having been given the rare chance to enjoy such a stunning piece of flesh, Paul was determined to do it justice.

With his hands he reached round and massaged Jodi's arse cheeks, taking a buttock in each hand, squeezing and pulling them apart, a finger exploring the hole hidden there. Again he could feel no hair, the skin between the cheeks totally smooth. Jodi was unable to hold still now, and with a huge sigh he thrust his dick down Paul's throat, letting him suck with all his power. The two were almost out of control. Paul's mind was a blur, as was his mouth, the rigid dick sliding back and forth in a frenzy.

Nothing else existed for them but the glory of the blow-job.

'Jodi. Are you there?' Both of them froze, as the handle of the dressing room door was rattled. Putting a finger to his lips, Jodi motioned for Paul to be silent, unable to see the humour of his request.

With my mouth full of your cock I can hardly shout too loud, can I? Paul thought to himself.

Jodi had become still, unmoving like a Roman statue, his cock totally hard. Paul started to suck again, slowly this time, just enjoying the friction building up in his mouth.

But Jodi had other ideas. Placing his hands on Paul's shoulders he eased him back, and stood away, his cock sopping with saliva and pre-cum. He fixed Paul with an intense glare from his clear, dark eyes, something on his mind, something he found it difficult to talk about.

'Would you ...' Jodi mumbled to a halt, the confident, charismatic TV personality but a shadow of his self. He had the air of a mischievous schoolboy, someone who'd been found out after committing some criminal act.

'What?' Paul decided that he would make this as awkward as possible for the man. Gorgeous as he was, he deserved to be made to sweat a little.

'I'd really like it if you... if you... if you could piss on me.' Dropping his eyes and looking at the floor, Jodi really did seem like a naughty boy now.

Paul didn't know how to answer. In all the few sexual escapades that he had had in his life so far, he would have described himself with the generic term 'vanilla'. He loved sucking and fucking and there his expertise ended. He had never wanted to go down any of the more extreme roads of sex – sadomasochism, leather, bondage or any messy stuff – none of this had any attraction. If you enjoyed the delights of the other person, why would you want to tie them up and beat them? The thought of pissing on another man disgusted him.

'Please...' The tone of Jodi's voice had changed to a wheedling, pleading whine. He squatted in the shower cubicle expectantly, looking up at Paul, his eyes now wide and hopeful. His cock was still hard, and with one hand steadying himself on the shower wall, he started to slowly wank, taking the whole length of the weapon from top to bottom.

Paul could feel himself becoming aroused again. Bending over, he unlaced his boots and kicked them to the corner of the room. Then in one swift motion, he stepped out of his trousers, standing before Jodi in his T-shirt and soft grey jockey shorts. The material of his underclothes was pushed out by the solidity of his cock, straining to be released, desperate for some attention. A drop of pre-cum had seeped out from the end of his cock, making a damp patch on the cotton garment, and Paul could see Jodi's eyes fixed on this.

In a glimmer, Paul had a bright idea. As the thought of peeing on another person repulsed him, and the notion of actually going through with the act made Paul squirm, he had come up with another alternative. Massaging himself through his pants, he stepped closer to Jodi, until his crotch was level with the presenter's face and only an inch or two away. With a will of iron and immense determination, Paul forced his bladder to open. Slowly at first he could feel a gentle stream of piss start to flow, the wet patch on the front of his pants spreading.

Jodi's eyes now widened even more, his mouth fell open, and his cock jerked with the thrill of the sight. Grasping his cock tightly, he began to beat off, jacking back and forth, fixedly staring at Paul's ever growing damp patch.

Paul had never known a feeling like it, the watery warmth, which spread across his crotch, flowing out and surrounding his still hard manhood, the wet material of his pants clinging to the contours of his cock and bollocks. He tried to ignore the musky, bitter odour and concentrate on the potential horniness of the scene, watching Jodi wanking ferociously, his hand wrapped about the stunning meat-pole, his breathing growing rapid, his body getting tense. As Jodi was at the point of climax, and he shut his eyes, Paul quickly slipped out of his sodden pants and grabbed his own cock.

Simultaneously they came, Jodi's load shooting up over his own chest, while Paul aimed at Jodi, bolt after bolt of hot spunk cascading over his face and neck. The orgasms were so powerful that both their bodies shook with the intensity, each giving out a cry of elation.

After a few moments, Jodi raised his eyes, a gobbet of sperm rolling down his cheek, then he licked his lips, lapping a drop of Paul's juice into his mouth, and smiling.

'Well, that was fun!' He stood and turned on the shower, letting the hot water burst over him. Pulling off his T-shirt and socks, Paul joined him, washing every hint of evidence from his body. As the water splashed down over them, Paul grabbed a cake of soap and started lathering Jodi, paying particular attention to his chest, stomach and crotch, the heavy cock hanging lifeless but impressive between his legs.

'You have a great cock.' Paul shouted above the roar of the water, weighing the bollocks in his hands, enjoying the size and feel, rolling them between his palms.

'Thanks. Yours is very nice too.' Jodi reached down and took it in his hands, gripping its semi-recumbent mass tightly, rubbing soap all over it, before letting the powerful jet of water wash the suds away.

Sensing that things could escalate again, Paul quickly finished off and stepped out of the shower, grabbing up a towel and briskly drying himself.

Jodi gave the shower control a sharp twist and joined Paul, taking the towel from him and placing it around his neck.

'I'd like to do this again sometime.' The young presenter slapped Paul on the arse, and gave a soft giggle, the laugh starting deep in his chest. 'Can I give you my number?'

This was certainly one of the oddest encounters Paul had ever had, but the chance to get his hands on that beauty of a cock was unmissable. He laughed too, as he sat down on the sofa, lacing up his boots.

'What's so funny?' Jodi asked.

'Everything. Out there today, you did your best to slime us, to make us sound like cottaging paedophiles, and yet here you are asking me for another session... wanting me to piss all over you. It's just extremely funny.'

Wincing, Jodi sat at Paul's side and watched his nimble fingers swiftly tying the laces.

'I guess it is funny. But when I was discovered and offered the chance to front this show, I jumped at the chance. My manager said I had to keep my real self secret. If anyone knew what I was into they'd fire me, and my career would be over in a flash. You can't expect girls to kiss the posters on their walls if all the time they know the boy on them is a piss-freak, can you?'

'I suppose not.'

Jodi paused. 'I really admire what you guys are doing... being out and all. I wish I could. It's just impossible.'

'Nothing's impossible, Jodi. If you are certain about something you have to do it. Look at me. I never thought it possible to end up in a boy band. Nick says we are going to be stars. How ridiculous is that? A gay boy from Watford ending up a pop star? But he says we can do it. No one will care about our sexuality, and no one will care about you... except perhaps a few evil-minded bigots, but that's the same in every walk of life. Just think about it.' With a tug, he finished tying his boots and stood.

Jodi watched him, the beads of water glistening on his body.

'Er... have you got a plastic bag or something?' Paul held up gingerly the sodden underpants, wrinkling his nose at the state of them.

'Sure, in that drawer.' Jodi motioned with his head to a small cabinet, then stood and also began dressing. Paul found a roll of disposable plastic bags, and ripping one off the roll, he placed his pants inside and sealed it with the metal tie. Pushing the bag into his jacket pocket, he turned to say goodbye.

'Thanks, Jodi. That was nice. Odd, but nice.'

The presenter gave one of his huge grins and took a card from a small plastic holder in the cabinet drawer. 'Here's my number. I hope you do call... I'd like that.'

Slipping it into his wallet, Paul smiled back. 'I will certainly try. And think about what I said, eh?'

'I will. Although I can't promise anything.' Jodi stood in the bathroom doorway, with the towel around his neck, drops of water forming a puddle at his feet, his hair damp and unruly, falling across his handsome face, the body looking like it should have been the model for one of Michaelangelo's masterpieces. How could Paul not want to see him again? He winked and slipped out of the door, closing it with a gentle click behind him.

The pub lunch had been delicious and filling, and the several pints of real ale had put Nick and the boys in an amiable frame of mind. Sitting in Nick's luxury penthouse flat, with full stomachs and a warm alcoholic glow, they awaited the broadcast of ROKTV's Sunday afternoon programme on the latest chart news.

Paul sat cuddled up with Joe on the big leather sofa, while Dean and Connor were stretched out on the floor, flicking their way through the latest edition of *16 Dreams* magazine, the premier publication for adolescent schoolgirls. A photographic session had been arranged for the boys late that week, and they wanted to see the kind of images that were portrayed in its pages. So far all they could find were articles on how to kiss for the first time, tampon advice and what to do if your boyfriend goes too far.

'Suck his dick!' Connor laughed, as they both read this article out to the others.

The centre-spread was of a popular solo artist, currently wowing the charts with his mix of rap and country music, pictured sitting on a bale of hay, naked except for a large cowboy hat over his groin.

'I bet he fills that hat.' Dean gave a chuckle as Connor joked again.

'Sssh.' Nick quieted them as he pushed the volume control on the remote, the giant wide-screen television growing in sound. 'Here it is.'

All five of them looked up at the picture, seeing Jodi looking confident, assured and incredibly handsome. Joe, Dean, Connor and Nick all turned their gazes to Paul, who looked at his nails, embarrassed. He had already told them about his encounter with Jodi, over lunch, leaving out the more intimate details.

'Lucky sod.' Dean's pang of faked jealousy instantly disappeared and he returned his gaze to the television.

Jodi was seated on the familiar orange couch and speaking to the camera.

'... And the trend is set to continue with several new artists and bands hoping for chart success. This week I spoke to members of new boy group BANNED. They are a group who want to be a hit, but have one drawback... their honesty. You see, all of BANNED are gay. But are we ready for such honesty from a group who want to sell music to unknowing teenagers? Do we want our youth buying records from corrupting influences? I wanted to know more about what the group got up to and was given some surprising answers from their manager, the Svengali of the pop world, Nick De'Ath...'

The picture switched to a close-up of Nick looking calm, while Jodi's voice spoke confidently.

'So tell me the truth about Joe, who is unable to be here today.

Is it true that he was gay-bashed because he tried to pick up some young innocent impressionable boy in a public lavatory?'

'I have no idea.'

'And have any of the other members of BANNED tried to pick up young boys in public lavatories?'

'This may surprise you, but unlike some managers, I don't keep total control over the group's lives...'

Nick sat forward, his brow corrugated with anger. The programme had rearranged what he had said and cut it together, misconstruing him totally. The impression given was that the boys were all deviant child molesters, who hung around public toilets.

'Bastards.' Nick stood and in an act of unfamiliar rage threw the remote control at the wall. The battery casing came away and the batteries flew out, landing on the carpet.

The boys just waited, completely lost for words. Even in their worst nightmares they didn't think that a simple TV interview would end up with such a black picture being painted of them. Did this spell the end of their short career?

Their eyes were burning into Nick's back as he stood looking out of the window onto the park, many storeys beneath. It seemed like hours passed before he spoke, spinning round to face the boys, a look of grim determination corrugating his features.

'Right. Yet again, in the space of a few days, I find I have to indulge in more damage limitation.' He looked sternly at Joe, who hung his head in shame and guilt. Dean gulped and gazed at Nick, trying to appear as nonchalant as possible.

'This programme is not going to be allowed to ruin us,' said Nick. 'I won't allow it. It wants to use sleazy, tabloid-type journalism to make us out the bad guys. Well, two can play at that game. If ROKTV want a fight, then they'll fucking well get one. We will smear them, more than they smear us. I'll get Melanie to see what she can find out about them, poor working practices, illegal contracting, personal scandals...'

His voice trailed off as a thought crashed to the front of his mind. Fixing his stern gaze on Paul, he spoke in a threatening tone, a tone that the boys had never heard before, and it worried them.

'I want to know everything that happened between Jodi and you, Paul, in detail. I will ruin that arsehole, before he gets the chance to ruin us. Talk.'

There was a real hint of menace in his normally placid voice that sent a shiver down Paul's spine. He now wanted success and fame so badly, but did he want it if it meant ruining someone else's life? Jodi was a good man at heart, he knew, and it was probably the editorial policy of the show's producers that decided on the content of each programme and the sleaze aspect. Did he want to succeed if Jodi was demolished in the process? It seemed he had little choice.

'Well...?' Nick stood, arms crossed, impatiently tapping the floor with the toe of his shoe.

Paul knew he had to speak, and so he did. In great detail he told about the encounter with Jodi, how the presenter had made the first move, and how he had a liking for watersports. He left out what he eventually did at Jodi's request, thinking that the public knowledge of Jodi's particular fetish was probably enough to finish him.

When he'd said all he could, Paul sat back and rubbed his eyes. Sometimes the world seemed a tacky and unpleasant place, and today was one of those times. For him and the rest of the band to climb to the top of the tree he had to kick away the ladder holding up everyone else. He had to kick a decent man like Jodi, and kill off his career, just so he could achieve his goals. He knew that this kind of thing went on all over the planet in many types of business, but now that it was so close to him he didn't like it.

'Right. Excellent. Now we've got that pretentious prick. I'll call Melanie now and she'll hopefully get this all over the front pages tomorrow. The fact that a well-known presenter gets his jollies by having guys piss on him is bigger news than some supposed rumours about you four. Yes... I can see the light at the end of the tunnel. It's not over yet guys, not by a long chalk.'

All the while, Paul sat watching Nick pacing the room like a panther, his arms gesturing wildly. As Nick reached for his telephone, a sudden illuminating flash of inspiration hit Paul. A possible way out.

'Er... Nick? Before you call Melanie, could I make a suggestion?' He watched as Nick halted in mid-move, the telephone receiver half-way between the table and his ear.

'What?'

'Now this might be a better solution. I don't want to ruin Jodi's career on television. He is basically a nice guy. I bet that the angle of the programme was an order from on high, from the producers. He can't be held responsible for what the show broadcasts. You can't shoot the messenger.'

Nick let out an exasperated gasp. 'And your point is?'

'Why don't you leave it to me? I've got Jodi's private number, I could call him and ask him to broadcast a retraction next week. I'll say that if he doesn't I'll tell the world about his fetish. He is scared stiff of being found out, and would probably agree. I don't want to finish him off like this. Please...'

The other members of BANNED looked at each other, unsure and nervous. Would Nick let Paul hold the future of the band in his hands? And would Jodi do what he was asked? It all seemed very uncertain. Nick sat down on the edge of his table, gently butting the telephone receiver against his chin. He was lost in thought.

After a few moments, he said, 'OK, why not? I guess a week is not long to wait, and a broadcast retraction will be so much better than a press release from us simply denying all the allegations.' He replaced the receiver with a soft click.

'All right. Call him.'

10: Roadie Rage

As the receptionist waved her fingers at the boys who sat waiting for Nick to see them, the four of them stood and filed down the corridor and into his office.

There was a palpable hum of excitement about the office of De'Ath and Lord Management, as today was chart day, when they would discover who had made the week's Top Ten.

Since the release of 'Only The Night', four weeks previously, the band had observed its slow progress up the charts, holding their collective breaths, watching and waiting, hoping that it would be the first rung on the ladder to success.

In its first week the single had sold reasonably well, with quite a few people wanting to buy its melodious delights. The retraction of Jodi Thorogood on ROKTV had helped clear the name of the band, with several of the less bigoted daily newspapers even publishing features on them, as 'a new kind of gay', calling them wholesome and non-threatening.

The presenter had appeared on his programme a week after the harmful edition was broadcast, looking rather strained and tired, to tell the world of the poor editorial decision made by the show's producers, in a blatant attempt to encourage ratings on a tide of sleaze and filth. The statement was brief, but to the point, and exonerated the band from any hint of impure behaviour, and ended with the surprise announcement that he was quitting as presenter at ROKTV to find a job with a station that had morals, and didn't desire to ruin careers for the furtherance of ratings.

At this shock pronouncement, a gasp of 'what the hell?!' was heard from somewhere off-set, as presumably this caught the show's producers unawares. The members of BANNED clapped and whooped with delight at this news.

Relieved and bursting with happiness, Nick sent a huge bouquet of roses to Jodi, with love and thanks from all of them, and wishing him every success. Jodi didn't have long to wait for this as he was immediately offered the job as host-cum-presenter on a new terrestrial magazine programme.

The single 'Only The Night' was released with as much fuss as possible, along with the video, which had screenings on many pop shows, including the popular weekend morning children's show, *Saturday Countdown*. Radio One had picked it for its playlist, and was giving it a fair amount of airtime. Melanie had arranged more interviews with various teen magazines, including *16 Dreams* to accompany the photos taken a few weeks before. The article had been well received, especially the photos, which had the boys frolicking in skimpy beachwear, surrounded by inflatable balls and straw donkeys, looking every inch the clean-living young foursome that they purported to be.

Connor was taken by surprise when he was asked for an autograph by a shy young girl, shopping with her mother in his local supermarket. Amazed, he happily signed the till receipt she offered up, and watched her go back to her mother's side, a huge grin of satisfaction plastered across her acne-ridden face.

In the four weeks that followed the single's release there had been a sudden rise in the number of discs sold, and it had made its first attack on the charts, sitting at number fifty-seven.

But now after a heavy week of press action on Melanie's part, and the boys' appearance on daytime TV's flagship programme

The Martin and Mary Show, they were hoping for a higher chart position. Nick was desperately wishing for the single to at least reach number twenty, for that would mean that the band had been noticed and a follow-up single should automatically do better.

All five men sat around the office, the walls laden with silver, gold and platinum discs, evidence of Nick's former glories, waiting for the fax that would contain the newly announced chart results.

'It's like waiting for the winner of the Eurovision Song Contest.' Connor sat back, his hands held behind his head, chuckling lightly. 'BANNED, nil points.' His French accent was atrocious and brought a hearty laugh from Nick who until then had been silent and contemplative. That broke the ice, and the air of tension in the room swiftly vanished.

'Let's have a drink for fuck's sake.' Nick stood and went across to the glass drinks cabinet by the door and poured out five shots of his favourite Slovakian vodka. 'Cheers.' He raised his glass in salute and tossed it back in one gulp, savouring the burning of the fiery liquid.

Hesitatingly, the four lads did the same, Paul bursting into a fit of coughs as the alcohol hit the back of his throat. Joe patted him on the back, and smiled.

'You never could hold your liquor.'

Through a barrage of choking coughs Paul retorted sharply. 'Thanks, sweetie. I'll do the same for you one day.'

'Do you know the best way to hold your liquor?' Dean looked angelically at the ceiling. 'By the ears.'

Nick burst out laughing again. 'Silly sod.' He stood behind Dean's chair and rested his hands on the lad's shoulders, giving him a brief squeeze. He had been immensely impressed by Dean's self-control. With only another couple of weeks to go before he could take the HIV test, he seemed composed, even serene, his sense of humour had returned and he gave the impression that he was the same fun guy as before.

The sudden electronic whirring of the fax machine made them all jump, and with a start Nick crossed to it, anxiously watching the sheet of paper that slowly inched from within. As it fully emerged, Nick grabbed it up and sat at his desk. His face gave nothing away.

'Well?' Connor sat forward, intent on Nick.

'Thirty-three.' With a sigh, Nick handed the sheet across the desk to Connor, who read it, his eyes rapidly scanning the few lines of information.

'Well, come on... that's not bad. It's not number twenty, but it's pretty good. Isn't it?' Connor looked around the room at the others who wanted to see Nick's reaction before making their own views known.

'It's excellent. Well done!' Nick stood and grinned at them all.

The lads jumped up and hugged, cheering and screaming at the top of their voices. They had finally made a sizeable dent on the charts. They hadn't reached a higher position but it was better than they could have hoped for at the start. With luck, their next release would achieve a more noteworthy spot. This had to mean the beginning of their careers, and the start of their assault on the heady heights of fame and notoriety.

'So what do we do now?' Paul asked, his voice still trembling with excitement. He was holding Joe's hand, enjoying the warm response of his boyfriend, who had his other hand around Paul's waist.

Nick sat back down and interlaced his fingers, watching the happy smiles of the boys. 'Well, we get the next single out quickly... capitalise on what we have here. Then we have to get you out there.'

He gestured to the cityscape outside the huge picture window, its towerblocks and churches, housing estates and shopping centres all wreathed in a fine, white mist.

'We go out on the road. Personal appearances. I have arranged for you to perform live in many of the country's shopping malls. Now this may sound a bit odd, but it is a vital step on the road to our success. Getting out there and letting the public see you in person is the next thing to do. It lets them get a good close-up look at you. Plus it shows you are happy to come to their town or city, and aren't just tucked away, not wanting to stray from the safe environment of London. Pack your bags, because we are off in a fortnight's time. First stop, Birmingham.'

The tour bus was quite spacious, with on-board toilet and shower facilities, as well as a large television and video. The boys, as well as Melanie and Nick and several technical personnel, settled in and made the vehicle as homely as possible. After all, they would be seeing a lot of it in the next month.

The first stop in Birmingham had gone very well, with the band doing the three numbers they'd already learnt, as well as having two more up their sleeves, the routines of which had just been perfected under Uri's watchful eye. They had been set up on a podium inside the Bull Ring shopping centre, and a large crowd had gathered to watch them. The redoubtable Melanie had done them proud with endless posters around the city centre, as well as features in much of the local press. You would have had to have been living as an ostrich with your head in the sand, not to know that BANNED were soon to be playing the city.

As the boys made their entrance from a side security door and onto the raised platform, they were amazed at the sight of so many people. Mainly teenage girls, some middle-aged shoppers, stopping to see what all the fuss was about, as well a sizeable quota of young men. This pleased the boys most of all. If they had a target audience in their minds, it was the younger gay consumer – the pink pound was vital to their success.

After Birmingham they travelled north, heading for Scotland, stopping off at Nottingham, Leicester, Sheffield and Manchester. This great northern city had known of the arrival of BANNED for some weeks due to Melanie's sterling work, and the boys were looking forward to seeing the place. They had heard about the infamous gay area, Canal Street, and were excited about sampling its delights. But first was their personal appearance. Work before play.

'Right, now my darlin's, this will be an important one, so give it all you've got.' Melanie stood with the boys, in a service corridor, waiting for the signal for them to start. Her lime green leather outfit and scarlet hair seemed a little loud for that time of the morning. Nick had returned to London to sort out some company business, leaving Miss Splasche in charge. Two security guards also stood with them by the door, keeping watch for any stray undesirables. After the uproar in Leicester, Nick decided that the boys would need some watching – that appearance having got out of hand with a bunch of about a hundred girls trying to avariciously tear the boys' clothes off.

Today the boys were wearing dark trousers and white T-shirts and had paid particular attention to their personal grooming this bright morning in Manchester. Joe wasn't sure if he had noticed an admiring glance from Stuart, one of the newly hired guards, who stood close by his side, looking incredibly horny in his tight black trousers, buttoned blue shirt and black peaked cap. Ever since he and his fellow guard, Jordan, had arrived, joining the boys on the tour bus, they had made themselves totally welcome. Both of them were funny, with amusing personalities. They had a wealth of captivating stories, but had the ability to turn on a menacing persona when engaged upon essential guard duty.

Of course the first thing the band noticed about the two as they arrived to take up their positions was their looks. Both guys were tall and well built, with obvious gym-trained bodies. Stuart was close-cropped with the general appearance of a squaddie, newly out of the armed forces, clear blue eyes, and a solid, square-cut jaw, occasionally lapsing into intense silences, while Jordan had a lighter air about him. His body was as well developed as Stuart's, but his dark eyes twinkled in a rounder, chunkier face, his hair gelled back from his forehead in the current fashion.

'Just keep an eye on where we are standing, and if there is any trouble just head for us.' Jordan patted Dean on the back, a gesture of matey supportiveness, sensing the nerves of the band members. 'Are you ready?' He caught the four lads' eyes and pushed the door open, a giant yell of glee crashing in on their eardrums.

The Arndale Centre was crammed full to bursting, as BANNED stepped onto the stage. As Connor stepped forward to start the first song, a loud cheer went up, which reverberated around the centre, almost drowning out the sound of the track. The Irish lad began to sing, his strong clear voice cutting through the clamour, willing every person there to look at him, and to appreciate what the group had to offer.

His wish certainly came true. At the end of the third song the place was in uproar. Girls and boys were pushing forward toward the makeshift stage, all wanting to get a piece of the four young hunks before them. Some were waving the pull-out centre-spread from *16 Dreams* magazine, some with autograph books or T-shirts. There was a fanatical gleam in some of their eyes, some with a determined air, shoving and pulling people out of the way, wanting to get close, wanting to be noticed by the four fantasy males made real here in Manchester.

All thoughts of an encore vanished, and each of the boys noticed the others' scared glances around. This was it, head for safety. But where were Stuart and Jordan? Dean caught sight of one of their peaked caps, just noticeable above the sea of bobbing heads, close to one side of the stage, and saw him waving at a security exit. Dean grabbed Connor's hand and they ran for it, butting their way through the crowd, ignoring the hands plucking at their chests and arms, trying to pull strands of hair from their heads.

It was an effort but they managed it, and threw themselves through the door, panting, watching Stuart throw the bolt across, barring further entry. They could see through the toughened glass that Joe and Paul had headed in the opposite direction and fled towards Jordan, at the other side of the stage area. A sudden sound of shattering glass filled the air, as the pressure of too many people finally gave way, and the front window of a small clothing boutique was pushed in.

Dean leant against the stone corridor wall trying to breathe calmly and failing. He had never seen hysteria before and it frightened him.

'Don't worry.' Stuart was implacable. His voice exuded coolness, and his face gave no hint of any panic. 'There is a back way to the centre's office where you left your stuff. We can make our way there at our own speed, and meet the others there. OK?' He put his arm around Dean's shoulders, watching as the lad bent double, breathing in lungfuls of comforting air.

Connor had slid to the ground, arms tightly grasping his knees, eyes shut, and head back, trying to blot out the images in his mind. What would have happened if those fans had actually gotten hold of them? It would have been nightmarish. If recognition and celebrity meant this kind of thing then Connor wasn't sure if he wanted it. The whole situation was far too alarming.

'Can we just wait here a while?' Dean's voice was shaky, as were his legs, and like Connor he sank to the floor.

'Sure. No problem.' Stuart stood by the door, peering through the frosted glass, watching as the shopping centre security guards tried to disperse the crowd. 'Still... it'll make a good news story. Miss Splasche will be thrilled.' A sardonic chuckle escaped Stuart's lips.

In another part of the shopping centre, Joe and Paul also waited anxiously. Having dashed to Jordan's side and been whisked out to another blank corridor, they wondered what was going to happen next. The door behind which they cowered didn't seem all that safe, and the flimsy lock didn't look like it would hold back the crowd surging against it. A deep voice boomed out through a loud-hailer, ordering the crowd to back off, to move away for safety's sake.

'This is getting nasty.' Jordan's brow furrowed, as he pushed his cap back on his head. 'This door won't hold forever. So I think we'd better move away.'

'But where to?' Joe gripped Paul's hand for comfort. They looked up and down the grey, soulless corridor and spied a large pair of doors at one end.

'There. That looks a likely place.' With authority and coolness Jordan strided off down the passage, with the two lads following close behind. As they reached the large double doors, a crash made them start and look round. The other doors had given way and frenzied people began to stream through.

'Quick, inside.' Jordan almost threw the two lads in behind the doors, leaping through himself and throwing the bolt. He flicked a switch and bright light flooded the room. Packing cases and boxes of supplies lined the walls of the store-room, as well as buckets, floor-mops and bottles of cleaning fluid. It seemed a safe haven from the frenzy outside. Paul pulled up a large straw skip with the words 'towels' painted on the side, and sank down on it, burying his head in his hands for a moment. With a look of alarm, Jordan noticed his shoulders shaking, and so gently he knelt by Paul's side and put a comforting hand on his thigh.

'It's OK... just a temporary setback. We'll be out of here in no time. There's no need to cry.'

Raising his head, the shaking of his shoulders continuing, Paul looked Jordan in the eye, tears rolling down his face, a huge grin plastered across his countenance.

'I'm laughing!' A roar of amusement burst out and Paul

collapsed in convulsions.

Perhaps there was a funny side to all this. The laughter was certainly infectious as both Joe and Jordan joined in, the loud roaring mirth acting in a cathartic way, taking away the edge of tension in the air, diffusing the danger in the situation.

'So I guess we're here for a while then.' Joe sank down on the skip next to Paul, his body still rocking with amusement. His leg was pressed up hard against Paul who reciprocated and pushed back. 'What shall we do to pass the time, then?'

Paul didn't answer his boyfriend's question with words. He placed his hand on Joe's thigh and stroked it, running his fingers up toward the groin, but his eyes were fixed on Jordan. The guard looked on amused, his beefy arms crossed, his cap tilted back on his head at a rakish angle.

'So I get a floor show, do I?' His voice was light and happy, his gaze strong and piercing. 'It's about time. I'm fed up with whacking off alone in my hotel room at nights.' He made no move towards the boys, just appeared content to watch.

Joe stood and moved to the front of Paul. Their eyes met and locked as Paul slowly unzipped and withdrew Joe's semi-erect cock, and gripping it firmly at the base, pulled back the helmet of skin at the end. He leant forward and started licking at the head. Joe gave a groan, enjoying the attentions of his partner, the endless nerve endings in his sensitive head going ballistic.

Paul kept glancing up at Jordan, seeing his reaction to what they were doing, and he noticed with satisfaction that the mound at the front of his tight black trousers was growing and becoming increasingly attractive.

Paul sat back and fumbled at the waistband of Joe's trousers, unbuckling the belt, and easing them down over his boyfriend's legs. He chuckled inwardly as he realised that Joe wasn't wearing underwear, and so he was free to get down to some intense sucking. Placing his lips around the head again made Joe squirm and so Paul knew he was doing good. He slid the pole down his throat and began to suck earnestly, taking the weapon down completely.

In the last few months that they had been members of BANNED and their relationship had entered a new and freer phase, he hadn't had too many chances for sex with his boyfriend, and now he relished the chance. It had been a while since Paul had been able to get his mouth around this fabulous piece of meat.

In a flash he had taken the whole of the swollen prick down until his nose was buried in the coarse dark pubes surrounding the solid pole. His own cock was beginning to swell and expand, pushing against his zip. Joe seized the moment and grabbed the back of Paul's head, fucking his mouth with increasingly faster strokes, becoming more and more urgent. Paul knew that in those few seconds Joe had been brought to the edge, his stiff cock now like an iron rod.

Not wanting Joe to finish too soon, he suddenly pulled away, and span him round, pushing him over at the waist. Joe's flat stomach tightened with excitement. Pausing a second to get his balance, Paul nuzzled in and started eating Joe's arse, giving great slobbering licks, alternating with little nipping bites at the skin around the puckered hole. His hand reached through and began to pull on the cock sticking up ramrod straight between the tasty thighs.

Gradually, whilst his tongue darted in and out, butting at the brown ring, sometimes just pushing the tip inside, Paul pulled the cock further toward him, until it was jutting backwards between Joe's legs, almost as if it was protruding from his arse. In this amazing position there was still plenty of its length to enjoy, and so Paul did just that. Joe gave another gasp as he felt his tender cock-head slip between Paul's lips and down into the warm mouth. He could hear the sounds of Paul's tongue slapping at the shaft, slurping loudly and contentedly at his most prized possession.

By this time Jordan could hold back no longer. He had reached in and freed his cock from its confines, and Paul's eyes widened at what he saw. The guard's cock was not very thick but extremely long, and in its erect state it curved gently upward, the pinky head already sticky with pre-cum. Jordan took the drop on one of his fingers and placed it on his tongue, savouring the salty sweetness of his own semen. He began to slowly wank his fist up and down his cock, encouraging it to its maximum size, his gaze glued to the actions of the two boys. Taking his eyes away for a moment he looked down and let a gobbet of spit fall down onto the head of his prick, giving his hand some lubrication.

This was for him one of the horniest things he'd ever witnessed. Although he'd always known he was gay, he had grown up in a fiercely straight household, where any hint of 'queerness' would have resulted in a severe beating. That guilt had stayed with him ever since, and made cruising for casual sex very difficult. Even with his dark good looks, Jordan was slightly afraid of making any move on another guy, for fear of violent reprisals if he had misjudged the situation. But here in front of his very eyes was an actual sex session going on. And if he wasn't mistaken, he was being invited to join in.

He kept watch on the boys, revelling in the sight of the chunkier one sucking the other's dick, and was rewarded with the sight of one of the most glorious climaxes. Paul was bent forward, eagerly sucking the long, thick shaft, now swollen and ready to burst. His tongue was flashing round the head, then darting back to the wettened arsehole, giving both areas his total enthusiasm. Jordan could see Joe's breathing increasing, and his face contorted into an anguished expression before he let fly. Paul let the cock go, as it sprang forward and up into its normal erect position, then a second later a great streak of cum erupted from the tip, a snowy white thread that shot out and up into the air followed by several rapid repeats. The spunk landed on the store-room floor, spattering in large globules.

The sight of this drove Jordan almost frenzied with excitement. He wanted some action now. Sensing this, Paul leapt up from his seated position and grabbed Jordan roughly by the shoulder. Joe – whose cock was still hard and had a trail of glistening juice dribbling down the trembling shaft – joined his partner, and forced Jordan to lie down on the lid of the skip. Jordan made a feeble attempt at protestation, but swiftly submitted, Paul pushing him down with surprising strength.

As he lay back he could feel Joe's fingers unlacing his shoes, then quickly yanking down his trousers, and throwing them to one side. As a cool burst of air hit his crotch he shivered, half with the cold, half in anticipation of the action to come.

Joe forced the guard's legs apart, holding him tightly under his knees, so that his legs were hoisted in the air and over his shoulders, pinning him to the skip. Paul held his arms back and knelt on his shoulders, leaving Jordan helpless, and unable to move. Paul had already removed his own trousers and underpants, so his cock was hanging precariously close to Jordan's mouth, but as Jordan put out his tongue he couldn't quite reach the moistened tip. He couldn't even raise his head, but as he lay there, pinioned, he could hear the tell-tale ripping sound of a condom packet being opened and the rubbery twang as Joe snapped it down his erect cock. Someone had come prepared. Another ripping sound and then the wet slapping of lube on rubbered meat.

With scarcely a pause, the head of Joe's cock pushed at Jordan's arsehole. Instinctively he tensed up and the hole snapped tight.

'Relax... you know you want this.' Joe's voice was cooing and soft, the antithesis of his hard brutal weapon, poised to plunder Jordan's sphincter.

Jordan tried to speak, but the pressure on his chest meant he could only whisper, and neither of the boys heard his plaintive cry, 'I've never been fucked before...'

The head again pushed at the ring-piece and, as it momentarily relaxed, shoved inside, Joe gasping as the circle of muscle clamped around the glans of his knob. He squeezed more lube from the sachet onto his shaft, hoping to provide some lube for his forced entry, not want to hurt the guard too much.

'Aaaah.' Jordan's cry rang out as Joe pushed further in. It felt like a whole arm was being inserted, and he desperately wanted the young guy to take the arm back. He couldn't bear it. A wave of dizzying pain coursed through him, a kaleidoscope of colours burst in front of his eyes, as he felt the solid tool slide deeper inside, filling him utterly.

Then without a second's hesitation, Joe began to fuck. Jordan was stuffed with the boy's cock, Joe's hands about his hips as he thrust in deep and pulled back until the tip almost plopped out, then he rammed it inside again. The lad was like a machine, a cold calculating robot, fucking the guard like a piston.

Jordan opened his mouth to cry out again, but found the tip of Paul's cock gently nuzzling against his lips, and without further warning it slid inside. The velvety head lay still for a moment, the meaty ridge sat on Jordan's tongue, waiting for attention. Paul's hands were cupping Jordan's head, encouraging him to suck.

Paul could tell that Jordan was somewhat of a novice when it came to oral sex and so he decided to take his time and make this a memorable experience for the hunky guard. Teasingly he didn't let his cock slide in any further, for a few minutes he just let the guy lick and suck on the head, working his tongue around the ridge, poking in and out of the slit, until he was completely familiar with its size and shape. Then Paul pushed down, at the same time easing forward, until every inch of solid flesh disappeared into Jordan's throat.

The muscular guard nearly choked as the cock nudged its forceful way down past his tongue, stretching his mouth wide, filling him fit to burst. But after a moment's panic had dissipated he realised he could actually breathe through his nasal passages without any problems. He could feel that Paul's dick wasn't too long, but its girth surprised Jordan. From his upside-down position he could see Paul's bollocks hanging very close to the bridge of his nose, and watched mesmerised as they swung before him massively. As the cock pushed itself fully down, they rested on his cheeks, covering his eyes.

Now that Jordan had become accustomed to the mass inside his mouth, Paul started to slowly withdraw, until the only head was touching his lips. Then he began to fuck Jordan's mouth in long deliberate strokes, softly at first, then increasing in tempo. The rhythm increased, and this combined with the fucking of his arse brought Jordan to undiscovered heights of ecstasy. The punishment he was now getting at both ends had him in an unparalleled state of joy. His own cock had swiftly grown to its biggest size yet, hard and throbbing, desperate to be used and enjoyed too.

As if Joe had read his mind, he grasped the cock which was waving with the rocking rhythm, and began rubbing it. The fucking and sucking really went into overdrive, all three of the young men writhing and squirming and groaning.

Paul was amazed at Jordan's abilities, he was giving some of the best head he'd ever experienced, almost engulfing his cock in a vacuum, sucking and licking, slurping and pulling, sending waves of pleasure coursing through every cell in his body. Looking down, Paul gloried in the sight of Joe fucking the guard, grunting with each stroke, filling him to the hilt. Jordan's stomach and chest were now glistening with sweat which ran along the muscular ridges, disappearing under his back. His body was a marvel, toned and firm, with broad, manly shoulders, tapering down to narrow hips, past the developed six-pack stomach. His legs were also muscular and covered in a light down of hair. A truly marvellous specimen of manhood. These thoughts encouraged Paul and with a determined grin he doubled his efforts, fucking the open, willing mouth, feeling the gentle slapping as his bollocks bumped against Jordan's nose with each thrust.

In this position Jordan experienced sensations he didn't know existed. For him this was a real first. The first time he'd ever done it in a public place. The first time he'd ever had two guys at the same time. And the first time he'd ever got fucked up the arse. His whole body was screaming, with both extremes of pleasure and pain. He didn't know which end to pay most attention to. As he started to suck harder to try and give Paul his best, his mind would switch to the cock banging away inside him and he tried to push back, matching each inward thrust. However hard he tried, he knew that this double punishment had to come to an end soon.

Jordan was the first to explode, shooting forth in a luminescent stream of cum. His arse muscles clenched about Joe's stiff cock, squeezing them to a state of climax also, the lad shooting forth in the depths of Jordan's innards. Paul shut his eyes and cried out in ecstasy, pumping his thick creamy load down Jordan's throat, the hunky guard swallowing every last drop, draining Paul dry, sucking and sucking even when the spasms of ejaculation had finished, coaxing the last dribble from his sated member.

As Paul sat back on his haunches, slowly allowing his cock to slip from between Jordan's lips, he shivered. The cool air in the store-room played across his naked body. He looked down in satisfaction at Jordan's body, his stomach wet with sweat and his own cum lying in a pool near his nipples, the prick still hard, but gently lowering towards the belly button, until it made contact, the head lying still, sticky and spent.

Joe grasped the base of his cock, holding on tight to the condom as he pulled out, enjoying every wince as each inch was extruded from Jordan's hole, his face contorted with bliss. This had been some fuck.

'Good job I keep a spare rubber in my wallet!' Joe grinned, carefully tying a knot in the sheath, and wrapping it in some paper towels. He reached for his clothes, stopping to admire the wonder of Jordan's body, images of this experience still dancing in his memory.

'Thanks.' Jordan sat up and looked about him. He grabbed up a wad of paper towels and with quick strokes began to wipe the pearly juice from his chest. 'That was incredible! I was nervous at first... but I loved it.'

'I could tell that.' Joe grinned at him. 'The way you held my cock in your arse was amazing. You must be an expert.'

'No. That was my first time.' Jordan looked sheepish.

'Fuck off!' An expression of complete disbelief crossed Joe's face.

'It's true. I look more experienced than I actually am. If we had a spare week I'd tell you my story. But right now I think we should be getting dressed and out of here. The others will be wondering where we have got to.' He leapt up and started picking up his strewn clothes, hastily dressing himself, his eyes on the two lads hurriedly doing the same.

Dean and Connor had taken some time to get their breath back. Eventually when they had calmed down and Stuart had assured them that they were safe, he led the way to the centre office where they had stowed their bags and got changed before the appearance. The centre manager had given Stuart the key to the office to ensure the four lads' privacy.

'Looks like we're the first ones back. I wonder where the other three got to?' Stuart locked the office door behind them, content in the knowledge that they hadn't been followed by any of the ardent admirers. He had just finished a spell in the Army, and was missing its cameraderie, its discipline and the hint of danger that goes with being part of Her Majesty's armed forces.

Today there had been that familiar tingle of adrenalin when the clamour began, he had the chance to use his wits, and to extricate the lads from a potentially sticky situation. They relied on him to get them to a position of safety, and thankfully he had done just that.

One thing he missed very much about his days of active service was the company of a particular sergeant, a tough, handsome, foul-mouthed guy called Tim DeMacchio. Early on in Stuart's career Sergeant DeMacchio had singled him out as a likeminded man, someone who he could cultivate in his own special way. At the start of an especially gruelling cross-country run, he kept Stuart back so he would finish last, which he did, ending up back at the bath-house long after everyone else had gone.

Switching from a regimental attitude to one of an old mate, the sergeant kept chatting cheerily to Stuart as he soaped himself down in the shower, leaning nonchalantly against the stall, a fierce eye fixed on Stuart's sizeable genitalia. He casually raised an eyebrow as Stuart towelled himself robustly, paying close attention to his privates, letting the cock begin to swell.

The sex that followed was rough and brutal. Keeping one eye on the door, they sucked and fucked each other in a variety of positions, and admitted afterwards that that was some of the best they'd had. For the next six months they had carefully begun a relationship, unbeknownst to anyone else, which naturally ran its course, and when Stuart left the regiment, the affair ended too.

He looked back on that time with real fondness, and would be eternally grateful to Tim for showing such interest, and revealing how much fun could be had between two men with healthy bodies, healthy appetites and a flair for invention.

Now Stuart sat back against the manager's desk and looked at his watch. With the state of things out there, the others could be some while in getting to the office.

'We might as well get changed,' Dean muttered as Connor sank into a chair, asking what they were to do next.

Pulling the T-shirt over his head, and revealing his torso

beneath, Dean kept his eye on Stuart, who although he wasn't directly watching him, seemed to have an eye on what he was doing. Dean stretched again in a mock yawn, letting the guard get a good look at his physique. He didn't particularly work out, but had a nice body, spare and meaty, with a nicely defined chest and stomach.

Stuart desperately wanted to lean forward, take Dean in his arms and smother him in kisses, licking sensuously down from his ear, round his stiff nipples and further south to what lay below. He wanted to put his hands on the lump at the front of his trousers, and squeeze, coaxing it into full, pulsating life. The thoughts of what Dean had stashed away were beginning to turn him on and he could feel himself becoming aroused. The tight black material of his trousers was pulled tight across his groin, and emphasised his growing manhood.

He kept his gaze down, not wanting to appear too obvious, but stealing swift glances at Dean, now shirtless and slowly unbuckling his own trousers, before letting them slip softly to the ground. He could tell that Dean was also stealing tiny peeks back at him. Perhaps he was interested?

Since he had taken the blood test and been declared negative, Dean's zest for life had returned a hundredfold. He had decided to enjoy every day as if it was his last and damn the consequences. After that brush with danger, he was ultra-careful with his sex partners, but the numbers of them had begun to increase dramatically. Now here was this attractive, well-made security guard giving him the eye. Without a second's hesitation he had made up his mind to go for it.

All this time Connor sat in the chair, hands in his lap, surveying the scene. He could see that there was some kind of electricity between Dean and Stuart. Were they flirting with each other? Ever since Dean had become a trusted and valued friend, Connor had decided not to look on him as a piece of meat, a handsome guy with a great body, a potential shag. But here he was getting turned on. What Dean and Stuart were doing was decidedly horny.

Connor let his hand sit on his crotch, the fingers resting along his slumbering prick, the slightest hint of contact enough to start the blood flowing into its length. He caught Stuart's eye and gently squeezed himself, just giving enough of a signal for the young guard to know his intentions.

Dean looked between Connor and Stuart, fully aware of the situation that was now building. If he wasn't mistaken both of the others were as horny as he was. Did this mean a fantastic three-way? He prayed that it did. Standing in the office in nothing but his tight underpants and his shoes, he waited. Stuart was now fully aroused as he could see the huge mound of his groin, and Connor was now pretty much the same.

'Well, what now?' Dean asked the empty air.

'That's up to you guys.' Leaning back on the desk, his trousers stetching tight, the cock enraged and ready, Stuart also waited.

'Should we do this?' Connor sounded a note of anxiety, his actions the opposite of his words, his own cock now hard and pushing to be released.

Dean hesitated before he spoke again. 'Well, Stuart, you could kneel down in front of me and take my cock in your mouth perhaps.'

The guard watched and waited still.

'You could swallow my cock down your throat, and suck it. Then you could do the same for Con, here. I bet you'd like to suck on our cocks wouldn't you, eh?' The tone of Dean's voice assumed a harshness, a tone that Connor had never heard before. Possibly it's a voice he uses for sex? Whatever it was, Connor thought it incredibly arousing.

'Would you like that?' Stuart hadn't moved, leaning back, his eyes darting between the boys, his crotch still large. 'Would you like me to suck your cocks?'

Dean didn't answer, and so Stuart repeated the question, harsher and more urgent. 'I said... WOULD YOU LIKE ME TO SUCK YOUR COCKS?'

'Yes, please.' The words burst out of Connor, unable to contain himself. Quickly standing, he leapt out of his clothes, until he stood at Dean's side, one of them naked and one in his briefs. Stuart raised an eyebrow sardonically, looking down at the white underwear, waiting for Dean to remove it.

As the lad dropped them on the floor beside him, he looked back at Stuart, not sure what the next move was.

'Good boys. Now I think it's time for you to do as you are told, don't you? I said... DON'T YOU?'

The angry edge to his intonation sent a small shiver of apprehension down the boys' spines. What did this man intend to do? And should they let him do it?

Before they could think further, Stuart made a decisive move. With a couple of quick flicks of his wrist, he had undone his trousers and peeled them back, reaching inside and heaving his cock free. Both boys looked at it in astonishment. The shaft was thick and veined, the head large and impressive, as it lolled in his hand, the bollocks the biggest they had ever seen, almost hairless, and hanging saggy and pendulous in their sac.

Dean wondered if it was one of those cocks that suffered from being too big, and never got fully hard. If it did, then he doubted his ability to take it all. Still he intended to give it a fucking good try.

'Come here.' Stuart's tone wasn't to be argued with. So without pause, the two lads moved closer. 'Kneel down.'

Sinking to their knees, both Dean and Connor licked their lips simultaneously, in preparation for this mammoth knob. Stuart leant forward a touch so that the huge mushroom-shaped head was just in reach of the boys' tongues, and like dogs they put them out, eager to lap at it. As the tips made contact, Stuart pulled back.

'Good boys. If you do as you are told you shall have it all. Do you understand?' He looked at them both sternly waiting for con-firmation. Waiting for the knowledge that they were going to play along with this scenario. Which they were both willing to do.

'Yes.'

'Yes.'

Dean and Connor nodded in approval. The reward wasn't far away. Stuart let them inch closer and one at a time begin to lick his cock. Dean started at the head, carefully letting his tongue slap around, slurping and wetting the massive tip, whilst Connor fell upon the shaft, getting his tongue around it, licking up and down, then falling on the bollocks with glee. He closed his eyes and sucked them into his mouth, stretching his lips wide to accom-modate them both. As he did this he heard Stuart groan, and shift slightly against the desk's edge. This was a signal for Dean to go into overdrive. Exhaling as he went, he let the colossal penis slide down his throat. For a few seconds he actually thought it would be too big, but somehow he managed it.

Stuart's eyes were tightly shut, his lips pursed and thin, and his breathing was getting faster, so the boys knew they were now the ones in control. Renewing their efforts, they gave Stuart the best blow-job of his life. Alternating between cock and bollocks, they sucked and licked, swallowed and nibbled. Saliva drooled over the exposed parts, helping with the lubrication.

Connor wanted his turn at the cock-head and so let each ball pop out from his mouth with a satisfying yelp emanating from Stuart's tight lips. He shifted slightly on his knees to give Dean access to the balls and so he could get a good run-up at the cock. In his sex life, Connor had one real delight, and that was being on his knees, worshipping at a mighty totem, pleasuring a meaty cock, and here was his dream come true.

He saw how Dean had struggled to take the thing, the vast girth almost proving too much for his friend. He was determined to have no such trouble. Like a snake unhinging its jaws, Connor opened wide, and let the giant purple head slip in, his lips clamping about it, savouring the size and texture. Then bit by bit, he swallowed, pushing his mouth further down the shaft, feeling it cram the oral cavity, his teeth brushing the sides, and in an instant he had done it. His mouth was tight about the base, with no real room for movement. Sitting back on his heels, he let his mouth slide up the monster, before plunging down again. In these positions the boys went mad.

Stuart writhed against the desk, gripping the edge with both hands, the knuckles white with the tension in his fingers. Never had he experienced such sensations. This would be one for the memoirs. A boiling surge began to build up in his bollocks and he could keep his climax back no longer. With a cry of exultation, he pulled his cock out of Connor's mouth and shot across the lad's face. Dean knelt in, wanting to catch a few drops of the precious fluid himself. As the spasms subsided, Stuart looked down at the spunk-covered faces and gave a rare grin.

'Very nice. With talents like that, you two should be on the stage.' He started to shove his still hard cock back in his trousers, when a catch in Dean's voice made him look up.

'We haven't finished yet,' announced Dean. 'Now it's our turn.' Jumping to their feet, Dean and Connor pushed down on Stuart's shoulders, jamming him to the ground. Their cocks were out and proud, both standing erect and waiting.

'Now you can suck us.'

There was going to be no arguing with Dean on this one. But Stuart had no wish to argue. Hungrily he fell to his knees, landing with a dull thud on the carpet. His tongue lashed out first at Dean then at Connor, exploring every inch of the lads' available tools.

Tim had taught him a few tricks about satisfying a man sexually, and he was only too happy to share them with these two willing participants. Starting with Connor, he took the lad in his mouth, pushing back the foreskin with his lips, then filling it with saliva and swirling it around the sensitive cock-head. He inwardly smiled as the Irish lad trembled, one of his knees shaking with the intense thrill. Then without a pause he let the cock slip out, before he blew gently on the tip, the short burst of cool air getting another extreme reaction from Connor. He repeated this on Dean, revelling in the joy of two young, smooth dicks all for him.

Quickly moving from one to the other, Stuart swallowed the cock down to the base, clamping his lips tightly around the shaft, letting his tongue slide out and lick at the ball-sac, and expertly he also sucked the orbs into his mouth. Holding these treasures in the warm wet depths proved too much for Dean, who without warning came in a gush, jerking as the salty sperm was poured down Stuart's throat, the guard thirstily swallowing every drop.

As his cock emerged from Stuart's throat, Dean looked on aghast as Stuart did the same trick with Connor, who in a few moments also shot his load, gripping the guard's head as he let fly.

All three looked up as someone banged on the door.

'Are you in there?' It was Jordan's voice. The sound of fumbling keys came loudly and the door swung open. Jordan stood flanked by Joe and Paul, and huge grins were plastered across their faces.

Dean and Connor stood back and stared in amazement, their colleagues and friends staring back admiringly at the naked bodies. Paul and Joe were especially impressed by the other two lads' youthful frames and pleasing endowments.

The sight of Stuart, cock out, and with droplets of spunk around his face, struck Jordan as hilarious and he burst out laughing. He had worked with Stuart on a couple of occasions and had guessed he was gay, but had been given no hint of a come-on – in fact Stuart had been rather cool and seemed uninterested in sex. Now here he was in a compromising position, with what looked like a very nice slab of meat himself, and it all became too much.

Sinking into a chair, Jordan sat, convulsed, the others watching amused, wiping themselves and dressing quickly, lest someone else should come along.

'Ah, there you all are.' The strident, nasal tones of Melanie rang out. She pushed open the door and entered the office, carrying her obligatory sheaves of notes and wearing a silly grin.

'This has been a great day. The national papers have leapt on the story, and you'll be all over the front pages tomorrow. You weren't hurt, I hope?'

She looked around the room, sniffing the air. 'Bit stale in 'ere, innit?'

The six men assumed an innocent posture and grabbed up their bags, hustling Melanie out of the door. A long sleep on the tour bus and a cold can of beer were now the only things on their minds.

11: The Camera Sometimes Lies

The middle-aged but still handsome receptionist looked up from the front desk and with a welcoming, beaming grin put out his hand.

'Good afternoon. BANNED, is it not? Welcome to the Carlton Palace Hotel. I am sure you will all be pleased with our facilities here, as pleased as we are to have you with us.'

His unctuous manner was not lost on Joe who gave him a wink, and held the handshake for a moment longer than propriety demanded, sure that he'd found another sister.

'Thank you, er... Sebastian.' Joe read the name from the receptionist's badge. 'I'm sure I'll be happy with everything you can offer me.'

In the year since BANNED's conception, the four members had grown in stature and personality, no longer afraid to speak their minds, or take a risk. Joe especially had become quite a character, always looking out for sympathetic gay guys to share a smile and a snigger with, and sometimes a shag. The other members had noticed his nymphomaniac qualities but not commented on it, preferring to let Joe have his fun... as long as he was careful and discreet.

The four young lads had assembled at one of London's premier hotels for a press conference organised by the indefatigable

Melanie, to announce the launch of their second album.

Representatives from the nation's newspapers were gathering in the Salisbury Ballroom where hundreds of chairs were laid out facing the top table, which was studded along with microphones and pitchers of iced water.

The four rising stars were taken by the bell boy to the lift, and then to an elegant suite on the top floor overlooking the River Thames, where they could relax and refresh themselves before facing the probing of the press. These occasions were becoming more frequent now that BANNED had achieved some degree of notoriety, and were looked on by the boys as a necessary evil, something unpleasant, but a task that had to be endured, if they wanted that useful article in the papers.

'All publicity is good,' Melanie had been heard to say at least ten times a week, knowing the value of getting the press on your side. Give them what they want, before they try to get it in sneaky ways.

There was a knock on the door to the luxurious suite, and in came Melanie, loudly clad in purple lurex with a white beret atop her purple hair, accompanied by a startlingly large young woman in a leather jacket, and an over-tight pair of blue denims that gave the impression of having been freshly sprayed on this morning, the total look completed by the absence of any hair on her head.

'Hello boys. Alright?' Melanie flashed a wide grin, showing a mouthful of sparkling teeth. 'Don't mind if we come in, do you?' She strode inside and flopped into a vast armchair, dropping her handbag at her feet. 'Come on in Debs, don't stand there like a spare prick at a castration.'

Her new girlfriend Debbie Whette had become a constant companion in the three months that they had been going out together. When the boys had learned that Melanie was a lesbian they were surprised, taking the news in good spirit, but the arrival on the scene of the statuesque and forbidding Debbie rather startled them. She hung around at Melanie's side all day, intently watching her every move, hardly saying a word to anyone. But they realised this was a small price to pay for having the services of the best press agent around.

And Melanie had done them proud. In the first year since BANNED's creation, she had arranged numerous interviews with the papers, got the shopping centre tour branded a huge success, negotiated many appearances on various television shows, including a spot on the weekly *Chat With Jerry* programme, the BBC's top chat host being obviously enamoured of the four hunks. Now she had pulled out all the stops to make this conference a good one. She had made sure that the reporters had been plied with wine and stuffed with a fantastic buffet spread, before the boys were due in front of them.

'Right then, if you're all ready... time to get down there.' Melanie stood and crossed to the door, yanking it open forcefully, and nodding to Stuart and Jordan who were on guard duty outside. The boys sighed and followed, heading for the lift.

'So how are you all today?' a weaselly-faced reporter asked first. His hand was clasped about a dictaphone ready to catch every word the boys uttered.

'Brilliant. Things couldn't be better for us.' Connor answered.

'So can you sum up the successes of your first year in BANNED?' The reporter asked, a glob of spit collecting at the corner of his mouth.

The boys looked at each other, wondering who would be the one to speak. Connor took the lead. 'It's been a great year. Since the band was formed we've gone from strength to strength. Our first single did quite well in the charts, our second got to number nine, and our third was the mega-hit 'In Your Eyes'. That was when we really hit the big time. Our debut album got to number five, and we are here today to celebrate the release of our second album, which we think is even better then the first.'

'But this last year has been fraught with difficulties, hasn't it?'

'I don't know what you mean.'

'The adverse publicity from the ROKTV show...'

'That was a storm in a teacup. There was no story there, and the programme knew it. Besides, they broadcast a retraction the following week, stating they had just been after gossip, hoping to smear our reputation before we'd even had a chance to establish ourselves.'

'What about the incident in Manchester, where a young girl was badly injured when a shop window was smashed and she was cut by flying glass?'

'That was a terrible thing, and we all wish her well. In fact we sent Mandy – that was her name – flowers when we heard about it. But we can't be blamed for that. There was inadequate security at the centre and things got out of hand.'

'OK, then what about the legal row over the song 'Only The Night'? Is it true that a disgruntled songwriter is suing because his tune was stolen?'

There was a murmur of interest around the room, and several hands were thrust in the air.

'There was some problem I believe with a young guy who thought the song was his. But as our lawyers pointed out, there were only vague similarities between them. He realised his error. Any other questions?' Connor looked about the room and pointed to a young man standing at the back, holding a notebook, but writing nothing in it. He had an assured air, his dark, Mediterranean good looks set off by a pair of astoundingly beautiful blue-black eyes, apparent even at a distance.

'Are you all still gay? Has any gorgeous girl managed to sway you to the other side yet?' A titter ran round the room.

Dean leant forward and tapped the microphone before he spoke. 'We are all still gay, and will happily prove it to any of you who'd care to come up after this press conference.'

A huge explosion of laughter rocked the ballroom. The young reporter who'd asked the question blushed, his tanned face developing a deeper reddened glow, and buried his head in his notebook.

'Next please.' Dean scanned the sea of waving hands and gestured to a young woman at the front, perched on a chair, holding a plate of vol-au-vents, a glass of wine and her recorder.

'What's next for you all?' She waited expectantly for an answer as if she'd asked for the meaning of life itself.

Joe leant forward. 'Where do I start? Well, the new album *Joy* is released next week. Then we have loads of press appearances to promote it. Then we'll probably have a few weeks off. There is also a great deal of planning to do for our first major tour, which will visit seven cities around the country, starting in London next April. That will be a great opportunity for the fans to see us live, and for us to get the chance to perform some of our favourite songs. It's gonna be fab!'

'So have you any further ambitions?' The handsome reporter at the back shouted out, his blushes now vanished, his voice ringing out again with clarity.

Paul took the chance to answer. 'At the moment to just do the best we can, to make music that our fans will enjoy, and to be as successful as possible.'

'So nothing could send your careers off the rails?'

'What do you mean?' Connor asked in a puzzled voice.

'Are there any scandals tucked away, that might blow up in your faces?'

'I don't think so. Besides, do you think we'd tell you if we had!' Another supportive laugh ran round the room.

The press conference struggled on for a short while longer, no one having any original questions for the boys, and so when it looked like things were beginning to get sticky, Melanie drew the proceedings to a close.

'Thank you everybody. That was great. If you see my assistant at the door she'll give you a preview copy of the new album.' She turned and motioned to Stuart and Jordan, who were standing at the side of the hall, to escort the boys back to their suite.

As the group waited at the lift, there was the noise of someone clearing their throat. The boys turned round to see Sebastian the receptionist, standing attentively by them.

'Er... I wonder if I might just... er... this young man wanted a word with you. He was quite insistent that I ask you.' At his side was the young reporter from the back of the hall, who stood close, his baggy jacket and trousers hiding what was obviously a very fit body.

'My name is Manuel, I write for the *Weekly Music News*. I wonder if I might ask a few more questions? I know it's a cheek, but I feel that we learned nothing new in that press conference, and that if you give me chance to ask some more probing questions I could provide a great feature in our next edition. I'm sure you'd like a good review of the new album, wouldn't you?'

The boys caught each other's curious glances, but it was Joe who spoke up first.

'Not so sure about this. What do you think guys? Melanie?'

The brash press agent shrugged her shoulders, and looked around the foyer for Debbie who had mysteriously vanished, finally spotting her sizeable frame heading towards her, carrying a plate of left-over sausage rolls and pastries from the buffet, stuffing them into her mouth.

'Why not? This young man looks like he might be a man of his word. And a good review in the *Weekly* would help enormously.'

'Alright, come up to our suite and we'll give you a few minutes.' Joe let the others cram into the newly arrived lift and waited for Manuel to follow, squeezing himself in tightly by the young reporter, pushing against his hard torso.

Once in the luxury suite, Melanie and Debbie decided to leave the boys with Manuel, and arm-in-arm, they went in search of some lunch.

Stuart and Jordan were at their positions outside the room, and so, feeling safe and secure, the boys sank down on the sofas and amchairs which peopled the vast suite.

Manuel perched himself on a stool and pulled his notebook from a shoulder bag. 'So to go back to my question this morning... are there any scandals that might break? Do any of you have any secrets that could threaten to destroy BANNED?'

The boys were slightly taken aback by this question again, and they racked their brains as to what he might mean. Everyone knew they were gay, and so that wasn't likely to be news. Joe still worried about his contretemps with Mitch those many months ago, but had calmed down since then, his anger at his rough treatment finally gone. No one else knew about it so that couldn't be what Manuel meant either.

'I don't know what you are getting at.' Connor stared at Manuel, perplexed, but inquisitive.

Manuel's expression was still, he was giving nothing away. Reaching into his shoulder bag he pulled out a video cassette. 'I see there is a TV and video player here. May I use it for a moment?' Without waiting for acknowledgment, he stood, crossed to the equipment, switched on the TV and pushed the video into the gaping slot.

A silent picture sprang to life on the huge widescreen set. It was footage from a security camera. It took the boys a few moments to recognise the location as The Bare Pit nightclub, where they had debuted successfully some nine or ten months before. The picture was slowly moving over the heads of the crowd, watching, spying, keeping its silent eye on the revellers. Then the images changed, as the camera moved away from the dancefloor and focused in on the control box, and onto Connor, having sex with JayVee and

Peter Q, the two house DJs. The picture was devastatingly clear, and the boys could see in a glorious close-up what Connor was doing with the two disc-spinners. Sucking their cocks one after the other, giving great head, and the two guys loving every minute. The five of them watched in silence as the DJs ejaculated and the picture suddenly went black.

Manuel pressed the eject button and placed the cassette safely back inside his bag.

There were distinct bulges in the guys' groin areas, including Manuel's, who waited for a reaction. But the one he got was surprising.

Dean stood and crossed to Connor's side, placing a wet kiss on his lips. 'Well done, mate. Great stuff!'

Joe joined him and slapped Connor on the back. 'If I'd known you gave such good head, I'd have let you have my knob long ago!' Paul also crossed and gave Connor a supportive squeeze of his cheek. 'Nice one,' he said.

All four of them were aroused by the video, and turning to face Manuel, they saw that he too had a hard-on.

'So did you like what you saw?' Connor asked. His face slightly reddened.

Manuel didn't answer at first, just watched the guys, his arms hanging nonchalantly by his side, the tell-tale bulge in his baggy trousers apparent to all.

'I liked it a lot. The question is what are you going to do about this?' He waited, the silence in the room could have been cut with a razor.

'Should we give Nick a call?' Paul sounded apprehensive, but his fellow band members appeared unconcerned.

'I don't think so. I reckon we can handle this ourselves. Dean, Joe?' Connor had assumed an air of superiority, taking control of the situation. The other two nodded their unspoken assent.

'Because I would hate to have to give this tape to someone

else... someone with less scruples than I have.' The guys weren't sure if there was a hint of a menace in the voice, although his meaning was certainly threatening.

'Any thoughts on the matter?' Manuel now believed he was the master of the scene, with these four young men in the palm of his hand. He was wrong.

'Is that the only copy?' Connor held the reporter's gaze.

'For the moment, yes. But I can make copies.'

'How did you get hold of it?

'Ah, well, I have friends in many surprising places, including night club management. I've been waiting for the right moment to show this to you, today seemed like the ideal opportunity. I had to get you alone, and my plan has quite evidently worked. Well...? I'm waiting for an answer.' The mound in the front of his crotch was still big, and the boys' eyes hadn't failed to notice this.

'I think you'd better let me handle this.' Connor's voice was hard and not to be argued with. Dean, Joe and Paul quickly left the room, then Connor pushed the door shut behind them and locked it with a resounding click.

Connor knew what he had to do. The reporter wanted something from him and wasn't going to go away until he got it. He shucked his clothes, peeling away the layers, taking it reasonably slow, making a show for the captive journalist, until he stood in just his underwear. Aware that the air-conditioning in the room was on, Connor's skin reacted to the currents of cool air wafting around them, developing goose-bumps, and he shivered.

It was Connor who took charge of the moment. 'I think you know what you want now, don't you? This is what you have been after all the time, isn't it?'

Manuel licked his lips. His eyes moistened and as he spoke his voice cracked, his throat dry and nervous suddenly.

'*Si*. Oh yes! I've dreamed of this for ever.'

Connor looked him straight in the eye, a mischievous glint there. 'You could have just asked me, you stupid fucker.'

Pausing no longer, Manuel ripped off his jacket and trousers, throwing them in a heap, then like the Irish lad, stood in just his boxer shorts.

'Come on then.' Connor waited, his hand falling to his cock, massaging it through his briefs, encouraging a hard-on.

The Spaniard didn't need to be asked again. He rushed forward, sinking to his knees in front of Connor, his mouth open. With his tongue he began to lick at the cock which was growing gently beneath the white cotton, feeling the blood rush into it, a noticeable throbbing in its length, leaving damp patches of saliva on the front of the pristine underwear. Connor pushed his crotch against the journalist's face. He looked down at the guy's body, muscular thighs, with a sturdy waist and hips, a beautifully chiselled chest and skin that had a healthy tanned, Mediterranean glow.

'Stand up.' Connor's voice now had a dangerous edge to it. If this bastard wanted the works then he was going to get it. 'Get naked.'

There was no mistaking his intentions and without a futher word, Manuel slipped out of his shorts. His cock was rigid and pulsating, and jutted out from the bush of dark hair surrounding it. The young reporter's prick was very nice, cut, with a large head, which overshadowed a long, thin shaft, sticking ram-rod straight out in front of him. It was lined all around with veins, which gave it some character. Its cut head oozed pre-cum. Connor placed his hand on it and it jerked at the touch. He could feel the shaft throbbing, the flow of blood pumping around its veins and arteries, swelling the erection to maximum. With one hand on the cock, he pulled gently, leading the Spaniard into the bedroom.

Manuel had only a few dark hairs leading up to his navel, and then a small patch around each nipple. Connor raised the guy's arm and put his face underneath. He inhaled deeply at the sweaty manliness, mixed with a sweet almost sickly smell of deodorant. Slowly they sank onto the bed, Connor's face still buried in the guy's armpit. He ran his tongue up to the ridge of the shoulder and then to his neck, lapping at the brown skin, and finally settled on the full, sensuous lips, pushing his tongue between them, and feeling Manuel's tongue respond in the same way. Their mouths were locked together, their bodies pressed hard against each other, now each enjoying the sensations the other was giving. Their toes were intertwined, the hairs on their legs bristled, and their cocks rose and butted, head rubbing against head.

With a sudden realisation that he actually wanted to experience hot sex with this handsome guy more than anything else, Connor began exploring every inch of his body, licking and sucking down from the lips and neck, spending much time on the nipples, biting and teasing the fleshy lumps, sensing Manuel's tense reactions. He moved downward to the feet, taking the big toe in his mouth, and sucking on it, teasing it like a cock. His tongue swirled around the toes, in and out of the crevices, hearing astonished gulps of delight issue from Manuel's throat.

It took only a few minutes more for Manuel to respond fully and they started to sixty-nine, Connor underneath, the handsome Spaniard on top. Connor put out his tongue and tasted the end of Manuel's prick. He was aroused by its saltiness, slowly taking the thick shaft inside his throat, feeling it slide down until it touched the back. Manuel's mouth was softly licking around the head of Connor's cock, before he too sucked it deep within. In unison the two guys began working on each other, Connor's head hanging over the end of the bed, to allow easier access, while Manuel's head bobbed up and down rhythmically, the power of his mouth's suction overwhelming.

Connor held tight to the shaft, as it thrust in and out of his mouth, working his wet tongue and lips around the head at each push. Manuel sucked greedily on Connor's meat also, varying the

the speed and direction with every stroke, wanting to give as much pleasure as possible. In this position they sucked at each other for ages, slowing down and easing the pressure every time they felt the other's balls tighten, not wanting an orgasm so soon.

Deciding to change the emphasis a little, Connor let the cock slide out from his mouth, and he pulled his face back and licked at the arsehole. He felt Manuel writhe at the contact, the pleasure taking effect. Again he took the stiff cock in his mouth, swallowing the whole engorged length, cupping the bollocks in his hands, gently squeezing and massaging them.

Then Connor felt a pair of hands parting his legs and raising them before settling on his arse cheeks, and so he looked up, peering between Manuel's bronzed thighs. He tried to get up but couldn't move, the weight of the young guy pinning him to the bed. The hands on his butt moved until they nudged at his balls, then one of them crept further up until it clasped his cock. Manuel's other hand poked at Connor's hole, probing and prodding.

This wasn't how it was supposed to be. With an almost Herculean effort, Connor pushed the guy aside, and rolled him over onto his stomach, pulling his legs down the bed until he was bent forward at an angle, his arse now available for plundering.

'In my bag,' Manuel said. Unsure of his meaning, Connor looked around, saw the shoulder bag and scooped it up. Inside was a packet of condoms and a tube of lube. He had obviously come well prepared for a good fucking. And that is what he was going to get.

Connor squirted some of the slippery lube on his fingertips and slowly he massaged the gel around the hole, which trembled and pulsed at the touch. The hole tightened as one of Connor's fingers tried to penetrate it. 'Relax, you'll enjoy it more...' Connor's voice now had a soothing lilt. The finger eased its way into the hole, spreading the lubricating balm around, working in and out, giving Manuel an exceedingly pleasing sensation.

The finger withdrew, and Manuel breathed out, waiting the main event, wanting and needing Connor's big cock inside him. He felt the rubber-coated cock-head rubbing against the arse cheeks, getting more and more slippery as it worked its way nearer to its target. Hands parted the cheeks and the head pushed against the tightly knotted ring of muscle, and with one thrust it entered.

Manuel bit down into the soft satin of the duvet, the desire to scream intense. The Spaniard tried to squeeze his arse muscles shut, to force the invader out, and put an end to the mind-shattering agony. He felt as if he was being torn asunder, as though a red-hot poker was being inserted. After several deep breaths, he did relax slightly, enough for Connor to continue on his inexorable way upwards.

Gritting his teeth, Connor pushed harder. He had never fucked such a tight, resistant hole before, and knew that Manuel must either be extremely sore or loving every second of the hurt. He pushed his thick cock forward another inch, gasping as the muscle ring clamped about the shaft, as if it wanted to squeeze it to death. Another couple of pushes and he could feel his bollocks brushing against Manuel's. He started to move in and out of the Spaniard's hole, backwards and forwards, the whole experience highly erotic and totally unexpected. Manuel thrust his arse up to meet each downward stroke, grunting every time the rigid shaft filled him.

With one hand, Connor felt around for Manuel's cock and balls, pressed against the bed cover, poking backwards between his thighs. Caressing them, Connor tried to match the regular strokes of his fucking, yanking on the balls then pulling on the cock. His own balls were banging against the skin above Manuel's sweaty orbs with each inward thrust. He began to get a little faster, looking down with admiration for the young journalist's capacity to take a good seeing to.

Manuel eased himself up the bed, moving away from Connor's pile-driver and spun over onto his back, throwing his legs over his shoulders, his hands stretching wide his arse cheeks, displaying his aching hole, wanting more of his punishment. The hole was opening and closing like a beating heart, inviting Connor in once more.

Kneeling up, Connor pulled off the condom and replaced it swiftly with a new one, and entered Manuel with one hard shove. They both moaned, as Manuel's hole seemed tight again, and needed coaxing, needed filling to help the muscles again become accustomed to the chastisement it was getting. Surprised at the constant tightness, Connor pumped hard, powerful strokes into him, again and again with the aggression of a fighter until he almost came, slowing down to stop the eruption of seed. Manuel was thrashing his head around in an ecstatic mixture of pleasure and intense pain. Leaning forward, Connor started to bite on Manuel's tanned nipples, taking them into his mouth, licking around the brown outer rim, nibbling and sucking, his eyes fixed on Manuel's face which was swamped by an expression of utter bliss.

Wanting the journalist to learn a lesson, Connor slapped him across the face. The young guy's eyes snapped open, astonished at what the lad had just done.

'What the fuck?' He spoke in deep breaths, matching the deep pounding strokes of Connor's cock.

'You... tried... blackmail...' Connor emphasised each word with a forceful push of his solid member. 'Never... do... that... again. Understand?'

Manuel nodded his head, and threw a fist up to his mouth, biting into the knuckle, his eyes moist with the exhausting exertions and the discomfort of his position.

Knowing that he had made his point, Connor took hold of the guy's cock and started to pump it up and down in his fist.

'Ohh, I'm gonna come!' Connor cried out just as the Spaniard did the same. His cock exploded, pumping into Manuel, as the journalist spurted out over his stomach and groin. Their breathing subsided, and the flow stopped, their two cocks shrinking back to their normal sizes.

They both lay side by side on the bed for a while. Manuel leant up on one elbow and gazed adoringly at Connor, his fingers gently stroking the limp cock. 'Thank you. I'm so grateful.'

'So you should be.'

'I am truly sorry for what I did.' Manuel looked at Connor, his dark, sensuous eyes filling up. 'But there was no other way. I have admired and wanted you since the first moment I saw you. I have tried many times to contact you, but the record company kept giving me excuses why they wouldn't pass on my letters. It's been like a constant nagging pain, wanting to somehow meet you, and have you. It has been the only thing I've dreamed of or thought about since that first glimpse.

'When that tape came into my hands, I knew it would be a way of getting close. And when I heard there would be a press conference today, well all I had to do was get hold of a camera, fake an ID badge, and bingo… here I am. I'm not really a journalist. I work as a masseur at a health club. Are you angry with me?'

Connor didn't speak for a moment, weighing up what they'd just been told. 'Yes and no. We don't like subterfuge or underhand behaviour, we want people to be honest with us. We aren't monsters, just regular guys. If you had come up and talked to me, tried to get to know me then we might have hit it off.' He paused and stroked the guy's thigh. 'On the other hand, we've just had a great time.'

Lowering his eyes, Manuel spoke softly, his fingers still paying attention to Connor's cock, as if he never wanted to let go. 'I tried everything to get near you. You don't realise the secure wall that's been thrown up around you guys. If the fans want to get to know you they can't... it's just impossible. It makes you all seem remote and unfriendly and uncaring, you know. Take my advice and relax things a little. The public will love you more for that.'

Pondering Manuel's words, Connor eased himself up onto his elbow, facing the handsome chap. 'I'll mention it to our manager.' He hesitated and put a finger under Manuel's chin and stared strongly into his eyes. 'You'll hand over the tape then?'

'Sure. It was never intended for the public, I just wanted to use it as a bargaining tool. And I think I got more than I bargained for.'

Connor smiled. 'You certainly did.' He looked down at the hand clasped around his genitals and felt the familiar tingle that showed an erection wasn't too far away. 'Are you in a hurry to be anywhere else?'

With a shake of his head, Manuel gave a hearty grin. 'Only a back rub for Mr Bergman. But he can wait. I'd rather give you a good rub. Lay face down, and you'll see how good I am.'

Connor decided that there was nothing else to do but agree.

12: Top of the Cops

The winter weather had definitely set in. Rain and wind buffeted the windows of Nick's office, making him shudder. He hated this time of year. Umbrellas, raincoats, boots, scarves, runny noses and flu. He was definitely a summer person, loving the opportunity to wear as little as possible, and to watch the capital's young men emerge into the sunlight, showing off their tight bodies, and muscular legs.

Now there was months ahead of unrelenting misery. He closed his eyes and pictured the forthcoming months of dreary negotiations necessary to get the boys' first concert tour up and running. But as he waited for the group to assemble in his office, he knew there was one bright spark in the approaching darkness.

BANNED was proving to be a bigger success than even he had hoped for. The second album had been a runaway hit, settling at the top of the charts and staying there for two months, earning a gold disc for massive sales. The band was now one of the country's top sellers, a phenomenon amongst boy bands.

Even the four lads had been taken aback by their rapid rise to fame. All the while they were being adored and screamed at by millions of doting fans, both male and female, they had kept their feet firmly planted on the ground. They hadn't let the heady heights of legend change them, or their attitude to life. Ever since the affair of the security camera, the boys had been inseparable, living in each other's pockets, always together, the bond between them stronger than Nick could ever have imagined. He had been told about what happened with that obsessive fan, and in a way disapproved of the method Connor used to handle the situation. But the fact of their strength and closeness was a contributing factor to their steady success. There was never a cross word between all four, harmony and cordiality abounded. Press interviews and television appearances were happy affairs, and every decision the group had to take was made with the least amount of argument possible.

Nick hoped that the telephone call he'd received early in the morning would make them happier still.

The intercom buzzed with its familiar insistent clamour for attention.

'Yes?'

'The boys are here.'

'Good, send them in. Oh, and coffee all round, please.'

He sat back and waited, a huge beatific grin lighting up his face.

The door opened and the boys poured in, chattering and bouncing with enthusiasm and energy.

'Hi Nick.' Paul beamed at his manager, sinking into one of the four chairs lined up opposite the desk.

'How are you today then?'

'Fab. What's this all about then?'

Nick was amazed at Paul's energy and zeal – in the last few months he had really come out of his shell, and was now far from the shy lad he used to be. In many group situations he even took the lead, and the others seemed happy to let him.

'I just wanted to tell you all personally about an up and coming bit of publicity that I think you'll like.'

The boys looked at each other, wondering what Nick could mean. In the recent past they had experienced every conceivable kind of publicity stunt, and interviews for myriad TV channels, newspapers and magazines. What was there left that they hadn't yet done?

'Don't keep us in suspense, what is it?' Paul leaned forward, hands clasped together in an attitude of deep concentration, his eyes sparkling brightly.

Nick took a breath and let them in on the good news. He smiled as he named the nation's biggest TV chart show.

'YES!' Paul exploded and sat back, grinning from ear to ear. For him it was a dream come true. Evere since he could recall he had sat with his mother watching the weekly stroll through the charts, revelling in whichever band were singing live, or appearing to be, keeping track of the top ten singles in his notebook. To finally be asked to appear on the programme was one of his ambitions and it was really going to happen.

'That's right. Next week. There will be a day of rehearsing at the studio then taping in the evening. They want a live performance of the new song. Any problems?' Nick waited for a response.

'None at all.' Connor seemed as delighted as Paul. A volley of nodding followed, showing the band's assent.

'Good.' Nick picked up a pen and scrawled something on a sheet of paper. 'Then go away. Have a few days' rest, and I'll see you at the studios.'

Seeing the studio set up sent tingles of exhilaration racing through the boys. As they stood in the doorway, watching the crew setting up the lights and cameras, they knew that they were in for a good day. They had arrived by limo, and been taken to the dressing room by a camp young assistant named Dom, who appeared completely overawed to be in the boys' presence, fawning madly, eager to make them as comfortable as he could.

'If there is anything you want, and I do mean anything, just ask and I'll do my very best to get it for you.' Dom almost drooled as he spoke, his sycophancy too much for the boys to bear.

'Some peace and quiet would be nice.' Dean gave the assistant a hard stare and closed the dressing room door firmly.

'At last,' Dean said, throwing himself onto the full-length couch. 'So when do you think we'll be needed?'

Joe picked up a call-sheet from the magazine-laden coffee-table, and scanned it rapidly. 'Well, it says here that we'll be on set for rehearsal at about two o'clock. Then free in the afternoon until six, and the taping starts at seven.'

'Excellent. Sounds like a plan.' Connor put his feet up on the dressing table, his hands behind his head, facing his reflection in the mirror. 'Call me when they're ready.' He closed his eyes and appeared to drift off in slumber.

'I think I'll go for a wander round and have a nose about.' Paul slipped outside.

The corridors were full of people, milling about, some with clipboards, some carrying articles of clothing. The walls were lined with portraits of many of the famous stars who had graced the programme, and as he looked at each one, Paul couldn't believe that he was actually going to be one of the hallowed crowd.

The studio seemed smaller than he expected, even with his newly found knowledge of television and its marvels. No experience had prepared him for the thrill of being here. He stood, leaning against a far wall, just watching the bustle, taking it all in, trying to commit everything to memory, when a hand tapped him on the shoulder. Paul spun round and found himself face to face with Jodi Thorogood.

'Well, bugger me.' Paul exclaimed, his eyes wide with surprise.

'Later, perhaps.' Jodi smiled and put out his arms for a hug.

'What are you doing here?' Paul asked as he clasped the young presenter to his chest, enjoying the feel of the warm body contact, and rather astounded at the fervour with which Jodi seemed to be hugging him back.

'I'm presenting tonight's show.'

'I don't believe it.' Amazed, Paul let go of Jodi who linked arms and started to stroll towards the canteen.

'Absolutely true. Scout's honour.'

'But were you ever in the scouts?'

'Once or twice.' Jodi laughed gaily, flashing his perfect set of teeth. 'It's a very small world in television.'

'Well, I'm glad to hear it.' Genuinely glad to see Jodi, Paul squeezed his hand and walked with him.

'Shall we grab a drink and catch up?'

'Why not?' Jodi led the way, and purchased two cups of tea, taking them to a table at the far corner of the canteen, away from everyone else.

'It is good to see you.' Paul smiled, ripping open a sachet of sugar.

'You too.'

'So how are things? How's the career?'

'Blossoming. Ever since I left that shit-hole ROKTV, I've gone from strength to strength. I got a regular job on a teen show, did some travel show stuff for a cable channel and finally hit the jackpot when they asked me to front this show.'

'So this is your first week?'

'Yup, and I'm scared stiff.'

'Join the club.' Paul took a sip of tea, grimacing at its bitterness.

Jodi suddenly went silent, stirring his tea slowly and thoughtfully.

'What's the matter?' Mystified, Paul placed his hand on Jodi's, comfortingly.

'I am sorry about what happened before... you know, what ROKTV did to you guys. It was a rotten thing to do, and I just wish I'd stood up to them a lot earlier.'

'You weren't to know what they were up to.'

'But I was. I knew the editorial policy of the station. Get as much dirt as possible on the guests, and smear them. According to them, that's what makes a good news story. I knew what they were planning to do, but because I was a lot more timid back then, you know, about my being gay and all, I went along with it. Meeting you and coming out was one of the best things that ever happened.'

'Seriously?' Paul tried to avoid looking smug, but he was delighted to hear what Jodi was saying. To have helped someone out, to have given them a hand escaping from the closet, made him extremely proud.

'Yes. And I'm glad to have this chance to thank you. I've wanted to call many times, but not had the nerve.'

'You should have.'

'I know. But we are here now. How's about we go out for a drink sometime?'

Paul swigged back the last dregs of tea. 'Absolutely. And if you don't call me, I'll call you!'

They both giggled like a pair of naughty schoolgirls.

'So would you like to come and meet the lads properly?'

'I'd love it. If they have truly forgiven me.' Again Jodi hung his head.

'Of course they have. They'll love you... believe me.'

'Right. After the rehearsal then.'

'It's a date.'

BANNED thoroughly enjoyed the run-through for the cameras, sensing that the whole studio was watching them, and tapping along to the jolly beat of their new single, 'Fun In The Sun'. Nick hung around, proud and happy, and Jodi sat back, smiling cheerfully, glued to their every move.

A spontaneous round of applause greeted them as they left the stage and headed for the dressing room, where they hung around drinking coffee and chatting with studio staff.

At a knock at the door, the boys looked up. Nick entered, his hand deep in the pockets of his leather jacket. He smiled at the assorted hangers-on and asked them to leave so he could talk to the boys in private.

'Well done guys. You'll be great. Now just relax and take it easy and save all your energies for this evening's preformance.' He crossed to where Dean was standing and gave him a peck on the cheek. 'You are all wonderful. And I am so full of pride that it is amazing! After the show tonight I want to take you all out. We'll go to a night-club, and have some drinks and a dance and see if we can't get an orgy together. What do you say?'

The boys all grinned simultaneously, the thought of a good night out suddenly very appealing.

'Excellent, then I'll see you all later. Have a good show. I'll be up in the control box, keeping an eye on the direction.' He gave a salute and left, leaving the door open. Dom, the floor assistant, poked his head round the door frame and tittered nervously.

'Anything I can get for you boys?' He emphasised the word 'anything', with a suggestive leer and a wink.

'No thanks, just shut the door and call us when we are needed tonight.'

'Will do.' He winked again and vanished. As he pulled the door to, the boys heard him talking to someone in the corridor, which was swiftly followed by a rapid succession of faint-hearted knocks.

'Come in,' said Connor.

The door was tentatively pushed and Jodi looked in, slightly apprehensive about meeting the boys again.

'Well, look who it is. Miss Trouble. Ruined any more reputations lately?' Dean's voice was mocking and his tone harsh.

'Come on,' said Paul. 'That's not fair. Jodi was only doing what the station ordered him to do. Besides, it all turned out OK in the end, didn't it?'

'I guess so,' Dean conceded. He put out his hand to Jodi. 'How are you?'

The presenter smiled and grasped the hand warmly. 'Great thank you. Look, I am so sorry about what happened. Please don't blame me... I got the retraction for you, and that should have cleared the whole mess up.'

Dean narrowed his eyes. 'Yes and we heard what Paul used as leverage against you. Glass of piss anyone?' The moment the words left his lips he was sorry he spoke them. 'Sorry, that was in bad taste.'

Jodi nodded, his cheeks flushed. 'I hope we can be friends. I'd really like to be. What do you say?'

The boys looked at each other for grudging consolation. Paul spoke up for them. 'Of course. We'd like that a lot.'

Looking thoroughly relieved, Jodi crossed and gave Paul a hug. 'Thank you.'

Squeezing back, Paul whispered in Jodi's ear, 'You're welcome.'

'Well, I'm dying of thirst. Anyone fancy a can of something?' Joe headed for the door.

Both Paul and Jodi looked up. 'Sure. We'll come with you if you don't mind?'

Joe smiled at his boyfriend and held the door open with a low bow. 'After you, ladies!'

The canteen was empty apart from a few assorted office workers, sipping tea and discussing whatever was on the reams of notes they had on the tables in front of them. No one looked up as the three young men entered.

'I'll get these.' Jodi collected three cans of ginger beer, paid and joined Paul and Joe at their table.

'This is nice,' he said, trying to fill the silence.

'Lovely.' Joe took a huge swig from his can and looked out the window, seeing the grey facade of the buildings opposite.

'I am a nice guy really.' Jodi put his hand on top of Joe's and gave it a squeeze. 'I am sure you'd like me.'

'Really.'

'Oh, yeah. Paul knows that, don't you?'

Popping open the can, Paul agreed. 'Right, Joe. He is a good man at heart, just got mixed up with an unsavoury lot. Give him a chance.' An idea struck Paul and he lowered his voice slightly. 'In fact I think you'd really enjoy getting to know him better.'

A puzzled expression crossed Jodi's face, but when Paul slid his hand up the young presenter's thigh and gave his crotch a squeeze, he understood the meaning.

'Come on. Let's take these back to your dressing room, Jodi.' Paul stood, scraping his chair back, and waited for the other two to follow.

Joe and Paul followed Jodi, striding insistently down the corridors to his large, comfy dressing room, and when they had settled down side by side on a long, velvet sofa, Jodi locked the door.

'So?' His voice had a thousand questions in it.

Paul leaned into Joe and let his hand fall on his partner's groin. As if a lightbulb had suddenly illuminated his mind, Joe realised what was going on, and a smirk crossed his features.

'I see. You horny little fucker.' He stared deeply into Paul's eyes before giving in to temptation, inclining his head and opening his lips, ready for a kiss.

Paul responded naturally, letting his tongue just flick across Joe's soft mouth before kissing him with fervour. Jodi pulled off his shirt and trousers and stood in just his extremely small, tight briefs, his cock and bollocks straining to be let out. He watched the two lads kissing and cuddling, running their hands over each other's bodies.

Paul and Joe hadn't been on intimate terms for a long time, and so their pent-up passion suddenly erupted. It was like a dam bursting its walls, so strong was their desire for each other. The sounds of the studio filtered through the walls, the regular, even beat of a ragged girl-group rehearsing their song for the cameras, stopping and starting over and over again. The air conditioning unit hummed, sending tiny gusts of cooling air about the dressing room.

Pausing for breath, Joe sat back and looked at Jodi, for the first time seeing what an attractive man he was. He scanned the body appreciatively, lingering over the crotch and the sizeable bulge in the micro briefs. Now that would be a very nice mouthful, he thought to himself.

He stood and pulled Paul to his feet also, then took off his clothes until he stood naked. Paul did the same and they waited until Jodi stepped out of his briefs, the three of them now hard and filled with nervous anticipation. The dark look in Jodi's eyes spoke of a deep, violent sexuality, someone who wanted something hard and fast. On the wall behind him was a large Disney poster, Mickey Mouse's beaming face surreally staring out over his shoulder.

Joe wiped a dry hand across his brow and smiled at the presenter, his eyes unable to stray from the cock which was now standing hard, curving high and proud, the thick shaft topped by a huge head, nudging the skin above his navel. Paul stared with admiration at this perfect penis, the memory of their first encounter at the front of his mind. He had adored it then, and somehow it seemed even more beautiful.

The sight of this hunk proved too much for Joe, who let his hand grip the shaft of his own cock, desperate for action, and started sliding his fist up and down.

Jodi couldn't hold back any longer. He came close to Joe, lifting a hand to his groin, cupping his bollocks, weighing and appreciating their size, running his thumb along the side of the cock. Joe was breathing quite heavily now, aware of the intense sexual tension in the room. The presenter began to pull down on the balls, squeezing a little harder, easing the hanging sac away from the body, seeing the cock get even stiffer. Pulling himself closer, Jodi let his other hand explore Joe's chest, running his fingers over the muscular pectorals, lightly touching the nipples which responded immediately by hardening. Jodi leaned in and pressed his lips against Joe's, the lad reacting in the only way he knew how, by opening wide and letting the invader's tongue slide in for a long, wet kiss.

This didn't last long, as Jodi spun Joe around, nuzzling into his neck so that his back was now toward Paul.

Joe was in a haze, a gentle dreamy trance, savouring the insistent nuzzling of Jodi's mouth and tongue around his neck and ears, but he started as he felt Paul's hands begin stroking his inner thighs, gliding over the downy hairs that led up to the crack between his arse cheeks. Joe closed his eyes and let the two other guys do what they desired. He could feel hands exploring his body, sliding down from his chest, to his genitals, massaging his buttocks, moving over every inch of his aroused torso and legs.

Joe became aware that a tongue was tenderly but adamantly licking around the tops of his thighs, between the creases of his cheeks, inching ever closer to the wrinkled hole that lay hidden. He gave a short gasp as the tongue found the object of its quest, and touched the pinkish ring. At the same time a tongue lapped at the head of his cock, lightly making contact, smoothly slipping around the lobes, and poking its tip into the generously sized slit.

Then the action began in earnest. Both mouths went into overdrive. His cock was swallowed whole in one gulping movement, taken to the back of a willing throat, before the mouth started to suck, giving and receiving, saliva covering every inch. The mouth at his arse began lapping and sucking too, the trembling tip forcing its way inside the tight muscle ring. Hands grabbed his butt cheeks, rolling them around, spreading them for the tongue's easy access. The double action was intense, he swayed, holding onto the back of the couch for support.

Jodi, crouched in front of Joe, took his time; sucking this cock needed some expertise, it would be a shame not to enjoy it. He could feel ripples of excitement through Joe's body, and hear small, rasping breaths escaping from his throat. He knew he was good at giving head, and he wanted desperately to give Joe the best he could. He knew he was succeeding. The cock filled his mouth, the pulsating head touched the back of his throat, pushing at the tonsils, eager to sink further down.

Jodi looked at the sight before him and saw that there was still an inch or so left before the base. Swallowing deeply and inhaling, he tried to actually unhinge his jaw, so that the totality of the weapon's length could slide into him.

A gasp of gratification burst out from Joe, stunned at this young guy's ability to take every inch of his cock. Somehow it had grown even bigger, the attentions from the striking young presenter blowing his mind as well as his dick.

Paul sank onto his knees, fervently lapping at Joe's hole. He was aware that this was one of his boyfriend's favourite activities, that he loved the feel of a warm, wet tongue slavering away at that tender opening.

For how long they stayed in this position, no one knew. They just enjoyed the activity whole-heartedly, giving as much joy to the other guy as possible. Then Joe's desire to be the top surfaced and he moved back, letting Jodi and Paul rest. His eyes devoured the sight of their impatient faces, smeared around with saliva and pre-cum juice. Their eyes pierced his, impatient for the next move.

'Stand up.' He stared at the two guys before him, his voice calm but authoritative. Both obeyed, standing sharply, cocks erect and tingling. Joe knelt and held the cocks, one in each hand, sliding his fist to the base, gripping each tightly. Then in turn, he began to suck them, taking each into his mouth, downing first Paul then

Jodi, in single, forceful strokes, sucking deeply, a harsh vacuum pulling on each boy's tool. Screams of delight came from them at his practised skill, as he tasted the rigid flesh of both boys. Stretching his mouth wide, Joe nudged Paul's leg so that he could reposition himself and take his cock inside at the same moment as Jodi's. Their eyes widened in admiration as Joe sucked on both their cocks, spit now drooling down his chin, running in rivulets across his chest.

This couldn't last, and all three of them knew it. The ball-sacs began to tighten, and the breathing started to become laboured. Joe stopped, not wanting this to end so soon. As if reading Joe's mind, Jodi got up and crossed the room, grabbing a holdall from under the dressing table. Unzipping, he held it upside down and threw a jumble of assorted items on the couch.

Paul's eyes grew wide as saucers as he realised what the items were. A large rubber dildo, a series of rubber balls on a string, a pair of handcuffs, a leather mouth gag, packets of condoms, a big jar of lubricant and tangled among them a chain with two crocodile-teethed nipple clamps on each end.

'One should always have something to do to pass the time.' Jodi gave a hearty guffaw as Joe began sifting through the equipment.

'This is a turn-up for the books,' Joe said, trying the clamps on his chest, and instantly releasing them as the teeth bit sharply into his nipples.

Jodi took the driver's seat and lay himself on one end of the couch, his head down and his legs hanging over the end, grabbed the chained clamps from Joe, and attached them to himself with an abrupt but piercing shriek as the teeth bit into his flesh. 'Use the balls on me, please.' His voice sounded strangled, and he gave a series of short, breathy exclamations of pain.

Caught up in the moment, Paul picked up the string of rubberised orbs and felt their weight, heavy and pendulous, but would they fit up that tight arsehole? He intended to find out. Pushing Jodi's legs over his head, he watched as the young guy held them back, around his knees. Joe had settled at Jodi's head and hovered, squatting over his face, his bollocks just inches from the open, panting mouth. Paul quickly unscrewed the lid of the jar of lube and grabbed up a handful, smearing it around the hole, pushing his finger inside to slicken the entry.

Taking the first ball, he also covered it with lube, and held it firmly at the sphincter for a few seconds, feeling and watching the hole pulsing, tightening and releasing automatically. As it relaxed he pushed the ball upwards, hearing a strident shriek from Jodi as he did. It slid inside, the musles snapping shut, tightly keeping the foreign object from being expelled. Small panting gasps were forced from Jodi's lips, as Paul then inserted another ball.

He looked up and saw Joe squatting lower, his bollocks touching Jodi's lips, eager to be sucked. As the presenter opened his mouth again, Joe let them slip in, enjoying their total swallowing by the wet mouth and tongue.

Again Paul pushed hard, powerfully forcing another hard rubber ball inside Jodi's screaming bowels. His eyes met Joe's and they locked, staring deeply into one another's souls, knowing that the other was experiencing the same deep thrill. All previous feelings had vanished in Paul's mind, all those nagging doubts, all the psychologically scarring jealousies that plagued the early stage of their relationship gone. No longer was he an immature boy, suffering pangs of suspicion every time Joe left the flat. Now he was a successful, attractive man in his own right, daily being adored by thousands, and with no need to feel insecure. He and Joe had reached a plateau of understanding and it felt good.

As Paul popped the final ball inside Jodi's arse, the lad arched his back, wanting to scream, but the bollocks in his mouth stopped him from doing so. Sensing that something was missing from this session, Paul looked about him, his gaze lighting on the giant dildo. Keeping his eye on Jodi's hole and the remaining length of string protruding from it, he slipped a condom down the length of the rubber phallus, wondering if he could actually take its extreme size. Slapping lube all over its increased dimensions, he positioned it at the entrance to his own arse. A groan of gratification made him look up as he saw Joe, eyes tight shut, roughly pushing his cock down Jodi's throat, the guy's head arched back, his hair touching his shoulders. The throat was now free for Joe's cock to slide right in, the top surface of the skin rubbing against the roughness of Jodi's slapping tongue.

Concentrating on his own pleasure, kneeling, with one hand grasping the string at Jodi's butt-hole, Paul sat slowly down on the dildo. Feeling the giant head butting against his sphincter, and willing it to relax, he pushed the tip inside himself. As he cried out, the wave of intense hurt rolling over him, feeling as if he had split apart, he gave a tug on the string. Jodi's arsehole bulged, the rubber ball forced against the tight muscle ring, but unable to get out. Paul pulled harder, and could see the muscles give way slightly and a hint of the red rubber peeking through. As it began to emerge, he slid his arse down on the dildo, experiencing the utter fulfilment of the phallus and the sight of Jodi's ring stretching, allowing the first ball to plop out, accompanied by a shuddering moan.

The dildo was now right up inside him, the cold rubbery texture of it filling him so completely, that he wondered if he would ever appreciate anything small again. He could clearly see Joe fucking Jodi's mouth, which made his own cock yearn for some oral attention. Still, bide your time. He started to ride the dildo, sitting up and falling back down, letting it rise inside him, relishing each thrust upwards, gasping as his own arse-ring relaxed and squeezed on the monstrous toy. Jodi was ripe for more and so with a vicious tug, Paul yanked another of the balls from out of the boy's hole, sensing that he would have screamed out in pain if his mouth hadn't been stuffed with Joe's dick.

Jodi didn't know what had hit him. He had bought the linked balls some months before, but never used them. Perhaps he was waiting for the right moment, with the right guy. As the first ball had forced its inexorable way inside him, ripping him apart, he'd wondered if he'd gone too far. If he could actually take them all. But then he had no choice. His mouth was full of Joe's beautifully shaped, heavy balls, and he sucked on them fervently, aware that the next ball pushed inside might actually make him black out. It felt like a football had been inserted, such was the blinding agony of his arse. Then as it popped in, the intense relaxation of the muscles was supreme, although the anticipation of the next ball sent shudders down his spine. Then it came. Pushing hard, wanting the sphincter to open and allow the intruder inside, and achingly it did.

Suddenly the bollocks had been withdrawn from his mouth and Joe's cock begged for entry. There had been nothing else he could do but accept the inevitable and open wide. The cock seemed bigger than before, it couldn't have added inches, that would be impossible, but somehow it had grown. It began pounding away, fucking with a purpose.

Jodi had started to experiment with harder and more unorthodox sex in the last six months, from his early fixation on piss-play, and had graduated to more sado-masochistic practices. But this was really proving too much. He desperately wanted to scream out at the top of his voice, wanting the violation at both ends to stop. But deep down he knew it wouldn't and he would have to take the punishment like a man. After all, he had brought out the bag of toys, and had begged for their use.

Another slippery rubber ball had been shoved inside him, and another until he felt that he was full of them. The desire to push and expel them all was overwhelming. Now he knew what childbirth must be like. Again he felt a scream rising in his chest, but the cock slamming away in his throat prevented it from escaping.

The undulating pain inside Paul's arse continued unabated as he rose and fell, sliding up and down the dildo, letting it push up inside, filling his entire being with pain and pleasure. Joe was also on another planet, the suction from Jodi's mouth was now greater than he ever imagined it could be, and his cock felt like it was trapped in some kind of vacuum, being pulled deeper and deeper into a sensual void. The power of Jodi's tongue and throat astounded him, this blow-job unlike any he had ever experienced. Every time a ball was pulled from Jodi's arsehole he gave a grunt of satisfaction and hurt, and his mouth seemed to clasp the cock harder within its maw, like a baby's dummy, comforting in times of stress and anguish. Occasionally Jodi would begin to sink his teeth into the prick plundering his mouth, but would draw back before he caused any damage. This sucking and biting action proved a killer and Joe felt a climactic surge beginning inside of him.

Paul watched and waited, before starting to wank his own cock, and with his free hand he started to jerk off Jodi's. With one ball left still firmly gripped inside the boy, Paul knew that he would be swamped with the most incredible sensations.

The hand that was tightly wanking his cock made Jodi's eyes bulge, and so with a deep, shuddering breath he doubled his efforts, sucking Joe off harder, if that was possible, letting Paul manipulate him to orgasm, feeling the inner pressure of the remaining ball, screaming to be expelled. It took a few more strokes on each of their parts before – almost as one being – they came. His body a mass of shakes, Jodi erupted, spewing out a load of his spunk, which shot high in a clear parabola, landing across his own face. Paul and Joe exploded over Jodi's torso, their juices falling over his muscled stomach and chest, each forcing the last few drops from their hidden depths, groaning and gasping for air.

It took many minutes for each guy's breathing to return to

normal. They stayed in the position, until Joe stood and flicked a small droplet of cum from the end of his cock, which fell amongst the lake of jism on Jodi's chest.

With a sigh, Paul eased himself off the giant dildo, standing, rubbing his aching leg muscles, trying to get the circulation going again.

'Help me up.' Jodi's voice was weak. He raised his arms and waited for Joe and Paul to come to his aid. Hoisting him to his feet, Paul saw that the string of rubber balls was still dangling between his legs, the final orb still inside his anus.

'Now you can't do the show with that thing in there.' Paul joked, feeling exhausted but triumphant.

'I know. But it's going to be painful getting it out.' Jodi looked worried, his eyes full of moisture and anxiety.

'Lean over.' Paul encouraged. Gently leading him to the couch, and bending him forward, Paul grasped the string and tugged, the ball inside refusing to budge. 'This might hurt a bit.' He tried again.

Jodi gritted his teeth as his sphincter muscles screamed in agony. The ball pushed against his ring, which finally gave way, and with one gaping movement, opened and snapped shut, letting the last ball pop out.

Jodi's head lolled forward onto his forearm, exhausted but intensely relieved.

'I should get some rest, if I were you.' Paul sat on the end of the couch, stroking the small of Jodi's back. 'You have a show to host tonight.' He looked up at Joe and signalled that they should get dressed and slip away before they were missed.

The taping of the show went even better than anyone expected. The studio audience went wild when the boys started their song, dancing with wild enthusiasm and cheering madly at the song's conclusion. If anyone doubted that they were a pop sensation, then this was the proof that BANNED were a success. It was onwards and upwards from now on. Nick knew that the next album would consolidate everything and open doors across the Atlantic, his dreams of managing a band who made it big in America filling his every waking thought.

The boys left the stage on a wave of euphoria, shaking hands, kissing cheeks, signing autographs. They knew that they had made it. Fame and fortune now was theirs for the taking and nothing could stop them.

They pushed their way down the corridor, through applauding crew members, and entered the dressing room, surprised to see two middle-aged men in suits and raincoats waiting for them.

'Can we help you?' Joe's face was wreathed in smiles.

'Joseph Turner?' The older of the two spoke with a quiet, but authoritative voice, his heavy lidded eyes giving nothing away.

'That's me. But I am signing no more autographs, my wrist is aching. And it's been a while since I've said that.' He erupted with a fit of the giggles, which was swiftly silenced as the man continued.

'I am Detective Inspector McGiveron, this is Sergeant Russell. Yesterday a Mr Mark Trevithick was arrested for possession of a significant amount of drugs, namely heroin, ecstasy tablets and marijuana. He has been charged with supplying these drugs to many record industry executives and personalities. Your name was in his diary, under the heading "Contacts". We'd like you to accompany us to the police station, to answer some questions.'

13: At the Queen's Pleasure

In response to the policeman's speech, the dressing room erupted. The other three band members protested Joe's innocence but there was nothing they could do. Faced with the insistent demand from DI McGiveron, they had to watch, appalled, as Joe was escorted from the room and out to a waiting police car.

Nick watched, ashen faced, as the whole ghastly scenario played itself out, unsure of himself for the first time in years, and with a feeling of utter helplessness.

As Joe was helped into the back of the car, his head pushed down to avoid hitting against the roof, Nick shook himself from his reverie, rushed forward, and called out to the worried lad. 'Don't worry. I'll follow on, and get our company solicitor there too.'

The car sped away, leaving everyone to watch the red tail-lights vanish into the distance.

Sitting immobile and fearful, Joe tried to look at the dark shapes outside, but his eyes refused to focus. The horror of the situation was crushing him beyond belief. If Mark was being done for supplying drugs, then they might think that he himself was one of Mark's customers. This could mean the end of his career, and a long spell in prison if they charged him. All he could think of was a bleak future, locked up for years, his liberty curtailed and his self-respect smashed to pieces. He had to convince them that he had no interest in drugs. He had to. His life depended on it.

The police station was a grey, forbidding block, and Joe was whisked through the doors and into an interview room. Inside was a table with chairs on either side, and a recording machine. There was no hint of comfort. He felt like a criminal, even though he knew he had done nothing.

He was suddenly very thirsty, his throat constricted and dry. The room was airless and claustrophobic, and the walls seemed to loom over Joe. He closed his eyes and tried to swallow.

Silently the door opened and DI McGiveron strode purposefully in, followed by Sergeant Russell. They sat opposite Joe and placed sheaves of notes and a diary on the table between them. Pressing a button, McGiveron switched on the tape recorder.

'Interview commenced at ten-forty pm. Present, Detective Inspector McGiveron and Sergeant Russell, and a Mr Joseph Turner. Right now Joseph, you can wait until your solicitor arrives or we can start things rolling now. What do you say?'

'Start now... I've got nothing to hide.'

'Right. Can you tell me how you know a Mr Mark Trevithick?'

'Yes, he works as a motorbike courier for the record company I record under.'

'And how long have you known him?'

'About two years, although I haven't seen him for about eighteen months or so.'

'When was the last time you saw him?'

'At a party at some friends of his, somewhere in Islington.'

'And that is definitely the last time you saw him?'

'Yes.'

'And were there drugs available at this party?'

'Yes, I think so.' Joe cast his mind back to the small, dingy flat, and the assortment of people there. 'I did see some people smoking joints.'

'Yes...'

'Wait a minute... when I went into the kitchen at one time I saw this horrid looking man, and it looked like he was doing a drugs deal with the guy whose flat it was.'

'Can you describe these two men?'

'The host was a guy called Scottie. Short, stocky, red hair, and the other guy was much taller, don't know his name, but he was bald, he had tattoos all over his body, and his chest was covered with big scars.'

The two policemen gave each other a significant glance at this information and Russell made a note on the pad in front of him.

'The man you have just described was well known to us. A rather unpleasant individual called Robertson. Dealt in drugs, porn, stolen vehicles. You name it, he did it. We know that he has been behind several large consignments of drugs coming into the country from South America. We were about to question him last week, but someone got to him first. Left small chunks of him all over his bedsit. Not a very nice sight.'

The picture painted by McGiveron turned Joe's stomach and he went very pale.

'Can you be certain that Trevithick had no drugs with him?'

'No.'

'Did he seem like a drugs dealer to you?'

'No. Mark was just a nice guy. I don't understand how he got mixed up in this. You are sure of your facts, I hope.'

'Oh yes, son. Trevithick was arrested last night, carrying a large packet of ecstasy tablets, which he was delivering to an address in Chalk Farm, the home of a costume designer.'

'Not Mitch something or other?'

'That's right. We had been tipped off about Trevithick's activities, using the courier job as a cover for his drug supply business. Of course he's been under surveillance for a while. We are following up all the contacts in his diary, including yourself.'

Joe couldn't believe what he was hearing. He had once thought Mark was a nice guy. But after the terrible ordeal at Scottie's flat he had decided not to keep up the friendship. Playing the scene over in his head, he knew that Mark was amongst the men holding him captive. He had pleasured himself on his helpless body, but as things started to get out of hand he had made a stand and tried to get Mitch to release him. A mixture of hatred and gratitude had filled Joe's mind, and after he'd woken up back at his flat, he never wanted to see Mark again. Anyone who could get involved with such scum as Mitch and Scottie deserved everything they got. Joe pondered momentarily if he should mention the kidnap ordeal, but thought better of it and remained silent.

'Would you like a cup of tea?' McGiveron was suddenly all smiles, switching off the recording machine and pushing back his chair with a high-pitched screech. He left the room, Russell at his heels, closing the door behind them, leaving Joe alone and shaken.

What had he got himself into? And what was going to happen to him? The whole thing was a mystery. But all he could do was wait and see what the police would do next.

After about ten minutes, the two detectives entered, carrying three plastic cups of tea and a plate of chocolate biscuits.

'There now. No need for this to be unpleasant, is there?' McGiveron was giving off an aura of chumminess, a total change from his earlier gruff persona. 'Now, Joseph, I want you to tell me everything you know about Mark Trevithick.'

'There's not much to say. We met first at a recording studio, and I went round to his place for... for a drink. Then we met up again months later and he invited me to the party I told you about.'

'So the invite to the party came from him?'

'Yeah. Although as I said, it wasn't his party. We were just guests.'

Russell made another note, then his eyes returned to Joe, the steely glare boring right through him. The lad looked down at the table, cowed.

'Now then... when you went round to Mr Trevithick's flat the first time, did he offer you any drugs?'

Joe hesitated. He wanted to prove his non-involvement in the drugs scene, but that meant making Mark seem more guilty. But it had to be done. He had let him down and had abused him in an appalling way, which was something Joe would never forget or forgive. 'Yes. He offered me a joint, but I didn't want any.'

'Have you ever taken drugs?

'No. I don't believe in them. Besides, it would ruin my career if I was found to be a druggie.'

McGiveron folded his arms. He leant forward so his elbows were resting on the table top. 'You are a homosexual?'

The directness of the question startled Joe, and he took a moment to answer.

'Yes. What has that got to do with anything?'

'And you had sexual relations with Mr Trevithick?'

'Yes. But what does this...?'

As Russell made another scribbled note, McGiveron raised an eyebrow in answer. 'We need to build up a profile of Mr Trevithick.'

'I fail to see what our having sex has to do with this drugs business.'

McGiveron said nothing, just watched as Russell finished his annotations. 'We would like to search your flat. Any objections?'

'None at all. I have absolutely nothing to hide.' Joe reached into his pocket and pulled out his door key. 'There. And I can tell you categorically that you will find no hint of drugs at all.'

'I am sure that will be the case... if you are the upstanding young man you purport to be. Now while we conduct the search I'm afraid we will have to place you in a cell. I'm sorry but that's the way it is.'

215

Joe's face fell. First being held for questioning, then to spend time in a police cell. He couldn't imagine the night getting any worse. He was wrong. Russell escorted him along a grimy hallway, past several locked metal doors, until he stopped at the end one, rattling a huge bunch of keys and unlocking the door. 'Sorry, Mr Turner, but we are very busy tonight. You'll have to share.'

Joe looked inside and saw a young man fast asleep on the only available bed.

'Don't worry about him. He'll be out for ages. Drunk and disorderly.' Russell spoke in an off-hand manner as if the only way he could remember people was by their crimes.

Gulping, Joe stepped inside and shivered as the door was banged shut behind him. The clanking of the lock being turned seemed to echo around the cell. He looked around and his heart sank at the grimness of his surroundings. The walls were grey painted brick, daubed with obscene graffiti. The only place to sit was on the bed, which was a thin plastic covered mattress, on an iron frame. He perched on the very end, just inches from the other guy's head, and told himself to breathe deeply and stay calm. This nightmare would have to end soon.

The young guy on the bed moaned and turned, in an uneasy sleep. Joe looked down at him and for the first time focused on his features. He was quite attractive, dressed in a suit and tie, the front of which was soaking wet. His mousy brown hair was mussed, and his strong face had the blush of too much alcohol. Hanging from one of his wrists was a pair of plastic handcuffs. Joe smiled as he realised the guy must have been out on a stag night, and got carried away with too much drink. Although why he was languishing in a cell wasn't obvious. And what his bride-to-be would say when he arrived at the church late was another matter.

Again the guy turned. Now face up, his jacket fell apart, showing the soaked shirt, which clung to the contours of a very nicely defined chest. If he had been on the dance floor at The Bare Pit,

Joe would have had no hesitation in trying to pick him up. As he watched the man slumbering, his mouth murmuring incomprehensible phrases, he saw the unexpected happen. The guy's cock began to grow, perhaps from an erotic dream, but Joe noticed a definite swelling within the plain grey trousers.

The sight of this handsome straight guy getting a hard-on really excited Joe, and he could feel a swelling in his own groin. All thoughts of his current situation vanished as images of this attractive young guy erect and naked filled his mind. Wide-eyed and amazed, Joe stared at the rapidly growing bulge, and his mouth dropped open when he saw that the guy's zip was undone and the head of the cock emerged, raging and already with a moistened tip.

The guy wriggled again and murmured, this time distinctly. 'Oooh, Nicky, yes... now.'

There was no indication as to whether Nicky was male or female. But whoever it was, they certainly were turning the guy on. His squirming on the mattress pulled his trousers tight across his groin and more of the cock was revealed, now totally erect and standing straight up. The foreskin had already eased itself back, to a roll of skin just below the tip, like a crew-neck collar. Joe longed to pull it back fully and let the head pop out, then go down on that very nice tool. And it was indeed very nice. The head crowned beautifully the thick, flat shaft, which made the cock appear very wide, rather than rounded. A real mouth-stretcher. A real straight boy's mouth-stretcher.

Joe licked his lips. All his gay hormones (or whoremones as Dean called them) raced to the surface, screaming at him, urging him on to commit the act. To forget his horrid surroundings and grab some pleasure, and fuck the consequences. The guy was obviously drunk, and in a deep sleep, and showed no sign of waking. It was risky, but was it worth the risk? The idea of taking this gorgeous heterosexual in his mouth and blowing him turned Joe on more than he ever imagined it would. Straight guys had an aura about them, a mystique that said 'look but don't touch'. And here was the opportunity to ignore that order. With one huge breath he decided to go for it.

Standing up slowly so as not to wake the sleeping beauty, Joe tentatively padded along the side of the bed, until he stood level with the guy's crotch. The cock still stood, proudly erect and available. His knees giving out a volley of creaks, Joe knelt by the bed and leaned forward, his face just inches away. He inhaled involuntarily and got a strong odour of beer and cigarettes, mixed with the heady aroma of maleness. He stared at the droplet of juice that rested at the tip of the cock, but as the guy shifted again it ran down the centre of the glans, disappearing into the folds of foreskin.

Joe put out his tongue to lick at the end, and drew back sharply as the guy murmured again, his voice now distinct. 'Yeah, do it...'

Joe didn't know if that was now an invitation to him, or to the fantasy dream figure, he was so caught up in the moment. Once more he inhaled, and holding his breath he reached out to the huge dick, touching it gingerly with his hand. He could feel it pulsing beneath his palm, and if anything, it seemed to respond, swelling to its maximum rigidity. Joe was utterly overcome with a strong desire to see and feel the testicles, but knew that to scrabble around in the guy's trousers could wake him from slumberland.

Bending his head forward again, Joe started to lick from the base of the cock, in slow circular movements, each time edging a little higher, marvelling at the size of the organ, wondering why stunning guys always had fabulous cocks. Was it a trick of fate, or just one of Mother Nature's balancing acts? He didn't know.

He mentally pictured his own swollen cock, every familiar inch, thinking back to his youth when he knew he had been blessed with larger equipment than the other boys at school. In fact they would cluster around him in the showers to get a good eyeful of his well-developed manhood. He even caught the games master, a snide indivdual called Mr Evans, sneaking admiring glances at it as he towelled off after the weekly sports fest.

Joe was always proud of the interest his cock engendered, willing to show it off to any boy who was curious, and he noticed that only a few of the others had penises that were in any way sizeable. He hoped he wasn't abnormal, but he revelled in the attention. As he grew up and entered puberty, it seemed to put on a spurt and get bigger and bigger. Hair sprouted, muscles formed, his voice deepened. And his cock increased. Every day he measured it, making secret notes in his private, lockable diary, and at each small increase he'd mark it with a red star.

At fifteen, when it measured five inches in diameter when soft, he knew he had something special, and daily jack-off sessions became the norm. He craftily stole a copy of *Playgirl* from the local newsagents, and the glossy photographs of naked men became his new obsession. The manly genitals displayed on every page aroused him intensely, and he realised his gay nature.

None of his other school mates would admit to wanking, and so he continued on his solo course of discovery, finding new ways to do it, with new sensations, using props or enjoying different feelings, rubber gloves, or scouring pads, butter and toothpaste. The last one proved too uncomfortable and he never did that again.

With the increased girth and length came an almost devastating shyness. He found that he couldn't approach any boy or girl for fear that they had heard about his endowment and would make fun. The assuredness of his earlier self vanished. In the years after leaving school and college, he made tentative inroads into the gay scene, often being chatted up by all manner of men, some nice, some not, but all of them attracted to the vast bulge in his jeans. Sometimes he thought that was all they were after.

It took him a while to realise he was in the position of control. He had the power to get men to do what he wanted. While they were forlornly aching for a sight and taste of his cock, he could get anything he wanted. A couple of miserable years of basically empty relationships followed until he met Paul, and fell in love with a young guy who was open and honest and cared for Joe as a person, rather than a cock on legs.

The guy on the bed gave a shudder, calling Joe back to the present. He opened his mouth again and licked, the flesh of the foreskin almost flinched at his tongue's approach, sliding away, coming to rest behind the silky-smooth head. Joe worked at the thick ridge of flesh that separated it from the meaty shaft, then toyed with the piss-slit, teasing it and poking inside. Opening his mouth as wide as he could, Joe lowered his lips to the awaiting skin, and he shivered again as the head slipped into his mouth.

Suddenly he was hungry for some action, inching down, bit by bit, until the head pushed at the back of the throat. Joe had to stop or he would gag. There was still an inch or so of shaft left outside, but in this position he couldn't take it all. With determination, Joe started to suck, taking the cock as far as he could before retreating until just the velvety knob was between his moistened lips. Then he went back down on it and found to his delight that he could get even further than the last time, feeling it pulsing and throbbing as he sucked.

A noise outside the door made him jump and, pulling away from the cock, he sank onto the floor, sitting hugging his knees, the position of his body hiding the hard-on from view. A hatch in the door slid open and an eye appeared, glaring at the two men. Then after a few seconds it snapped shut and the sound of footsteps receded. Joe turned back to the inert body on the bed. The noise hadn't seemingly disturbed him at all. Kneeling again, he gently began to unbuckle the guy's belt, and undid the hook fastener, allowing the top of his trousers to fall away, noticing with a

rueful grin that the guy wasn't wearing underwear. With the trous-
res now fully undone, and loose, Joe let his fingers tenderly slip
inside the crotch area and lift the bollocks out. Again he marvelled
at their size. Leaning in close, he nuzzled against the hairy sac, his
tongue curling around one of the extraordinarily heavy balls and
bringing it into his saliva-filled mouth.

Pulling it into his mouth, Joe began to lick it with his tongue,
feeling it moving around inside the skin, responding to each
caress. The other one was hotly throbbing against Joe's cheek, and
so opening his lips wider he sucked it inside, gently easing it in
with the tip of a finger. Joe pushed his face right up until his lips
were pushed against the underside of the guy's cock. Then with
gusto he started working the nuts back and forth in his mouth.

He looked up quickly, checking that the guy was still asleep,
and saw his eyes tightly shut, and so he reached up and grasped
the cock shaft once more, enjoying its solidity and size. Moving
his hand up and down, masturbating the hefty organ, Joe got into
the rhythm, sucking and stroking as one. When his mouth started
to ache a little from the huge bollocks inside, he let them pop
wetly out, and moved his attention back to the cock. The warm
wetness of his mouth engulfed the weapon till it was sliding down
into his throat again. The guy gave a moan, and stiffened.

Joe stopped for a few seconds, his gaze focused on the guy's
face. He looked as if he was still heavily sleeping. Resuming his
previous position, Joe started again, blowing the whopping dick
for all he was worth, increasing his speed, and almost willing it to
jerk out its juice. The cock began to buck wildly inside Joe's
mouth, and without warning he felt the sharp, salty taste of semen
splash down his throat. He pushed his face all the way down as the
guy shot again and again.

The cock started to soften immediately and so Joe pulled away,
wiping his lips, eager to remove any trace of the guy's spunk.
Quickly he settled back on the bed, leaving the guy's rapidly

shrinking cock and balls hanging out. If he was as drunk as he seemed then he'd not care if he was on display.

Joe looked at his watch. An hour had passed. How much longer would they keep him cooped up?

Nick rang the bell at the police station reception. Serena Wicksteed, the record company solicitor, accompanied him, impatiently drumming her immaculately painted nails on the counter. A fresh-faced, blond-haired, blue-eyed constable appeared from the back office and smiled in a friendly manner.

'Can I help you, sir, miss?'

Serena took command. 'Yes you can. You are holding a client of mine for questioning, Joe Turner. I would like to see him, please.'

'Just a moment, miss.' The constable turned away to consult a clipboard, and then faced Nick with an even bigger smile. 'We are waiting for DI McGiveron to return. He shouldn't be too long. If you could wait in the room over there, I'll let you know when you can see him.'

'But has my client been charged with anything?'

'No, miss. But if you'd just wait until the DI gets back... then he'll let you know how he wants things to proceed.'

He turned away, replacing the clipboard on a hook, and went back to reading the evening paper.

Serena stifled a curse and strode into the waiting room, Nick following at her heels like an attentive puppy. Her towering hairdo and dazzling black eyes usually cowered even the most macho of men, but they had had no effect on the jolly constable. She sat with a sigh of disappointment and withdrew a packet of cigarettes from her capacious handbag.

Lighting up, and studiously ignoring the large red 'DO NOT SMOKE' sign, she puffed away for a few moments, before turning to Nick. 'If they have no evidence he is a user, then they can't hold him. I'll get him out of here, don't worry sweetheart.'

Her assured air comforted Nick. And he needed plenty of comforting. At the very moment BANNED were on the brink of trans-
Atlantic success, it looked as if it might be snatched from under his
nose. If it turned out that Joe was a drug user, and had been buying this stuff, then he'd be finished, and so would the band. In the
drugs-conscious twenty-first century, more and more teenagers
were aware of the dangers of illegal substances, and turning away
from being fans of stars who indulged. There was no way BANNED
could continue with a confirmed drug addict in their midst. Deep
inside, he knew that Joe was clean, and had no involvement with
these things, but a nagging doubt still persisted. He shook his head
and leaned in toward Serena.

'Got a spare ciggie? We could be in for a long night.'

Three hours had passed before the cell door was unlocked and Joe
was escorted back to the interview room. As he walked down the
dingy corridor, he was gladdened to see Nick standing at the far
end by the reception desk. His manager gave a small but encouraging wave before Joe was taken inside, and sat at the now familiar table. A statuesque woman in a purple Chanel suit, with a head
of hair laquered into a fearsome tower, sat in the accompanying
chair.

'Hello, Joe. I'm Serena, your solicitor.' Her extreme appearance
worried Joe slightly, but if she was Nick's solicitor she was probably the best in the business.

DI McGiveron and Sergeant Russell appeared, wreathed in
smiles. McGiveron deposited Joe's keys on the table.

'Thank you.'

Joe looked up. 'So did you find anything?'

'No. Although we did give your flatmate a bit of a scare.'

'My boyfriend actually.' Joe stuck out his chin defiantly.

'Quite.' McGiveron shifted in his seat. 'Well, there really is not
a lot more you can tell us. It seems clear that you were just an

acquaintance of Trevithick and not one of his regular drug-buying contacts. Thank you Mr Turner, you can go now. We'll be in touch if we have any further questions.'

Relief washed over Joe, and he managed to croak out a word of thanks before a flood of tears poured from his eyes.

'Sorry, it's just the relief of knowing I'm in the clear.' He sniffled and took the handkerchief that Serena pulled from her bag.

'Come on, let's get you home.' Serena stood and helped him to his feet, pulling open the door, and ushering him towards reception.

Nick hugged him as he emerged, linking arms and leading the way outside to a waiting taxi. The car park was thankfully free of reporters and photographers, so this incident was still secret. And it looked like remaining so. Certainly if Nick had anything to do with it.

At this stage in BANNED's life they needed a clear run at the future. Having seen off a few minor skirmishes, including the ROKTV vendetta, the boys were still thought of as having a good, wholesome image. And that needed to remain so. With plans now fully underway for their first concerts next spring, they had to keep up the momentum of their sales, and stay in the public consciousness. That couldn't be too hard, could it?

14: In the Flesh

According to the tabloid newspapers, from the moment the telephone booking lines opened they were deluged with thousands of calls for concert tickets. The telephone system was forced to grind to a temporary halt, and so vast numbers of fans were unable to actually buy the small squares of embossed card allowing them entry to the first series of concerts by BANNED.

It became apparent to Nick that the concerts would be a smash hit, exceeding all his expectations, when the ticket sales fiasco hit the main news, and the front pages of the press. Photographs of lines of patient people, standing at the Arena box office, filled the pages of the daily papers, interviews with jolly schoolgirls and their world-weary parents made up many column inches. In all, so much less important than the story of fraudulent dealings at the Bank of England, but something which relegated that piece of news to the publication's inner pages.

Knowing that the biggest of the phone call-centres selling the tickets was under much strain and needed cheering up, the four members of the band staged a surprise visit, with copies of the current album and signed photographs for the beleaguered workers, a tactic which proved so successful that the telephone agents went back to work with renewed gusto, endeavouring to do their best for these four handsome and friendly guys.

It was decided to stage their first appearance at the London 'Chocko-pops' Arena, a vast concert venue, unfortunately named for its major sponsors. The stage at one end looked out over an auditorium of eighty-thousand seats, all of which the show's backers confidently expected to be filled. The week of the concerts had thankfully been warm and dry, the first rays of spring sunshine helping the country to relax a little after the harsh winter with its storms and constant flooding.

'Testing, testing... one, two, three,' Dean's voice rang out loud and clear through the PA system, followed by a piercing screech, making him pull back and drop the microphone from his lips. The sound check was going badly, and was taking longer than expected. If the first concert was to open on time the following evening then the technical drawbacks would have to be sorted out sharpish.

'That's so boring. Say something else.' Connor stood next to Dean, hands on hips.

'Like what?'

'Anything...' Pausing for a moment, Connor moved in close to his microphone and spoke. 'There were these two nuns and a goat... One nun said...'

'Thank you, Connor, that'll be fine.' The voice of the sound engineer, Gaz Leitner, boomed around the stage, from his remote-controlled mike. 'If you could start the first song, then we'll see how it all sounds. Oh... and just be a bit careful on stage... there are still loads of cable and wires lying around, we don't want any accidents.'

As the orchestra struck up the first notes, the boys all experienced a tingle of exhilaration which coursed through them. The notion that they were standing on the stage in this immense showground, preparing to play to a huge audience of screaming fans took their collective breaths away. The sound of the musicians playing their hits in a stylish, orchestral manner was also a surprise, giving a new gravitas to the numbers.

Connor started to sing, his strong, natural voice filling the auditorium. At the moment the boys joined in with the melodic harmonies, a crackling noise boomed out.

'Stop there.' Crossing the stage, Gaz took Paul's mike from its stand and checked the lead.

'Probably just a bit loose. I'll replace the connection later. For now, try not to touch it, baby.' He smiled at Paul and gently pinched his bottom.

'Sex maniac.' Paul blew a kiss at the sound engineer, watching his retreating back, admiring the arse and legs in their skin-tight denim. The rest wasn't bad either, he thought: quite a lean body, which seemed to complement the lack of height, but his face certainly appealed... round and cheeky, with an almost permanent lop-sided grin.

The music started once more, and the boys launched into the song, feeling their voices soaring and filling the Arena with their perfect pitch. At the final climactic notes, there was another crackle and an ear-splitting scream. Everyone turned to Paul, who stood, holding the microphone lead, his eyes wide, his skin deathly white. For a second more he just stood, still as a statue, and then he fell back, landing on the stage floor with a dull thud.

Gaz rushed on from the side of the stage. 'Don't touch him! He's had a huge shock from that cable. Someone call an ambulance... quickly!'

All around the stage was utter commotion. Stage hands rushed about, not knowing what to do. The stage manager grabbed up his mobile phone and called for help. Joe crouched by Paul's side, helpless. He looked on at his boyfriend's inert body, his eyes fluttering, the breath coming in short, ragged bursts.

The stage manager ran up to the group. 'The ambulance is on its way, it'll be here in about ten minutes.'

Joe stared up at the stage manager, horrified. 'Ten minutes? What if he dies in the meantime? I couldn't bear it.' Tears started rolling down his face at the awful prospect of losing Paul. Throughout their shaky relationship, they had always loved each other deeply, and the thought of being without him chilled Joe to the core.

'Come on Paul, hang on in there. Keep with me. Try and focus on what I'm saying. Come on... come on...'

There was a hubbub at the side of the stage, as Nick appeared, flustered and ashen-faced. 'What's happened? Oh, my God. Paul...'

He sank down and placed his hand on the stricken lad's forehead. It felt scorchingly hot. His skin was slowly resuming its normal colour, faint reddish roses beginning to blush on his cheeks. His eyes fluttered open.

'Paul, it's me,' Joe said comfortingly. 'Don't try to speak. You've had an electric shock, and we are taking you to hospital.'

Paul's mouth opened and shut, but no sound came out. Unable to speak, he grasped Joe's hand tightly.

'I understand. I won't leave you. I'll be with you all the time.'

The tight grip on Joe's hand relaxed and Paul went limp.

Joe had never seen so much fearsome equipment before. The hospital had surged into action the moment they carried Paul's unconscious body from the ambulance, whisking him straight through to an emergency room. The machines hummed and beeped, wires protruded, and electronic read-outs fluctuated.

'I'm afraid you'll have to wait outside.' A pretty Asian nurse took Joe's arm and guided him from the room.

'No, I'm staying with him... I promised.'

She was adamant. 'It's hospital regulations. I'm sorry.'

By this time Joe was again on the verge of tears. Anger welled up inside him. 'I don't care about your fucking regulations. That is my boyfriend in there. If he is going to die, then I want to be with him.'

'I won't be spoken to like that, whoever that is in there.' She gave Joe a furious stare and continued. 'The doctors are doing their best to help him. Now please, sit in the waiting room, and I'll fetch you as soon as possible.' The nurse propelled Joe forcefully out of the room and shut the door in his face.

'I'm sorry,' Joe said. But nobody heard him. He watched through the window as green-gowned medics worked on Paul's motionless frame. Tearing himself away, he made his way ponderously down the corridor to the waiting room, slumping down in a hard plastic chair, ignoring the open-mouthed stares of a couple of young women, one nursing a bandaged wrist. Joe closed his eyes and tried to hurry time forward, willing the doctors to speed up. A hand touched his shoulder and Joe jumped. He looked up and found himself staring at Nick and the rest of the group. The manager's face was corrugated with concern.

'How is he?'

'I don't know. They won't let me see him.'

'I am sure they are doing all they can.' Nick sat beside Joe and put an arm around him.

'They'd better be.'

Nick looked around at the rather run-down waiting room and sighed. 'When he is able to move, I'm checking him into a private hospital. Nothing but the best for Paul.' He raised his glance to Dean and Connor who stood by the door, not knowing where to put themselves. 'Look, you two guys go home. There is nothing you can do by waiting around here. I'll call you when there's any news.'

Dean nodded. 'But what about the concert? What do we say to people?'

'Say nothing. We'll postpone the concert. I'll make all the necessary arrangements and Melanie can handle the press.'

The two lads shook their heads in disbelief at the situation and headed for the exit.

'Thanks. I couldn't have handled having them around. I love them dearly but it would have been a strain.' Joe sank against

Nick's strong chest, the warmth and the comfort just what he needed right now.

Nick held him close, not caring about the startled glances of the two young women. 'I'm sure he'll be fine. He just has to be.'

Joe realised he must have been dozing against the solid muscle of Nick's chest, when a hand tapped him on the shoulder. It was a young male orderly, dressed in a white coat, with the obligatory stethoscope hanging round his neck. His fresh-faced beam instantly told Joe that Paul was alright.

'You can go in now. Last ward at the end of the corridor, first bed on the right.' He gave Joe a reassuring pat and turned away. At another time Joe would have been tempted to chat the guy up, but now all his thoughts were with Paul.

'I'll stay here.' Nick waved Joe off, and sat back crossing his arms. 'You should be alone with him now.'

Unable to argue, Joe set off, almost running, his eyes scanning the wards and the beds until he found his partner. He was unprepared for how bad Paul looked. His skin was a ghostly white again, and his eyes were closed; tubes and wires were connected to him, an array of machines surrounding the bed. Moving close, and trying to bite back the tears, he sat on the edge of the bed and took Paul's hand. There was no response. A doctor appeared around the door and came to Joe's side.

Joe stared up, his eyes brimming, at the doctor who picked up the chart hanging on the end of the bed, made a few hasty scribbles and turned to Joe.

'How is he, doctor?'

The man smiled, his dark eyes trying to be positive. His face was kindly and the grey hair seemed to be just right on him.

'He experienced a bad shock. His heartbeat is still irregular, and so we'll be keeping him in for observation. Things should settle down in a day or so.'

'Thank you, thank you so much.' Joe squeezed Paul's hand once again. This time he exclaimed with relief as he felt a squeeze in return, not strong, but still there.

Another white-coated individual with a shoulder-bag entered the ward, checking the charts at several of the other beds and then stopping at Paul's. He leaned in and spoke to Paul, in a soft, soothing voice. 'Paul... Paul... can you hear me? Can you open your eyes for me?'

The stricken lad slowly raised his eyelids, his gaze weary and unfocused.

'How are you feeling, Paul? A bit groggy I suppose?'

Paul nodded.

'And how long will you be here, do you think?'

Joe was puzzled by this question. Surely the staff at the hospital would know how long he would be in their care.

A gentle shake from side to side indicated Paul didn't know the answer to that one.

'And what will happen about the concerts? Will they be cancelled?'

This time Joe was even more concerned.

'Look, what has this got to do with you?' His tone was one of rising anger.

'Joe, can you tell me exactly what happened to Paul today? Is it true he got a shock from an electric cable?'

'Who are you?' Joe stood and angrily faced the man. Sensing that his time was running short, the stranger reached into his bag and pulled out a camera, aiming the lens at Paul and hastily taking a couple of shots.

Scrabbling to his feet and running around to the other side of the bed, Joe grabbed the undercover journalist by the arms and shook him violently.

'You bastard. Have you got no feelings?'

'Hmmm. Reporter assaulted by pop singer... should make a

good story. I'd let go of me if I were you... don't want to make things worse, do you?' The slimy journalist smoothed out the sleeves of his white coat and replaced the camera in his bag. 'Thank you, Mr Turner.'

Joe raised a clenched fist, the temptation to punch the guy on the nose was inordinately strong. Sensing that he was in danger of getting hurt, the guy hurried from the room.

Joe slumped back on the bed and took Paul's hand. 'I'm so sorry about that...'

The only response from Paul was another confirmed squeeze of the hand.

The Asian nurse entered the ward and came to the side of the bed. 'I need to check him out again. So if you could...'

'I know, I know.' Joe stood and faced her, sheepishly. 'Look, I'm sorry about earlier. I was upset.'

The nurse smiled. 'Don't worry. I've had a lot worse, working here, I can tell you. There's a coffee machine down the hall. If you could give me five minutes?'

With a nod, Joe was about to leave when a high-pitched beep issued from one of the machines. The nurse looked anxious and rushed to Paul's side. Reaching up she pressed the emergency button for assistance. The electronic read-out on one of the machines had slowed to a single, unfluctuating line.

All hell broke lose. Several doctors burst through the doors, pushing Joe aside. They pulled back the covers and started prodding and pulling at Paul. They spoke in insistent voices, but just low enough for Joe not to hear them. A trolley was wheeled through the doors, with a frightening piece of medical apparatus on it. One of the doctor picked up the two metal paddles and shouted at the room, 'Stand clear...'

Joe had seen such procedures on many hospital drama series on the television. He knew they were trying to restart Paul's heart. That meant that it had stopped beating, and technically speaking,

Paul had died. Joe hugged himself tight and started to pray.

The jolt of electricity surged through Paul making his body give an involuntary jump. 'Again.' The doctor sent another burst of electricity into Paul's chest. Helpless, Joe stared at the awful scene, unable to move, wanting to look away – but his eyes were fixed on his boyfriend's pale face.

The doctor looked up at the assembled medics. 'We're losing him...'

Joe didn't sleep at all that night. At around midnight, the nurse had told him to go home.

Paul had reacted to the third bolt of electricity, and his heart had started beating again. He was now slumbering heavily and would probably do so until the following morning. There was nothing for him to do, so he had better get some rest. Besides, he'd be of more help to Paul when he was awake and feeling refreshed. The night itself was windy and the sound of squally gales kept him from falling asleep. Also every time he closed his eyes he saw Paul lying in the hospital bed, grey-skinned and unmoving. He kept his eyes on the clock, counting the hours until he could return to his partner's side.

Paul on the other hand slept remarkably well. He had been given a sedative, and so fell into a deep unconscious state, waking at eight the next morning. As he came to, he experienced a minor panic when he failed to recognise his surroundings, but in a few seconds pictures and images flooded his mind, and he remembered what had happened at the Arena.

He gazed about him, taking in his situation. Next to the bed, machines whirred and buzzed happily. He realised he must have been in a large ward because the pale green curtain had been pulled around the bed giving some small amount of privacy. With a large stretch and a yawn, he shook his head and gave himself the once-over. Bearing in mind the terrible shock he had had the day before, he felt remarkably fine. There were no aches or pains. No burns or scars. In fact he felt perfectly fit and well. The curtain drew back a couple of inches and a head poked round. It was a young male orderly, with an open, friendly face, a mop of brown hair that seemed to possess a life of its own, giving the impression that its owner had been sleeping rough for many days.

'How are you feeling today?' The young orderly stepped through the curtains and took Paul's wrist, checked his pulse and made a note on the chart at the foot of the bed.

'Very well, actually. I think I feel really good.' Paul watched as the medic looked at the machine's read-outs intently.

'Well, that's excellent news. You had a big shock, you know.'

'I know. But why do I feel so well, then?'

The orderly sucked on the end of his pen, and smiled down at Paul, one eyebrow raised quizzically. 'Who knows? Perhaps the shock gave a jolt to the system, sort of like a computer rebooting itself, and it gave your body a lift... I really don't know.'

'So can I go home?' Paul looked up at the orderly from under his eyelids, giving the pleading look that Joe found so hard to resist.

'I don't know about that. It's up to the doctor in charge of your case. Normally we should keep you in for observation for a few days at least.'

'But I feel fine. I do, honest. Cross my heart and hope to die...'

'Don't say such things in a hospital!' The orderly beamed at Paul, his face lighting up, showing a twinkle in his eyes.

'I could do with a shower, though.' Paul scratched his head, feeling a bit grimy and unclean. 'Can I take one?'

'Not until you get the all-clear from the doctor. It's bed baths only for the moment.'

Paul pursed his lips and gave the orderly a winning smile. 'And who does the bathing, precisely?'

He thought he detected an imperceptible pause before the

orderly answered. 'Generally speaking it's one of the nurses. But... er... if you want, I could give it to you...'

The intention couldn't have been clearer. Whatever shocks Paul's body had been subjected to, he now felt awake and raring to go. His loins stirred, and he could feel a rush of blood to his dormant member, lying across his thigh.

'I'd like that very much,' Paul said.

Placing his pen in the top pocket of his white coat, the orderly leaned in towards Paul, his lips brushing the tip of his earlobe. 'Don't go away...' The voice was husky and oozed sexual overtones, its implications stirring Paul's cock further.

He parted the curtains and stepped through, pulling them behind him.

After about five minutes, he reappeared, with a plastic bowl of warm soapy water, a sponge and some towels.

'Got everything?' Paul gave an inquisitive glance at the young man.

'I have.' Placing the bowl down on the bedside chair, he started to roll the blanket and sheets down the bed until Paul was completely uncovered. 'Could you sit up?' He helped Paul to lean forward, allowing him access to the tied ribbons, holding the medical gown closed behind Paul's back. He slipped the gown off and gazed appreciatively at the naked young lad lying in front of him.

Paul's hand was strategically placed across his crotch, just hiding the semi-hard dick, giving a semblance of propriety. The orderly then lay some towels along Paul's sides, tucking them underneath his torso. Without a word, he then dropped the sponge in the bowl, and squeezed some of the soapy suds onto Paul's chest. Slowly, but extremely thoroughly, the orderly began washing. Using the sponge in small circular movements, he lathered up, gently caressing the skin of Paul's chest and stomach, then moving up around his neck. He eased Paul upright so he could get to wash his back, smoothing the sponge over him. Then, deftly, he picked up a dry towel and began drying the newly cleaned areas, letting Paul lie back down.

Squeezing out the sponge, the orderly moved down to Paul's legs, lifting them tenderly and giving each a thorough washing and towelling. Then both men knew that there was only one area left untouched.

The orderly hesitated, until Paul spoke in a dry-throated voice. 'Well, finish the job then.' He moved the covering hand away and sat up on his elbows, parting his legs slightly, seeing the wide-eyed gleam of the young man, staring admiringly at the thick cock, which stood up, almost erect, bending forward a little, eager and waiting.

The orderly dropped the sponge in the bowl and left it there. He swished his hands in the soapy water and moved close. With nimble fingers, he started stroking the skin of Paul's inner thighs, moving inwards and upwards, until the tips of his fingers brushed the underside of Paul's scrotal sac. The lad gave a short inhalation of breath at the contact, and smiled encouragingly, urging the attendant to continue. His hands slippery with soap, the orderly stretched his grip around the bag, pulling the bollocks away from the body, emphasising the growing cock, which reacted in the only way it knew how, stiffening and standing to attention. With his free hand, the orderly stroked the soft skin of Paul's dick, running his fingers along the underside, following the swollen ridge from base to tip. Then he ran his gentle touch over the head, feeling every bit of the purple monster, watching Paul squirm with joyous anticipation.

Knowing that time was of the essence, the orderly wrapped his fingers around the shaft, taking a tight hold, and began to move it up and down, feeling his fist glide smoothly from top to bottom. He could see that this was being enjoyed, Paul's eyes had shut and his head had fallen back on his shoulders. With intense concentration, the orderly increased the speed, and soon was wanking

Paul's cock with vigour. It didn't take too long for Paul to feel that familiar boiling in his balls, as they were manipulated expertly by the young guy's hand. And in a grunt he let fly, shooting out a stream of cum, landing across his newly scrubbed chest.

The orderly picked up a towel and wiped the semen clean, giving Paul a conspiratorial smile. 'That was very naughty, you know.'

'I know. And I feel like being even naughtier. Come here.' Paul waited as the orderly moved to the head of the bed, and with one practised motion, Paul unzipped the man's flies and pulled his cock out.

'This'll have to be quick, so brace yourself...' Paul took the cock in his mouth, clamping his lips around it. The cock was very thin, with a head that was as narrow as the shaft, but it was exceedingly long, too long for Paul to take all the way down his throat. Sliding his mouth down as far as possible, he started to suck, rigorously slavering at the guy's erection. The orderly gripped the edge of one of the machines, his breath rasping out shortly.

Paul knew that he was an expert cock-sucker, and he gave all he could, swirling his tongue around the shaft, nibbling around the head, pulling the foreskin forward, and then sliding it back with his fist, emphasising the smallish mushroom head. The sound of approaching nurses increased Paul's sucking and in a few brief strokes he brought the orderly to climax, letting the spunk shoot out over his face and neck.

Hastily zipping himself up, the orderly threw a towel at Paul. 'Here, wipe up quickly. I'd better be gone.' He grabbed up the bowl and vanished through the curtains, reappearing momentarily, his face beaming. 'Thanks.'

Nick was surprised at how well Paul seemed when he arrived at the hospital that afternoon. Joe sat on the side of the bed, weary but relieved at the state of his partner.

'I feel absolutely fine. Really.' Paul was adamant that he didn't want to stay in the hospital for a moment longer.

'It's up to the doctor, not me.' The manager waited for the grey-haired physician to speak.

Folding his arms and peering over the top of his half-moon spectacles, the doctor seemed content. 'Well, we cannot keep you here. If you feel fine then you can go. On the condition that you make an appointment and come back in a week for another look at you. And if you feel strange in any way, come straight back.'

Paul nodded. 'I will. I promise.'

'Good, then off you go. And look after him, won't you?' He directed a stare at Nick who stared back unintimidated.

'Right, let's get you home. A few days' rest will do you the world of good.' He opened the bedside cupboard and passed Paul's clothes to him.

'I've said I feel terrific. I want to do the concert tonight.'

Both Nick and Joe gaped open-mouthed at what they had just heard. Shaking his head, Nick said, 'That is absolute lunacy... after what you've been through. I won't allow it.'

Paul gritted his teeth and spoke with a determined thrust of his chin. 'Look, Nick. I'll be the judge of what is good for me, and right now I have never felt better. How can I let down the thousands of fans who have paid to see us tonight? Feeling as well as I do? I'd be a fraud, I just know it. I couldn't face them again. I mean this, Nick. Get everything moving because I want to do this. Or I walk. I'll leave the band and never come back.'

Even though he knew the contract wouldn't allow Paul to leave BANNED, Nick could see the seriousness of his intentions. Perplexity engulfed him, and he had to sit down for moment and think. What if he let Paul perform, and he collapsed again? He could die. And that was unthinkable. But on the other hand, Paul seemed perfectly fit, fitter than he'd been for months. Perhaps he should just bite his tongue and let the boy do it.

'OK, you win. Come on, I've got a lot to organise. The press will have to be told immediately. And the Arena. Jesus Christ... you boys don't make things easy for me.' He pulled his mobile phone from his pocket and started dialling, striding down the hall to the exit, leaving Paul to throw on his clothes and follow, tugging Joe along in his wake.

Almost every seat was full at the Arena. Those who hadn't heard the news of the concert's reinstatement would be offered tickets for one of the following nights or a complete refund if they couldn't make it. Paul knew that there would be some disappointed fans, but he put that from his mind. The sound check had been done again, but with extreme care. Gaz, the sound engineer, looked so ashamed and guilty when Paul stepped on stage for the rehearsal, that he had to go over and give him a hug, telling him not to take the blame.

The other three members of BANNED had crowded around Paul when he arrived at the Arena and emerged from the taxi cab. They were protectively helping him and making him comfortable to such an extent that he had to say something. 'Hey, guys... look, I'm OK. Stop clucking round me like a bunch of worried hens. Let's just get this show on the road. If I need anything, you'll be the first people I ask.'

The guys' nerves didn't begin until just before the start of the concert. The sound of eighty-thousand fans chanting and cheering, clapping and shouting out the band's names suddenly filled them with dread. They had never played to such an immense crowd. And doubts began to emerge. Dean was the first to speak.

'What if they don't like the show? He paced up and down, not knowing the answer. 'What if they hate us? What if we fall over, or the sound gives out?'

Paul, who was the calmest of the four lads, chipped in. 'Look, life is full of "what ifs". You can't go around worrying about what happens to you. Look at me. Apparently I nearly died yesterday. So today, as I'm still alive and fighting fit, I decided to just go for it: have fun, enjoy everything I do, and fuck the consequences.'

There was no arguing with that, and as the time for the concert to start was almost upon them, the four lads stood together in the dressing room in a group hug, eyes shut, hoping for a successful performance.

They needn't have worried. From the moment the lights dimmed on the stage and the first throbbing, pounding notes of the orchestra matched the pulsing of the lights, they were a winner. The crowd cheered triumphantly as a giant staircase lowered itself from the stage roof, and four spotlights picked out each individual member in their brilliant beams. In unison they marched step by step down the staircase, in time with the beat of the song, until they stood on the stage, each in metal-capped boots, leather trousers, white T-shirts and fringed black leather jackets. They looked sensational.

As Connor started the first song, a gigantic wave of warm applause rippled around the auditorium like a Mexican wave, ending up flowing over the four performers, bathing them in its glory. Looking out at the audience, the boys saw a sea of nameless faces, getting smaller and smaller as they receded into the distance, until they were tiny moving pin-pricks, undulating in time to the rhythm. Enormous balloons bobbed over their heads, as did huge painted placards, bearing phrases like 'CONNOR I LOVE YOU!!!', 'DEAN I'LL TURN YOU STRAIGHT!!' AND 'BANNED FILL MY HEART'. People waved torches and cigarette lighters giving the appearance of a vast, moving lake of tiny lights.

Never in their lives had the boys seen such a sight, and nothing could have prepared them for it. All they could do was perform the best concert they were able to give, the fans deserved nothing less.

A string of security guards stood at the front of the stage, at ground level, to stop any of the more excessive fans making a run for the stage. The boys could make out the darkened shapes of Stuart and Jordan among the assembled guards and knew that they would be doing their best. In front of them, pushed against the barriers, were many screaming fans, mainly men, all having lost any semblance of dignity, waving their arms, blowing kisses and screeching out their favourite band member's name.

Nick, Uri and Melanie stood in the wings at the side of the stage, all holding hands, unable to comprehend the scale of the boys' success, and all grinning ecstatically. For them their futures were assured. Melanie knew that she had the best job of her life, representing a top band, for as long as they continued to scale the charts, and Uri also knew that without him the show wouldn't be as slick and stylish as it was. His routines had made the boys look athletic and graceful as well as sexy, and his part in their continued success was obvious.

Nick had managed many bands before, some achieving chart recognition, but none had been as big as BANNED. He would soon be rolling in money, and so would the boys. At last they had reached a pinnacle that would provide for them and their loved ones for the rest of their lives. There only remained one goal in Nick's mind, and that was to conquer America. He had put out several feelers to music agencies over there, and had a pleasing response. The first single by BANNED, 'Only The Night', had been released earlier that summer, but plummeted without trace. Keeping his faith in the boys' abilities intact, Nick was convinced that if they actually went over to that country for a long spell and made many personal appearances, then with the backing of the right American agent, they could crack the potentially huge market.

As he focused his gaze on the four performers on stage, a large burst of laughter erupted from his chest. The guys were loving every minute of the show. During the 'Fun in the Sun' sequence, where the boys were all wearing skimpy swimwear, Paul was generating gales of hysterical mirth, having placed a potato down the front of his speedos. At the end of the routine, as if of one mind, the boys all turned their backs and dropped their swimming briefs, showing their arses to the crowd, who sent a huge cheer thundering towards the stage.

At one point Dean's microphone failed during one of his solo spots. Smiling broadly, he walked to the wings and picked up another and carried on as if nothing had happened, behaving like a real professional. The lads did not stop for two solid hours, giving each number their all, rushing offstage to leap into the next set of costumes for the following section. There was a dodgy moment when Joe failed to fasten his pin-stripe trousers properly for the gangster number and they slid gracefully to the stage floor, leaving him in a jacket and jockstrap, and trousers bunched around his ankles. Raising his eyes heavenwards, he hitched them up and swiftly hooked the fastener.

During the concert's slushy finale, the stage was deluged with hundreds of teddy bears, of varying hues and sizes. Many carried love notes attached by strings or rubber bands, and at one point, a stage hand had to run across the front of the stage and clear a path for the boys to walk through. The back of the set was now an immense red heart, in which a door swung open and one by one the boys filed through, leaving a single spotlight on it, which got smaller and smaller until it eventually vanished.

The audience was elated. They didn't want the evening to finish, but grudgingly they accepted that it had, as the auditorium lights slowly faded up. The crowd left behind tons of rubbish, and headed for their cars, or coaches, trains and buses, to make their euphoric way home.

The boys ran, full of adrenalin, to their dressing room, chattering and hugging each other, unable to contain their excitement.

'I can't believe what just happened!' Paul burst out.

'Neither can I!' Joe picked Paul up and swung him round, nearly knocking into Dean.

'Watch it!' Flopping down on a chair, Dean ran his fingers through his sweat-drenched hair, and looked up as there was a knock on the door. Nick entered, wreathed in smiles and carrying a magnum of the best champagne.

'Well done boys, you were magnificent... I am so proud... I just don't know what else to say.' There were tears of joy in his eyes, and with a sigh of delight he began opening the bottle.

'Can I come in?' Uri stood in the doorway, Melanie's vivid purple head poking over his shoulder.

'Of course!' Connor hugged them both and led them to the centre of the room. 'Have some champagne!'

Soon the alcohol was flowing, and after the boys had finished off the bottle, they made their weary way to the waiting limousines, which whisked them away to the central London hotel that they had been inhabiting for the last two weeks.

As they entered the lobby, there was a spontaneous eruption of polite applause from the assorted suited and bejewelled ladies and gentlemen standing around.

Struggling under the weight of flowers and gifts, the boys made their way to their rooms, four adjoining suites on the top floor, dropping all they carried and slumping exhausted on their beds. But the night wasn't over yet. It held one more astounding surprise.

15: Fourgy

Having made an excursion to the mini-bar, Dean sank back onto the plush king-sized bed, kicked off his shoes and switched on the television. Even with the presence of dozens of satellite channels he could find nothing interesting to watch. Dull documentaries about nomads in the Sahara Desert vied with dreadful programmes about beach babes in Ibiza, none of them able to hold his attention.

Dean looked at the clock on the bedside table. Five minutes past midnight. And he was still wide awake, the rush of adrenalin still pumped around his system. The mixture of all the champagne he'd drunk earlier and the two miniature bottles of brandy from the mini-bar seemed to be having no effect on him whatsoever. Listlessly he stood and crossed to the window looking out over one of London's vast, plush areas of parkland, seeing a small group of dedicated fans standing below, waiting for a glimpse of their pop idols. They'd probably be there all night. Silly sods.

He picked up a book he was half-way through and started to read. After five minutes when he realised that he'd read the same sentence ten times over without the sense of the words sinking in, he threw it down on the bed beside him. This was ridiculous. What he needed now was company.

★

Joe and Paul lay back on the bed, their arms and legs entwined, wearing only white towelling robes. Soft music from the clock radio played.

'When I thought I was going to lose you, I couldn't bear it,' Joe whispered tenderly in Paul's ear.

'Stop thinking of that. I'm here now and fine. There's no reason we shouldn't be together for years to come.' Paul tweaked Joe's nose, and planted a kiss on his lips. 'Another drink?' Disentangling himself, Paul crossed to the mini-bar and popped open another half-bottle of champagne. Pouring some for each of them, he sat back on the bed and raised his glass. 'Well, here's to the future.' They drank down the bubbly, and looked around the room.

'I'm not in the slightest bit tired,' said Joe.

'Neither am I.'

'So what could we do to pass the time?' A devilish glint twinkled in Joe's eye.

'I just can't imagine.' Paul reached down and placed his hand on Joe's crotch, patting the mound of flesh beneath the fluffy towelling. With one finger, he hooked the dressing gown apart, revealing Joe's cock, which lay across his thigh, fat and tempting, an object of beauty.

'Hmmm, what have I found?' Paul had an expression of mock puzzlement on his face. Then he licked his lips and lowered his head.

A knock at the door made him pull back. Sighing, Paul called out, 'Who is it?'

'It's me, Dean. Can I come in?'

Paul padded across to the door, his feet sinking down into the luxurious pile of the carpet. He pulled the door open and smiled at Dean, who stood carrying a couple of half-bottles of champagne.

'I couldn't sleep. Fancy some company?'

All thoughts of blow-jobs vanished from Paul's mind. He was genuinely glad to see his friend.

'Sure, come in. We couldn't sleep either. Pull up a bottle and join us.' He led the way back into the bedroom. 'We have a visitor.'

Joe looked up and a big smile corrugated his features. 'Dean... come in... make yourself comfortable. We have.' He gazed down, following the line of Dean's excited stare, and hastily pulled his robe closed.

'I hope I wasn't interrupting anything.' Dean fixed his eyes on both the lads, sure that he'd barged in on the beginnings of something sexual.

'Don't be stupid,' Joe answered. 'It doesn't like being cooped up, it needs a little air now and then.' With a flourish, he pulled open the robe again, giving both guys a good look at his slumbering penis.

Dean sank down on a plush sofa and surveyed his two friends. 'You seem a lot happier together these days.'

'We are.' Paul plumped himself down beside Dean, curling his legs up underneath him. 'I think that because of all we've gone through, we have a stronger relationship.'

Dean smiled wistfully. 'I wish I could find a relationship as strong as yours.'

'You will. I know it.' Paul squeezed his thigh appreciatively. 'Mr Right is just around the corner.'

'Perhaps. All I seem to meet is Mr Shallow-But-Hung.'

'Nothing wrong with that! Now are you going to open that champagne or am I going to have to smack your little botty?'

Dean grinned childishly, and started to unwrap the cork on one of the bottles. 'Don't make offers you can't keep...'

'Who says?'

'I do.'

'Well, fuck you. Look, why don't you get comfortable? There's a couple of spare robes in the closet. Throw one on... you'll feel better out of those clothes.'

Standing, Dean made a bee-line for the closet, shucked his clothes quickly and wrapped himself in the comforting, all-enveloping material.

When he returned to the bedroom, Paul had poured out more champagne for all three of them.

'Cheers.' They downed the glasses in one gulp.

Joe looked thoughtfully at the other two. 'There's one thing missing here, you realise?'

Both Paul and Dean chimed out, 'Connor.'

As if in answer, there was a knock at the door. All three burst out laughing, as Paul rushed to the door, and threw it open.

'Come in Connor, you took your time!'

The Irish lad looked bemused. 'Eh? I couldn't sleep and wondered if you felt like some company. I knocked on Dean's door but there was no answer. I guess he's got his head down.'

'I don't think so... well not yet anyway.' Paul led the way back to the bedroom, and with a wave of his arm, gestured toward Dean and Joe, now snuggled up together on the huge bed.

Connor giggled like a naughty child. 'So is this a private orgy or can anyone join in?'

'Help yourself.' Paul gave him a hug and then threw himself down on the foot of the bed. 'Grab a robe and come to the cabaret, old chum.'

The three others watched as Connor took off his clothes and put the robe on, pulling the belt tight around his waist.

'Have some champagne.' Joe waved his empty glass in the air. 'And you can top me up too.'

'I'd better catch you guys up.' Connor raised the bottle to his lips and finished off the final drops. 'Good job I brought some more with me.' He picked up his trousers from a heap by the door and pulled two half-bottles from the pockets. 'This should keep us going.'

'Hooray. More booze!' Paul was now lying down on the bed, dangling his legs over the edge. His dressing gown had slid up around his thighs, and the front was slightly open. As Connor handed out more drink, he looked down and saw a glimpse of Paul's bollocks, beautifully rounded and smooth.

'Hey, look what I can see.' The Irish lad quickly knelt and with one hand gave the ball-sac a friendly tickle.

Paul raised his head, and instead of flinching or pulling his robe closed, just stared straight at Connor, with a clear, sober gaze and said, 'That's nice. Don't stop.' He sat up, letting the robe fall open, displaying his cock and bollocks.

Suddenly embarrassed, Connor stood, watching Joe's reaction, then realising that Joe wasn't reacting at all. In fact he was lying back, his arms tight around Dean, watching the unfolding scene through hooded eyelids; then he looked down at Dean who raised his eyes and stared back.

'This is nice.' Dean spoke low and intense. 'I never realised how much you guys mean to me. I hope we'll be friends forever.'

Joe ran a hand down Dean's chest, slipping it inside the lapel of his dressing gown and gently stroking his finger up and down one of his nipples, lightly brushing the tip, encouraging it to full erection. 'Just friends?'

Dean didn't know what to say.

The four lads collectively drew in their breaths and froze. Never in the twelve months of BANNED's life had they looked at each other in an extreme sexual way, except for the obvious relationship between Paul and Joe. Dean and Connor had had sex before with Stuart at the Manchester shopping centre, but even then they hadn't really looked at the other one as a sex object. The four of them were colleagues, fellow band members and mates, but suddenly, in this plush hotel suite, a switch had been flicked on, and here and now they were aware of the sexuality and eroticism of the other guys. All four knew that they had reached a significant moment in their collective friendships. Once they crossed the bridge into thinking the others were freely available sexual beings, there would be no turning back.

Did they dare? And what would happen to them if they did? There was only one way to find out.

Joe and Dean began to kiss, as did Connor and Paul, their tongues meeting and darting fully in each other's mouths. It was their first real such contact and they enjoyed the sensation, just falling into the wetness, exploring the cavities, delving deep.

Paul reached down and felt Connor's cock, fingers squeezing and fondling. Connor reacted accordingly and did the same. Their chests collided as they took each other in a warm embrace. Connor licked at the soft skin of Paul's neck, around his ears and chin, nibbling at the earlobes, feeling Paul sagging with ecstatic delight at the sensations. He had found Paul's weak spot.

Spending some time on his ears, Connor lapped and licked, then worked his way slowly downward to his chest, paying close attention to his nipples, his tongue reaching out and moistening the tips. He let it swirl around the surrounding darkened skin, before biting gently at the hard mounds, taking his time, flicking them, then sucking them deep inside his mouth. After he had pleasured himself this way, he headed south, pausing at Paul's navel, where a small pool of sweat was beginning to gather. He let his mouth rest on the patch of skin just below, dangerously close to his genitals, inhaling, loving the heady scent of talcum powder and man.

Paul was too excited to wait any longer and he grabbed Connor's head and forced his face into his groin. He spread his legs wider, allowing Connor easier access, feeling the hot licking of his tongue at the newly aroused areas. His friend's wet, lapping tongue licked between the thighs, faintly touching the base of his balls.

The hard-on that Paul now sported was protruding from the robe, the head poking out dramatically. With his fingers Connor pulled at the strip of towelling belt and let the robe fall to the floor in a discarded heap, allowing the cock freedom, so that he could suck it properly. Which he did. His mouth closed around the end, then let the entire shaft slide down his throat. The cock filled Connor's mouth, and he continued to enjoy sucking his friend for some time, lost in the heightened passion. Paul's eyes were closed, his hands gripping Connor's hair, tugging at the very roots, unaware that he was actually causing him some pain. Sucking through the discomfort, Connor continued.

The rising and falling of his mouth, the regular rhythm of the sucking were more than Paul expected. He was stunned by the expertise of Connor, amazed that he was finally being blown by one of his closest friends. He opened his eyes and looked down, watching his cock disappearing down the lapping orifice. He looked up and saw with a smile what was happening between his other two friends.

Joe and Dean were still kissing, but one of Joe's hands was feeling Dean's arse, cupping the buttocks, moving them in a circular rubbing motion, stroking the fleshy cheeks. Dean moaned softly and shifted around on the bed. His cock was getting stiffer all the time, and he badly wanted Joe to suck it. Joe's other hand, lightly tweaking Dean's nipples, moved down and ran across his stomach muscles, which were now becoming slick with nervous sweat. Dean's breathing spasmed, and his stomach muscles rippled beneath Joe's touch. Then he felt Joe's fingers fondling the robe around his crotch, pulling it open, lingering around the head of his cock. The stiff meat bobbed up, falling into Joe's grasp, and without warning he began to wank it, rubbing the tender head, which was sticky and waiting.

Taking this as an invitation, Joe knelt by Dean's side and bent forward, licking at the head, sensing the lad tense up. With one hand he fondled Dean's thighs, feeling for the heavy hanging balls, his mouth moving toward the weighty meat of his dick. He turned his head slightly so he could lick at the underside of the throbbing glans. Dean watched in fascination and desire as Joe's lips sucked at the head, slipping his tongue around it, then pulling back so it rested on his lower lip, all the time the tip of his tongue flicking at the tiny slit, coaxing out the ambrosial pre-cum. Suddenly Dean pushed up at Joe, forcing him to swallow all of his broad, solid flesh.

Joe began forcibly rubbing his lips up and down the rigid tool, at the same time reaching inside his robe for his own cock. Dean could see it was big and thick, an incredible size, in fact one of the biggest Dean had ever seen. It was beautiful. How he had never looked at Joe as a sexual object until now puzzled him immensely. He watched, enthralled as Joe wanked at his own cock, increasing the speed and pressure of his mouth at the same time. His free hand pulled at the ball-sac, manipulating them, squeezing and stretching.

This double attention sent shivers coursing through Dean's body. This was astonishing. Joe's tongue and mouth were feeling so good on his cock that he just had to keep him going. All he wanted now was another mouth and tongue on his arsehole and that would be utter heaven...

Connor was so caught up in the sucking of Paul's cock that his legs began to go numb. When he shifted slightly to ease the pressure, it made Paul realise that he was uncomfortable too. Kneeling himself, he pulled Connor to the ground and they lay on the carpet, legs wrapped around each other's hard bodies, until Connor pushed Paul away and got to his knees, forcing Paul's legs up in the air, exposing his parted cheeks. Connor wanted so much to push his cock inside that pulsing hole, but without protection he daren't.

'I've got some in there.' Standing up and hurrying to the bathroom, Paul emerged with a couple of packets of protectives and lube. Taking one from Paul's hands, Connor ripped the packet open and rolled it down the length of his now rock-hard dick. He waited for Paul to settle on his back on the carpet, knelt up close and tickled the hole with the end of his cock, rubbing up and down against Paul's waiting knot.

Paul closed his eyes, his arms wide, his fingernails scratching at the soft, woolly feel of the carpet, enjoying its luxurious texture, his mind full of the imminent invasion. He could feel the head pressing impatiently at him, and with a shove it pushed past the tight ring of muscle. Paul cried out with a mixture of shock and delight, arching his back, grasping himself around the knees, allowing Connor easier access. In this position, the Irish lad fucked Paul, slowly at first, increasing the pace and momentum as Paul got gradually accustomed to the size of the monster within him. Connor's hips slapped wetly against the buns of Paul's arse, then he gently pulled Paul toward him so that the boy's back was resting on his knees.

Squirming around, encouraging a deeper fuck, Paul groaned with pleasure. Small squealing sounds emitted from his throat, as he was unable to form words, the intense anal battering robbing him of his ability to speak. Then, unbelievably, Connor leant over and took the tip of Paul's cock in his mouth, his agility surprising even himself. He rolled the swollen head around his mouth, and slowly and surely, as Paul hefted his hips higher, he could slide more inside. In this amazing stance, Paul was sucked and fucked at the same time. The more Connor leaned back, forcing his cock deep within Paul, the more he thought the cock in his mouth would snap from the impossible angle it was at.

The pace of the fucking increased. His breathing also got quicker, rasping and blowing with the exertions. Beads of sweat were now dropping from Connor's brow onto Paul's smooth stomach, rolling away and disappearing under his arms. The carpet was beginning to graze his shins and the tops of his feet, but he didn't care. All that existed was this moment and the wonderful connection between the two of them.

On the bed, Dean was also enraptured, feeling the semen beginning to stir deep in his bollocks. Sensing this, Joe stopped his sucking and eased himself creakingly to his feet. His own cock was in need of a little love, and so slipping out of his robe he placed a hand on Dean's shoulder and pushed him, unresisting, to the floor.

Unable to ignore such a tempting sight, Dean fell upon the stiff pole, sucking the rigid flesh inside him. He licked at the sides, gripping the shaft at the base, running his tongue around the swollen head, savouring the droplet that oozed from it, a bitter-sweet promise of what was to come. He stared at the neatly shaped bush of curly hair that perfectly framed the immense organ, watching its outlines fade and come back into focus as he slid down the shaft and then pulled back. Shifting on his knees, assuming a more comfortable position, Dean held the cock-head between his lips, gazing down in awe at the fearsome length of the weapon.

The bond that now held the two men together was unbreakable, perhaps the strongest that can be had between two men. Dean gazed up at the abdomen towering above him, the well-toned ridges of muscle undulating and covered with a light sheen of perspiration. Several times Dean paused in his cock-sucking to take the balls into his mouth, drawing them in, gently pulling on the sac until the skin would give no more. His eyes looked up at the cock, now standing proudly over his face, beautifully hard and perfectly formed, a real work of art. Then Dean started to suck with an intense fervour. Joe was in flights of ecstasy, gripping tightly to Dean's shoulders, his legs rigid.

As Joe looked down on Dean slurping at his cock, trying to take it all in his accommodating mouth, and succeeding, going down on him with speed and vitality, his gaze was drawn to Paul and Connor, engaged in a mighty tussle, the Irish boy slamming away, fucking Paul's arse as if his life depended on it. He could do with some of that. It had been a while since he'd filled a tight arse.

Perhaps Dean would oblige. It certainly was a nice arse and he was sure Dean would be a great fuck.

As if reading Joe's mind, Dean's eyes swept across the room, seeing the other two, and then registering the situation. Pulling his lips away from the cock in front of him, he stood and took up the opened packet of rubbers, ripped a sachet with his teeth and handed it to Joe, who smiled, rapidly sliding the protective down his enlarged dick, which stood up at a fierce angle. Ready to do what its master wanted. He lubed it up.

Lying down on the carpet, his cock now sticking up in the air, Joe grinned at Dean, who didn't waste a second more. He sank down, straddling Joe's thighs, and positioned the cock at the aching ring of muscles, the touch of the mushroom head making him shiver in anticipation. Joe's hand caressed Dean's chest as he sat down on the cock, letting every thick inch slide up inside of him, his sphincter clenching tight and relaxing with each push down. Dean was now moaning pleasurably, his hand wrapped around himself, beating off with utter enjoyment.

Joe could feel the strong muscles gripping the whole length of his cock, urging it higher and deeper, almost swallowing him up to the hilt. He stared wide-eyed at this handsome man, this dear friend, who was riding his cock, taking it all inside of him, and loving every minute.

'I want some of that.' Paul's voice rang out. Joe looked up and saw him standing over the pair of them, Connor at his shoulder, his swollen dick in his hand.

Dean realised it was time for a change of position so he eased himself off Joe's cock and got to his feet.

Without being asked, Paul lay down on the bed, his legs spread, held back behind his shoulders, waiting. Dean, Connor and Joe seemed all of one mind. Picking up a fresh condom, Joe slid it down his cock, slathered it with lube and pushed it at the aching hole.

Paul gave a cry of pain as Joe's cock slid inside. It was bigger than Connor's and so stretched the ring of muscles more. Even with all the times he had been fucked by Joe in their relationship, it was still painful at the first thrust. Joe now gripped Paul's ankles, his legs separated and unable to move. Grunting, Joe began slamming away, filling his boyfriend's hole with his stiffness. Pumping back and forth, Paul experienced the exquisite sensation of the warm, solid meat being crammed inside him.

Connor and Dean moved around to either side of the bed and knelt up at Paul's side. Inching themselves closer, they positioned their cocks just by the lad's mouth, letting his tongue slip out and start lapping at the two enraged heads.

Kneeling in even closer, Connor and Dean started to kiss, exploring each other, tongues meeting and caressing. Sliding forward, they let Paul have greater access to their cocks, which he started to suck, one after the other, turning his head left and right, giving even attention to both, revelling in the two rigid dicks, taking both deep into his throat, slavering them with saliva. The two cocks butted each other as they were taken down and lovingly sucked, the bollocks in the two hanging fleshy bags swinging and slapping against the side of Paul's chest. Reaching over, still intently kissing, they let their fingers run over each other's chests, feeling the manly contours and tweaking and rubbing the trembling nipples.

Joe was tremendously turned on as he fucked his boyfriend hard and his boyfriend sucked their friends, sucked on their two big, thick poles, while they all watched each other.

Then as if they had all had the same thought, Joe pulled back, watching Paul's muscle ring retract as it let his invasive weapon slide out. Connor and Dean picked up condoms and slipped them on, the Irish lad first to slap lube along the length. Letting Joe move away, Connor knelt up and pushed at Paul's hole, feeling the ring give way and admit him, sighing with pleasure as he entered.

Paul was one of the best fucks Connor had ever had, obliging and sensitive, knowing when to push down and when to squeeze his muscles tight, clamping, vice-like, around Connor's cock.

Unable to believe what was now occurring, Paul just let it all happen. He was having sex with his best friends, and it was fantastic. Connor was delivering a great fuck, as good as Joe, and it felt amazing. His powerful thrusts filled Paul, driving a deep lungful of air out of him with each upward thrust. He could feel Connor's balls slapping against his arse, and he suddenly gave out a cry of ecstasy as both Dean and Joe fell upon his chest, taking one nipple each, sucking and teasing, running their tongues around the outer circle, then sucking hard, pulling both muscled breasts into their mouths. The suction was intense, and the sensations too delicious for words. All he could do was emit groans and grunts, his whole body aflame with lust and passion.

Dean and Joe caught each other's eyes and knelt up. Now it was Dean's turn. He watched as Connor pulled his hard cock out of Paul's arse, then saw that Paul's hole was opening and closing, almost like a breathing entity, covered with lube. He grabbed Paul's ankles, anchoring his legs wide apart and high in the air, and let his cock-head rest at the hole for a moment, almost savouring the moment of anticipation.

Paul was desperate. He wanted to be stuffed again, needed that cock inside him, to fill his body and make him feel whole. He really wanted to give Dean a good time, to show his friend that he could accommodate his hard weapon, to give him the ultimate experience.

Sensing that the time was right, Dean pushed. With very little resistance, the cock slid in. Dean gasped at the tightness around his dick, sucking him deeper, pulling his manhood up the greasy hole, until it filled Paul totally. His eyes wide open and his teeth clenched, he started to fuck. He could see why Connor and Joe had had huge grins on their faces as they gave it to Paul. He was now feeling the same waves of pleasure, and the rippling of Paul's muscles as they coaxed him higher and deeper.

Joe and Connor knelt either side of the bed, their heads forward. Joe nuzzled his face into Paul's thighs, taking the bollocks into his mouth, watching with an astonished glance as this seemed to encourage the cock to expand further. Taking this as an invitation, Connor put his lips to Paul's cock, sliding the head inside his mouth, and began to suck.

Now Paul was riding high, flying over heights of ecstasy he never thought possible. The multi-sensations from the three other lads were mind-blowing. His arse was aching so much from the punishment it was getting that he thought he would always have an ache there, while the oral action he was getting seemed better than ever. The triple attention felt unreal, and he wanted it to go on forever.

But sensing it was time for another change, Dean slowed down and gradually pulled out. He pulled the condom off and rapidly replaced it with a fresh one. Not letting Connor and Joe finish their attack on Paul's cock and balls, he grabbed him by the waist and flipped him over, so he was kneeling up on the bed. Connor mirrored this position so he and Paul were now face to face on the mattress. Joe rubbered up, and sat up, holding his cock ready for entry, heading for Connor's hole, while Dean similarly got ready to continue his assault on Paul.

Paul and Connor started to kiss, as simultaneously Joe and Dean resumed, pushing their unyielding meat inside the two suppliant lads. The desire to cry out was deadened by the insistent kissing, Paul and Connor lost in the joy of each other's mouths, breathing deeply through their noses, pushing their hips back in unison at the pounding they were getting.

Both Dean and Joe seemed to have achieved the same rhythm, speedily banging away for all they were worth, wanting to give their utmost, to fill their passive mates' arses utterly.

How long they stayed in this position, they didn't know, and didn't care. All that mattered was the moment, and the deep, hot, punishing, incredible sex. Each of the boys had had plenty of sexual encounters, some good, some bad, but they all knew that they had never had such a sensational session before. Somehow they had become more sexual beings, more sensual and more imaginative. Never before had they been with anyone else that they desired so completely to satisfy.

All four of them knew that this couldn't last. The depth of emotion and lust being expended between them had soon to reach a shuddering climax. Joe and Dean could sense that their cum was boiling, and would soon erupt. Both Paul and Connor wanted to see the explosion of the other's cock, and so gently eased themselves off the pounding dicks.

They all knelt up on the bed, in a circle, each beating themselves to orgasm, watching intently each other's exertions, glorying in the sight of the four hardened cocks, fists clamped about each, jerking furiously, willing the spunk out.

It didn't take too much longer. Paul was the first to come, giving a grunt of relief, as his jism shot out, flying across the circle, landing in irregular blobs all over Joe's chest and neck. One small globule fell directly on Joe's lips, and Paul watched entranced as he licked it clean away.

This sensual act made Joe come too, erupting furiously, a yell of delight escaping his tightly pursed lips. His seed spattered on the duvet cover, almost invisible on the cream-coloured satin. Strings of stickiness dripped from his fingers, slicking the length of his cock.

Connor and Dean then came together, fiercely jacking off, both firing out their hot, white juice, which shot high in the air and landed on the bed, mingling with Joe's already spilt jism. They wanted to produce more of their semen than they ever had before, to prove, if possible, that this was the most significant orgasm they had ever experienced and certainly the most draining. As each boy came, their bodies were overwhelmed, consumed with a shuddering convulsion. Heads pounded, and cocks jerked, backs arched and eyes bulged, as each boy felt the life essence draining from the end of his throbbing penis, his body racked with exhaustion and overcome with emotion.

'JESUS CHRIST!' Connor screamed out at the top of his voice, utterly spent, dripping with perspiration, slowly pulling on his cock, his fingers now coated with his own spunk, still holding in his other hand the condom he'd been wearing, then throwing it to one side.

'Wow!' Paul had nothing else to say. He could feel his arsehole aching, a dull pain there, testament to the mammoth pounding it had just received, as he sank back on his heels, his prick still sizeable, lolling at half-mast, gazing dreamily at his three mates all shagged out, and looking the horniest they ever had. 'Why have we never done this before?'

'I don't know.' Connor sat back too, breathing heavily, the impact of what had just happened not lost on him. 'I guess we were so caught up in getting the band off the ground, making it a success, that we ignored the fact that we are all still young men, with our drives and juices intact! Today just happened to be the day we realised that.'

'I guess so.' Joe lay back down, his head against the soft, plump pillows. 'I never really thought about you guys as sexy. I knew you were attractive, and I knew you all probably had rampant sex-drives, like me and Paulie here.' He smiled and put out his arm toward his boyfriend, who smiled back and clambered up the bed, snuggling at Joe's side, using one of the towelling robes to wipe his sticky fingers and dry up the traces of semen from his cock.

'But it was only tonight,' Joe continued, 'after the excitement of the concert, and the pure rush of the audience's reaction, that I looked at you in a different way.'

Dean took Connor's hand and drew him close, hugging him

from behind, his arms held tightly around the Irish lad's chest.

'I know what you mean,' he said. 'I could never have imagined doing something like this with all of you.' He squeezed Connor tight, adoring the warmth of his body and the smooth texture of his skin as it lay against his own chest, fitting together perfectly like the pieces of a jigsaw. The memory of the sexual escapade with Connor and Stuart at the Manchester shopping centre filled his mind. 'I will admit to having had a threesome, but I could never have imagined having sex with three other guys at all. It's like some Roman orgy!'

Bending his neck, Connor kissed Dean's forearm, the happy memories of that same encounter fresh in his mind too.

Paul piped up. 'I have never had anything like that happen to me before. When you all took turns fucking me, I couldn't believe it. I still can't. After all we've been through, it seems like we've wasted so much time.' He raised his eyes and kissed Joe on the lips. 'No offence baby, but it feels like I've got three boyfriends now... three beautiful, handsome, well-hung boyfriends. Life doesn't get any better than this.'

A tear welled up in his eye, and with a swift motion, he wiped it away with the back of his hand.

'What are you crying for?' Connor looked concerned.

'I don't think I've ever been so happy. With you three, and the band's success, this is more than I ever dreamed of.' He patted Joe's cock which lay bloated and fat across his thigh. 'Do you remember how I used to be? A jealous, neurotic queen? Thank God I've changed.'

Joe kissed his forehead. 'Hear, hear! You are so much more sexy now that you've grown up. Isn't he, boys?' He winked at Dean and Connor, who both winked back and nodded effusively.

'Oh, yes, a real stud-muffin.' Connor crawled toward Joe and Paul, settling himself at their sides, throwing his arm across them both, and hugging them.

'I would definitely say he is a total hunk, and a great fuck too!' Dean joined the others, and they lay back, a tangled heap of naked flesh, arms and legs entwined, feeling the delicious afterglow of their wonderful sex.

Unexpectedly there came a knock at the door.

'Who is it?' Joe called out.

'It's me, Nick. Can I come in?'

The boys looked down at their appearance, and decided that Nick seeing them like this was probably no big deal. In fact he'd seen them in a lot more inflamed positions than this.

'Come in if you're naked!' Dean giggled as he shouted out at the suite's door.

Stepping inside and closing the door behind him, Nick entered the bedroom, and his eyes widened with amazement.

'Well... no need to ask what you've been doing!' He sat on the edge of the bed, drinking in the sight of the four handsome lads, unclothed, obviously indulging in some post-coital relaxation.

'Why didn't you ask me to join in? I could have done with a good fuck tonight.'

The boys looked at each other, all with the same thought dominating their minds.

Joe spoke. 'It was something we had to do between ourselves. No offence, Nick, 'cos it would have been fun to have a fifth. But we had to do this... It has sort of cemented our friendship... and brought us closer together.' He paused and licked his lips provocatively. 'But now if you'd care to get that gorgeous cock of yours out, I'm sure we could find some place to put it.'

Nick said nothing, but grinned, showing his perfect white teeth. 'That's a very tempting offer, and one I may take you up on. But first I have some business.'

The boys rolled their eyes.

Noticing their reluctance, Nick patted Dean on the thigh, leaving his hand there, feeling the soft hairs, and the heat of his skin.

'If you'll just listen for a moment, I've got some interesting news.' He moved his hand higher, lightly brushing the underside of Dean's bollocks. 'I have just been checking my e-mail, and I've had a message from Wally at Hall Associates in New York. They have heard about the phenomenal success of tonight's concert, and want to fly us out for some preliminary talks about releasing a new single and possibly doing some concerts over there.'

He surveyed the boys' blank faces. 'Well? This could be the chance to make our mark on America. Who knows... some day soon you could be performing at Carnegie Hall.'

'Nah,' said Connor. 'That's for oldies. I think we should at least do a show at the Hollywood Bowl. If it's good enough for John Cleese and co, then it's good enough for us.'

Connor burst out laughing, his stomach rising and falling, and soon all three other boys were trembling heaps, their laughter filling the room, whilst their manager looked happily on.

Also by
Sam Stevens

The Captain's Boy

This tale of homosexual lust centres on Robert, long-limbed lusty son and heir of Lord Marchant. Robert has had a privileged childhood at Marchant Hall, during which he has only scratched the surface of his sexual capabilities. Now a fine, handsome young man, his sexuality begins to fully awaken. When his father discovers him deep in the gamekeeper's boy, his horror knows no bounds. He insists that Robert join the Navy forthwith or be disinherited. Unwilling to comply, Robert runs away, only to fall foul of the ruthless press-gangs who roam the ports seeking such unwary victims and forcing them into the service of His Majesty. At sea, Robert finds he has much to learn about the sexual tastes of seafaring men – and when he and his crewmates are captured by pirates intent on regular man-on-man orgies, he discovers just how far men will happily go in order to satiate their carnal desires.

UK £7.95 US $11.95 (when ordering quote FIC 20)

*Prowler Books are available from bookshops including
Borders, Waterstone's, Gay's The Word and Prowler Stores.
Or order direct from:
MaleXpress, 3 Broadbent Close, London N6 5JG
FREEFONE 0800 45 45 66 (Int tel +44 20 8340 8644)
FREEFAX 0800 917 2551 (Int fax +44 20 8340 8885)
Please add p&p – single item £1.75, 2 items or more £3.45, all overseas £5*